2Sp

2Sp

The Eve of War
Torquere Press Publishers
1380 Rio Rancho Blvd #1319, Rio Rancho, NM 87124
Copyright 2014 by Rae Gee
Cover illustration by BSClay
Published with permission
ISBN: 978-1-61040-757-1

www.torquerepress.com

**If you liked The Eve of War,
you might enjoy:**

Mars on the Rise by Rae Gee

Selling Mars by Rae Gee

The Eve of War

The Eve of War
by Rae Gee

Torquere Press, Inc.
romance for the rest of us
www.torquerepress.com

The Eve of War

DEDICATION

For Bertie,
the cat-on-loan who never seemed to go home.
I miss you, my furry little muse.

Dedicated to the memory of John Smith and John Pratt.
"The grave will soon close over me and my name [be] entirely forgotten." - John Smith
May your names never be forgotten.

The Eve of War

CHAPTER 1

The once manicured lawn had become a war zone, the grass covered with the slain bodies of Erus' horses. Entrails spewed from sliced stomachs and the stream ran red with blood. Birds circled the carcasses, picking at meat and intestines. At the heart of the carnage lay a pile of heads, the final insult to the magnificent steeds. As they disembarked, Erus gave another howl, the air turning blue as he cursed life, gods and the person he suspected of the carnage.

For dangling from a roughly built gallows, its head nearly torn from its neck, was Erus' prized dapple-gray stallion. Cedo felt his own heartbroken cry begin as his eyes fell upon what was once his horse. Metal legs torn from their joints and its head at a strange angle, his beautiful iron horse hung beside his Master's. Its pistons and delicate wiring had been torn from its carcass, spilling from its sides in a final insult against the glorious machine. It may only have been metal, but Cedo felt the heartache as if it had lived.

The butchery was a message, and, like Erus, Cedo suspected he knew who from.

Trying to hold back the bile which threatened to burn his throat, Cedo followed Erus across the stream, Billy and Francis trailing behind them. The acidic stench of death and excrement filled the air and Cedo covered his nose. Erus seemed not to care, striding through the destruction, his hands running over the flanks of his dead animals. The birds scattered before them, squawking at the disturbance.

Panic stopped him amid the wreckage, a single thought in his mind.

Misty.

Frantically Cedo looked around himself, searching the nooks and crannies of the garden.

"Misty!" His voice echoed pathetically. "Misty!"

Other than their small party, there was no movement. Everything was eerily still. Agitated, he hurried after Erus, following as his Master slammed through the rear door of the house and down the servants' passageway.

"Mr. Black?" Erus bellowed. "Mrs. Sugden? Mr. Morris?"

Their footsteps thudded heavily against the bare boards and Erus stormed away, angrily calling for staff who never responded. As they stepped into the hallway, Cedo's Master stopped, tossing a glare that had Cedo stepping back. The redhead's eyes narrowed, flicking left and right as he listened. The house was still.

Too still.

Never had the house felt so oppressive, a strangling feeling which threatened to snatch their lives away after they had battled so hard to stay alive. It did not feel good to be back.

Suddenly, the study door opened and Erus swung around, shoulders stiffening as the Patron stepped out.

"You," he hissed.

"So nice to see you, Erus." The Patron smiled a sickly smile and offered a hand, which Erus chose to ignore. "Please, come and join me. Your young friend can remain here."

Erus stepped into the abyss, the door thudding shut

behind him. Nausea rolled through Cedo, and he silently stepped up to the door, listening for scraps of information.

"I'd come away if I were you."

Francis and Billy stood behind him, Billy looking more forlorn than before. Cedo did not want to leave the door but his snooping was garnering him no information. Those inside the room knew he was listening and were keeping their voices to hushed whispers. Taking Billy's hand, Cedo glared at the door, daring the Patron to confront him.

Billy did not shake him away, which mildly surprised him. But he did not look at him either. He just stared straight at the door, face stony and blank. He was obviously not prepared to let Cedo know whatever was going on in his mind.

"Where are the staff?" Cedo deliberately kept his voice low.

Neither Billy nor Francis replied. Time moved slowly onward, the house so quiet that the ticking of the dining room clock could be heard from their post by the study door. They remained frozen to the spot, sentries awaiting the return of their commander. Cedo took slow, deep breaths, silently sending up prayers for his Master. He knew not what went on behind the door, and the silence left him with an uneasy sense of dread. There had been something darkly sinister in the Patron's smile.

Eventually, the door opened and the Patron walked out, a drawn and weary Erus following him. Replacing his hat on his head, the Patron nodded toward them.

"Welcome back, gentlemen. Erus."

Erus gave the Patron a small nod and escorted him to the door. As it swung shut, Erus slumped against it, head lowered and the heels of his hands rubbing at his eyes. For a while, he remained as he was, hunched over and silent. It was worrying, sickening even, and Cedo walked toward him, eager to be with him. Instead, his Master lifted a hand and waved him back, never looking at him.

"Go." He sounded tired. "Freshen up and rest. Francis, Cedo shall show you where you can rest."

They slid away like ghosts, Cedo leading them up the stairs. Their return should have been joyous and triumphant, a grand entrance. Instead, it was everything but. Opening a door across from his own room, Cedo showed Francis in. Previously, the doors had been locked but in the Guards' search and their subsequent flight to the Dynasty, the bolts had been forgotten.

Beyond the door was a modest bedroom, which appeared to be having alterations done. Needless, it had a bed and all the amenities Francis would need.

The bespectacled man gave him a small bow. "I thank you."

Cedo returned it with a weak smile. "I shall be just across the hallway should you need anything. Anything at all, just knock."

With another bow, and a smile, Francis retreated into the room and softly closed the door. Closing his eyes, Cedo laid his head against the wall. His eyes felt dry and his limbs felt heavy. He tried to explain it away as side effects of the drugs, but he knew that it was weariness. It had been so long since he had properly rested. Finally his exhaustion had caught up with him, and he felt, quite literally, sick and tired. Beneath him, his knees gave way and, gratefully, Cedo began to sink to the floor, only too happy to let sleep take over. As he settled against the wall, strong arms wrapped around him and spirited him away to bed.

As quiet as a mouse, Billy had taken care of Cedo, undressing and washing him before laying him on the bed. It was an act of tenderness Cedo had not expected, and one for which he was grateful.

Stretching over the cool, clean sheets, Cedo turned his head and looked at his mate. Billy was sitting on the edge of the bed, silently giving Cedo his back, head cradled in his hands. An empty sadness swept over Cedo and he slid closer, resting a hand in the small of Billy's back.

"Come to bed. It will make you feel better."

Billy's shoulders rose and fell with deep, even breaths. Desperately Cedo wanted to feel the blond man beside him. To feel his lover's arms around him and lips against his skin. Like an impatient child, he gave a tug on Billy's shirt. Finally, the blond man rose and shed his clothes before sliding into bed. A small smile flickered over Billy's lips and Cedo felt himself return it. Unable to help himself, Cedo ran his hands through waves of sun-blond hair, savoring the feeling of being able to perform such menial tasks away from prying eyes.

"I am sorry for what happened on the journey," he softly whispered.

Cedo was sure he could see a glimmer of happiness in Billy's blue eyes.

"'S all right. I just want you to respect my opinions an' wishes."

Taking Billy's hand, he gently stroked it. "I do. It is just..." Pausing, Cedo sighed. "I have never been in a relationship such as this."

Billy's fingers tightened around his own and he looked into curious blue eyes. "'Ow do you mean?"

Stroking his thumb over the back of Billy's hand, he studied it. They were the hands of a man, strong and rough with thick veins dancing beneath the skin. Hands that were capable of bringing either life or death.

"I have never been in a relationship where I have been considered an equal. Never have I ever really had to consider the feelings of another, and the change is difficult." Cedo looked back at Billy's face and smiled. "And I thank you for your love and patience. The way you stand beside me means a great deal."

Billy's lips turned up in a tired smile and he opened his arms, beckoning Cedo closer. Filled with a renewed happiness, Cedo slid into the welcoming embrace. He rested his head beneath Billy's chin, arms wrapping around his friend. He was finally home.

The hours slipped by, silent thieves of life and day. Cedo and Billy awoke at sunrise the following day. It felt like a million years had passed since their time in the dungeon.

Leaning into the pillows, Cedo listened.

Silence still filled the air. There was nothing, no footsteps or voices. No grating of machinery or clanging of metal. It was a painful silence, filled with loss, and he dared not leave the room.

Then it came, a sound that set his teeth on edge and instantly filled the house with anguish. It went on far longer than its carrier should have been able to sustain. So loud was the cry that it woke Billy with a start. Lurching from the bed, they made for the door. Francis was already standing in the hallway. The trio stood and listened to the wail. It was one of heartbreak and bereavement, the never-ending siren of a broken soul.

Cautiously, they picked their way to the stairs. The sight that met them froze Cedo to his very core.

For there, at the bottom of the stairs, knelt his Master. Head thrown back and hands wrenching his hair, he cursed unseen gods. It was both pitiful and terrifying, a sight he never thought he would see.

Leaving Billy and Francis at the peak of the stairs, Cedo quietly walked toward him, laying a gentle hand on Erus' shoulder. Erus flinched away, as if he had been burned, skidding across the floor.

Hunched and staring at Cedo from beneath flame-red hair, he hissed, "Leave me."

His face was a mess of anguish and anger, dark and twisted. Dark circles bruised Erus' eyes, and he looked haggard and sallow, as if he had not slept. Shaking, Cedo retreated to the safety of the stairs, watching the troll-like monster.

"Master..." His voice trailed off as the creature pulled back its lips and bared yellowing teeth.

"I said, leave!"

Crawling back to Billy's safe embrace, his eyes never left the bastardization of his Master. Under the fierce glare, they retreated to their rooms and firmly battened the doors against the impending storm.

Falling back to the bed, Cedo watched as the sun rose over the Downs. He allowed his thoughts to consume him, thoughts of terror and horror, thoughts of what went on in his Master's mind. Billy knelt behind him and wrapped his arms around Cedo's waist, holding him tightly. Billy said nothing, yet Cedo could not relax.

Gentle kisses touched his shoulder and Cedo shivered beneath his lover's lips. He so wanted to fall to the bed and relieve all his stresses through Billy. But his mind was elsewhere, trying to decipher what was happening. The atmosphere in the house was septic, rotting from the very core. Cedo knew he would never know the full truth, and it angered him. There were three of them, ready and willing to help, yet his Master's damned pride would never allow them to extend that hand. All they could do was sit and wait for the storm to break.

Billy's hands began to work at his neck and shoulders, knuckles rubbing at tight knots of muscles. The warmth of relaxation began to tickle him, spreading from the easing muscles and flooding his body. Groaning, Cedo rolled his head forward and let his eyes fall shut. Worrying would get him nowhere.

His lover's fingers kneaded and worked, getting into every crevice and working their magic. Quietly Cedo purred, never lifting his head. Instead, he fell into a blissful trance, swept away by the constant ministrations. When Billy's hands fell away, Cedo remained where he was, traveling away to a different plane. He never wanted to surface, never wanted to face what sat at the foot of the stairs.

It was a knock at the door that pulled him to and, upon his weary "Enter," it opened, Francis stepping in. His hands were clasped before him, face pale and ashen, looking the part of the bearer of bad news. Cedo felt the panic rise.

"He has worried about this moment," Francis began. "He knew it would come, yet he buried it and fell into his work."

Billy rose from the bed, placing himself between Francis and Cedo. Expecting the worst, Cedo reached for Billy's hand.

"Don't you be bringin' bad news in 'ere."

Closing his eyes, Cedo tightened his grip and murmured, "Billy, please."

There was a flash of blonde hair and blue eyes bore down into him. "Cedo, I refuse to let anythin' 'appen in 'ere. We've been through a lot of bad stuff an' if 'e's goin' to pile it on, then 'e can go."

"I'm afraid there will probably be nothing but bad news for the foreseeable future," Francis started. "No matter how far we bury our heads in the sand, we will unfortunately have to face it at some point soon."

"An' this bad news is?"

Beyond Billy, he saw Francis step closer. His face was still set like stone. "I fear Mr. Veetu has had his wings clipped."

Dropping his head to his hands, Cedo allowed his mate to take the lead. It seemed simpler, especially as he felt at a sudden, wrenching loss for words.

"'Ow do you mean?"

He heard Francis take a deep breath. "I mean that he has, no doubt, had all of his research and work taken from him. The Patron cannot be seen to have had someone executed only for them to return alive and well and carry on. Unless he can get his folios back into his possession, he will have to start from scratch. He is a broken man, Cedo, and needs you now more than ever. Go to him and be by his side."

Billy's hand stroked over his hair and Cedo lifted his head to look at the blond-haired man. Worry lined his lover's face, his normally serene blue eyes filled with pain.

"Do you want to go?"

Nodding, Cedo took Billy's hand before pulling himself to his feet. "I must. I have an obligation to him, and I am afraid he must think that we do not care about him."

Giving them both a weak smile, Cedo began to dress, not caring whether the clothes matched or were clean. He had no idea where any of his belongings were and it gave him a strange, disconcerting feeling, as if everything he held dear had been stolen. Running his fingers through his hair, he took out as many of the knots as he could before looking in the mirror. He looked far from perfect, but he would have to do.

Apprehensively he walked to the study. Disturbing Erus, especially in the throes of grief, was a nightmare he did not want to face. Yet he realized he needed to be by his Master's side, a beacon of hope and strength in the dark hours. The door to the study stood ajar, and Cedo's heart rattled in his chest as he cautiously approached it. When he heard deep, soul-shaking sobs, he stilled, the sound breaking his heart. Gently he nudged the door open and stopped at the sight that met him.

Hands flat against the desk and hair hiding his eyes, Erus shook with the horror that tore through his mind. Approaching Erus slowly, Cedo brushed his fingers over his Master's shoulder, only for Erus to dart away. Eyes wild and heavy with tears, Erus pressed himself into the window before he slowly sank to the floor. Heart wrenching, Cedo caught him and lowered them both to the floor. Erus did not look at him, refused to acknowledge him and Cedo could only imagine what was running through his mind. To break down, especially before his bonded, was a crime in itself, something which should never be seen. Beneath Cedo's fingers, he shook and shivered, whining and sobbing, yet he never pulled away. Instead, he allowed himself to be held and rocked in the manner of a wounded child, each sob tearing at the fiber of Cedo's being.

It was horrific, like listening to very heart of a person being torn apart. In essence, Cedo presumed, that was exactly what was happening. Holding his Master close, Cedo whispered sweet nothings. While his heart tried to heal his beloved, his eyes took in the cause of the anguish.

The study was a shadow of what it had once been. The shelves, once crammed with books, stood empty barring a few, lonely scraps of paper. Erus was mourning, and it was not a grief that could be healed through words and affection. There was a great deal of work to be done, not just to restore his Master but to restore what they needed to protect their country.

Running his fingers through filthy, matted red hair, he whispered, "What of the war room? You have plans stored in the safe."

An energy began to crackle through the air, one which Cedo recognized all too well. He refused to back away as it touched his skin, raising his hackles. Raw, green eyes looked up into his own and chapped, bloodied lips took irregular, shaking breaths. He would hold his ground, would not run from the monster. Their time below ground had shown him so much more about himself and Erus.

Fingers topped with cracked, grime caked nails slid over Cedo's chest to his throat. They teased over his skin, making him shake, inklings of fear beginning to taint his mind. Wrapping around him, they pulled him down, closer to the Inferno he held in his arms. Death stinking breath stained his nose and Erus' face twisted into a horrifying sneer.

There was no time for the fear to take hold. In the blink of an eye, Erus was gone, sweeping from the room, a man possessed. Cedo barely had time to catch his breath before the house was filled with the sounds of slamming doors. Rising from the floor, he walked to the door. From the opposite hallway, Billy and Francis emerged. Both wore wide-eyed looks of shock.

"What in Inferno..." Billy watched as the shadow of Erus disappeared deep into the house.

"Apparently something had jogged his memory," he softly replied.

Billy nodded. "Look, we've just been to the kitchen, scoutin'. Looks like the place ain't been empty long. There's fresh veg, some stuff in the icebox an' 'alf a farm of dried meat."

"Mostly fresh," Francis interjected. "But, should you care to join us, we're going to cook."

His stomach rallied at the words; it felt like an age since he had last eaten and, with a nod, he followed them.

With a fire stoked on the open hearth, they set about preparing a meal. While the store cupboards contained very little, it would far surpass the meals they had eaten while incarcerated within the Dynasty.

A heavy, soot-covered pot hung over the fire, its contents of broth gently bubbling away. Leaning against one of the counters, Cedo watched as Billy set about cutting vegetables. With great concentration, Billy bent over the stone surface, a long knife nimbly peeling and scraping. The sight made him smile and warmed his heart and something stirred within him. There was something decidedly pleasant about watching his mate cook him a meal.

Sliding from the counter, Cedo stepped behind Billy and laced his arms around the taller man's waist. Resting his chin on Billy's shoulder, Cedo watched him work. Billy chuckled, never lifting his eyes from his task.

"You are good to me," Cedo said.

Billy gave another husky chuckle, and Cedo tightened his arms around the other man. He never wanted to let go, never wanted to give up the man he held. He had been gifted with someone who was as close to perfection as he was ever going to see. It chilled him when he remembered what his Master had sacrificed for him. Erus had risked everything to make him happy.

"Perfect," he whispered, lips kissing Billy's ear. "You are living, breathing perfection."

Billy stopped and lifted his head, peering over his shoulder. "I wouldn't say that, but I'm grateful that you think so. Warms my 'eart, it does, listenin' to you talk."

A smile tugged at Billy's lips, and Cedo moved to give him the gentlest of kisses.

"You goin' to let me get on with this? You can't live on fresh air an' a 'appy 'eart."

Grinning, Cedo slid away and seated himself on one of the counters. A sense of helplessness that he had felt many times before fell over him. For the first time in many months, he felt that he was more than a mere ornament to be appreciated by another. He had hoped that he and Billy would do things together, but it was as if his mate had taken on his Master's mentality. *Look, but do not touch.*

Slipping back to the floor, he faced Billy. "Can I help?"

Looking up, Billy flashed him a bright smile, a smile which Cedo had not seen in many moons. Eyes the color of sapphires sparkled with a flare of happiness.

"Yep. You can eat the finest stew this side of Svenfur an' tell me 'ow good it is."

Sadness pricked his heart and he leaned against the stone surface. "Do you need any help with the cooking?"

Billy looked to Francis and Francis looked to him.

"Can you make dumplings?"

His hopes of being helpful were dashed away and he sadly shook his head. Wistfully, he smiled. "I can make lemonade."

Francis' eyes widened and he puffed his cheeks. Beside him, Billy gave a long whistle and cracked his knuckles.

"Right, Cedo, time for a little life lesson."

The dumplings were a little too golden and far from perfect, but Cedo had made them with his own hands. Rather than take, he had created something for those he loved. Such chores had never featured in his life. Once there had been servants to do the work for him. It was a completely different matter now that they were alone.

Seated around the stone island, they ate in silence. The only noise came from cutlery scraping crockery, and it echoed off the walls of the large kitchen. Billy had been right; the stew was the finest on the coast, full of flavor and color. Cedo decided that, should he only be allowed one meal for the rest of his days, the stew it would be.

Quietly, he asked, "Where do you think the servants are?"

The others mulled over the question before Francis chanced an answer.

"They could be anywhere. In another household or in a prison camp. They may even be dead. They may return, they may not. Who can tell?"

The thoughts made Cedo feel ill, and he placed the spoon to one side. "But why? Why empty a house?"

"I fear that the Patron may be making a point. Mr. Veetu is now a non-person. As far as the country is concerned, he's dead. No doubt all of his papers have been seized. Whether it is an attempt to stop the experiments, I don't know. Although, from what I can gather, he was rather coerced into performing them by the very government who paid him. My guess, and I wouldn't take it for an educated one, is the government has decided to cut out the middleman. They wish to drive Mr. Veetu to the sanitarium with the madness of grief. Emptying the house is part of the process."

"And if they need more machines?"

Francis was quiet for a moment before his eyes bore into Cedo's. "They'll no doubt purchase them from the enemy."

Silence fell over them again, the words slowly sinking in. In the blink of an eye, the world had changed. There would be no more stages, no more stories, no more adoring applause. Now they were at war with an enemy that appeared to be unstoppable. Cedo had seen their arsenal up close, and as far as he knew, they had nothing that could match it. Nothing unless Erus could emerge from the recesses of his grief.

"Aye-up." He followed Billy's eyes to the door behind him.

An unadulterated relief washed through him as the door was nudged open. Misty padded in and gave an ear-splitting cry. Face aching from grinning, Cedo slid from his seat and scooped her up. He ignored her impatient wriggles as he cooed and stroked. She was alive and, for that moment, it was all that mattered. Hugging her close, Cedo walked back to his seat and placed Misty gently on the table. With a gaze that could have frozen water, she gave him her back, set her tail in the air and daintily walked over to Billy. Scratching her ears, Billy patted his own shoulder, grinning at Cedo when she hopped up, her tail winding around his neck.

Picking over his food, Francis chuckled. "Cats. Such fickle creatures."

Just like his Master.

"Cedo!"

His back snapped straight at the call of his name, the quiet, post-meal bliss shattered. Across the table, Billy and Francis looked up, shock settling over their previously relaxed features. Misty lifted her head and flicked an ear before resettling around Billy's neck.

"Cedo!"

His Master's voice echoed along the hallways, reverberating off the walls and to the kitchen. The sound of it sent tiny icicles of terror through him. The door crashed open and Erus clutched the doorframe, eyes and hair wild. Quickly he took in the diners before staring straight at Cedo, chest rising and falling as he caught his breath.

"Come. I need your help. We haven't a moment to waste."

CHAPTER 2

Cedo gave Billy and Francis an apologetic smile as he slid from the stool and followed Erus' billowing black coattails as they made for the study.

As they rounded the final corner, Erus instead swept into the dining room. Already its large table had vanished beneath piles of paper and a few, meager folios. Slabs of blank paper and boxes of scientific instruments and sticks of graphite were stacked to one side. Along one wall stood several wheeled blackboards, their faces as blank as a starless night.

Erus gestured around. "The boards need to go around the room. Side by side, if you please."

Gripping the frame of one, Cedo eased it around the table and pressed it against the wall. Behind him, Erus chattered, the complete opposite of the man he had encountered earlier. Now he was calm but animated, thoughts forming logically. He spoke of attacks and counter defenses, of how and when James would strike and the weaponry he would use. Erus spoke of building an arsenal which bettered James'. Still, they had to prepare themselves for losses, either material or human. Talk of war made Cedo's blood run cold. All too often it appeared to be a fruitless exercise in one-upmanship. But faced with the fine details, he began to realize that, in some cases, it was a necessary evil.

"He won't come for us. Despite our connection, he will make for the capital. That doesn't mean we can let our guard down. He will still damage us because so many of the weapons factories are here." Pushing the piles of papers to one side, he unfurled a map across the table and traced a finger along the coast. "We must fortify the coast as he will believe that we won't think to do so."

"And how do you propose to do that? We have over seven thousand miles of coastline. It shall be impossible!"

Erus snaked an arm around Cedo's waist, fingers possessively running over his hip. Moving them closer to the map, the redhead swept his fingers over the blue swells of sea.

"We shall electrify the waters. It's about time this country dragged itself from the dark ages and into the cleaner, faster age of electrical power."

Cedo kept his eyes on the map. Erus' fingers began to explore the hollow of his hip, and Cedo felt his breath hitch, his skin puckering beneath the touches.

"And you plan to do this by using it to kill people, do you?"

Erus' chin sank into his shoulder, his breath tickling Cedo's cheek. "Is there a better way to show people its power than to use it to protect our great land?"

His Master's arm tightened around him, drawing him to Erus' firm body.

"And how shall you electrify the waters?"

Cedo was finding it difficult to maintain his balance. All he wanted to do was sink to the floor and beg Erus to take him. But now they were playing an entirely different game, a game that had seen the slate wiped clean. Now they began the race to see who would wind up on top.

"Are we going to have this entire conversation in questions?" Erus asked.

His hand slipped from the map, fingers inching over

Cedo's necklace before lying threateningly over his throat. Closing his eyes, Cedo felt the guilt begin to rise.

"Billy..." he hissed.

Erus growled, the hand at Cedo's throat tightening and drawing his head to the redhead's shoulder. Opening his eyes, Cedo looked up into harsh, green ones.

"I'm not your toy. Tell me what I am."

Still staring into Erus' face, Cedo felt a lump form in his throat. The game was up and, without any effort, Erus had won. There was nothing left but to give himself over. Erus continued to stroke his throat, reminding Cedo of his place. He did not want to open his mouth, did not want to speak. But he knew that, unless he spoke, the cruel fingers would only strangle him.

Finally, he whispered, "You are Master."

"Good." Erus pressed a gentle kiss to his forehead and released him. He returned to the table, poring over sketches and folios, face suddenly hidden behind a curtain of hair. He waved his hand nonchalantly in Cedo's direction.

"I should like some food and drink. And when you've done that, draw me a bath. Otherwise do not disturb me. Play with your toy or something."

Vexed, Cedo skulked from the room and back to the kitchen. All that remained of their meal was a pile of clean crockery and a half-empty pot of stew. Snatching a bowl from the sink, Cedo filled it with meat and vegetables before slamming it onto a tray. The sound echoed around the kitchen but he did not care who heard. This was not how it was supposed to play out. Erus was not supposed to step back into his former habits. They were allies, all equal and with their own skills. But, as before, his Master would be a sly bully, forever making demands and roughly taking him when the desire rose. A war was about to rise and Cedo was useless. His talents had no place in the midst of battle.

Fear gripped Cedo and he leaned against the sink, fingers closing around the cool, white porcelain. Would he be tossed from the house now that he had no place in Erus' little hierarchy? Would he be freed and left to drift along the paths and roads of the coast? What would become of Billy? He did not want to leave his beloved mate behind but, with his deft fingers and unstoppable attitude to work, Billy had no doubt climbed to the top of Erus' ladder.

Dashing the thoughts from his mind, he grasped the gilt-edged tray and made his way back to his Master.

Erus completely ignored him as Cedo quietly deposited the tray on the table. Without so much as lifting his head, he waved Cedo from the room.

Scowling, Cedo made his way back to their room, a rage burning in his belly. He desperately wanted to be more than a slave. Wanted to be more than the silent being that stood and knelt and bowed. Despite the atrocities suffered at the hands of his own Master, nothing had changed in Erus. If anything, it had only added fuel to the fire. Erus was not just determined to protect his country, he was determined to end James' existence as well.

Cedo could see why James was nothing but an oppressor. He was a man who had let power and riches go to his head. A man who wanted to rule the world.

The rage began to wane, replaced by an aching weariness as he pushed open the bedroom door. Weeks of constantly living by his nerves were catching up with him. Yawning, Cedo fell to the unmade bed, savoring the silence. He removed his shoes and buried his toes in the linen, balling it over his feet and legs. His eyes became heavy, eyelids slipping over gritty eyes. Drifting into his mind, Cedo saw only a comfortable, welcoming blackness.

Linen riding over his skin woke him. Soft lips suckling his hip caused him to open his eyes. Smiling tiredly, he gazed down at the figure curled beside his legs. Sodden hair hung in tendrils around Billy's face, and his lightly golden skin was speckled with water. A gleam danced in Billy's eyes, the corners of his mouth twitching into a grin. Running his hands over the damp curls, Cedo pulled the naked body to him, linking his arms around muscular shoulders and gifting his mate with hungry kisses. He felt starved and barren, as if he had been left out in the sun to wilt.

Their lips melted together, and he cared not for the dampness that seeped through his clothes. Tongues slid between their lips, each tasting the other. Wandering hands slid beneath his shoulders and lifted him from the bed. The kisses, as simple as they were, told him so much. Told him that he was wanted and needed. Loved from the depths of another's heart.

Panting and with bruised lips, Cedo regretfully pulled away. Sliding back to the bed, he looked at his lover, beads of sweat now mingling with droplets of water. Running his fingers over Billy's face, he cupped his jaw, stroking soft stubble free skin.

Smiling, he whispered, "I wish to taste freedom before it comes."

Billy frowned. "Before what comes?"

"The war." Gently he pulled Billy's lips back to his own. "I want to see what our world is like one more time, before it is inevitably turned to rubble."

Billy rested on his elbows, face filled with confusion. "'Ow do you know it's goin' to be reduced to nothin'?"

Cedo felt himself become wistful and he gazed past his mate's shoulders. "Because I have read the history books. I have seen what becomes of countries which engage in such conflicts." Returning his attention to Billy, he grinned. "Let us go. Let us go and see what lies in the city. What delights we will find this time."

"An' are you goin' to tell Erus that we're doin' a runner?"

His smile remained in place, the anticipation growing. "Of course. I am sure that he will not deny us this. Besides, he is so busy that I am sure he will not miss us."

Billy raised an eyebrow. "You're sure you want to do this an' risk 'is wrath?"

Draping his legs around his lover's waist, Cedo pulled Billy close. Pushing the damp hair from Billy's face, Cedo stared into his lover's clear blue eyes. "Let us do it. Just this once. And you did promise that I could meet your mother."

Sighing, Billy shook his head before pressing the gentlest of kisses to Cedo's lips. "On your 'ead be it."

Cedo had dared not outline their plans to Francis. Now that he had won Billy round it was far easier to quietly leave without having to rise to the challenges of another. As much as he adored Francis, Cedo knew, deep down, that the bespectacled man would do his best to talk them out of their escape. Best just to slip into the night without so much as a word. Besides, someone needed to remain behind to care for Misty.

Dressed all in black and hidden beneath Erus' heavy cowls, he paused at the foot of the stairs. Holding his breath, he listened for his Master. Through the silence it came, the minute sounds of a pen scratching against paper. Pressing himself to the wall, Cedo glanced through the gap of the study door. Light spilled from the desk, his Master hunched over it. He looked pale in the lamplight, red hair roughly pulled back from his face. Gently Cedo knocked and waited.

The scratching paused, and Erus looked toward the door. His eyes were dark and heavy, exhaustion written into his flesh.

"Yes?"

With his heart pounding, Cedo pushed the door open and walked to the desk. Erus gazed up at him, face expressionless.

"Billy and I should like to return to Svenfur to see his mother. Would you be so kind as to allow us to leave for a while?"

From beneath the mask of exhaustion, a small smile cracked his Master's lips. "Once upon a time you would never have asked. You would have just left. For this, you can leave but I want you back here within twenty-four hours."

The excitement grew, sweeping over Cedo and sending a shiver along his spine.

"However," Erus continued, "if you do not return within the day, then I shall come after you. And trust me, you do not want to take me from what I'm currently doing. You do plan to return, don't you?"

Cedo felt his heart drop. Could he do that after the promises he had made? Could he run and never return? Or was Erus just as fragile as the next person, forever wondering when his beloved would leave?

"As you wish, Master."

With a nod, Erus returned to his work before glancing up. "Are you leaving now?"

Cedo nodded. "No time like the present. As we no longer have horses, we intend to walk across the Downs and be there before dawn."

"Safe travels to you both."

"Thank you, Master."

He returned to Billy and they made for the servants' quarters and the door to their freedom. As silent as shadows, they slipped through the darkened building.

Under the pure moonlight, the detritus of the garden glimmered. Piles of metal and rotting flesh remained where they had fallen, fluids solidifying and slippery. Deftly they stepped around and over them, Cedo feeling bile rise at the vile stench.

Black shards of shadow snaked across the ground, harsh and menacing. A biting breeze swept off the Downs, picking up the hem of the cloak. The alien moonlit world stretched away before them, showing miles of cruel, unforgiving Downs.

Stepping over the stream, Cedo stared at what lay before them. Somewhere, over the undulating ground, lay Svenfur. A chill ran through him, his skin prickling beneath the layers of clothing. Billy touched his elbow and he looked to his lover. Silently, Billy nodded toward the rolling hills. Taking a breath, Cedo took one last look over his shoulder. Behind him, the sprawling house stood in darkness, the wrecked airship the only indicator that anyone was in residence.

"Ready?"

He nodded and turned to face the darkened Downs. "Ready."

The night drew on, an inky, unending stain. Chills rippled over the hills, carried by the sea to his bones. Clutching the cloak to him, Cedo walked, Billy never far from his side. Mostly they walked in silence, picking their way carefully over pot-holed ground.

"How far?"

He heard Billy lick his lips. "Ten, twelve miles as the crow flies."

Cedo grunted a reply and lowered his head. His

eyes strained to pick out the crevices that were hidden among the grass. If stepped in, they could be lethal and time needed to be taken to find the holes which lay in their path. Through the grass and over the trees flowed something that piqued his interest. It tickled his nose and brought a flicker of life to his cold body.

The sea. He could smell it on the breeze, its salty scent wrapping around him in teasing tendrils, drawing him closer.

Straining forward, Cedo rose to the brow of the hill and looked down. A lump caught in his throat as he gazed across moonlight-dappled waves. In the distance the pier stretched out into the water, a steely finger lit with thousands of colored lights, all gently swaying in the breeze. Inching toward the sea was the city he had called home for so long. Lamps wound along the streets, picking out the areas that could afford to light up the darkness and plunging those that could not into a permanent midnight. Here and there fires and simple lamps lit the poorer areas, lighting the way for the innocent.

Billy stood by his elbow, gazing at the snarl of buildings before them. "Wish I could see the 'ouse from 'ere." His voice was wistful, tainted with longing. "Can just about see Sea View from 'ere though."

It was there, in the furthest reaches of the city, a place so tainted with blood that its presence was rarely mentioned.

Gently Billy touched his shoulder. "Come on. If we keep goin' we'll be there before sun up."

Nodding, Cedo gripped the cloak and stepped forward. Everything ached; his joints screaming in the cold. They had walked for hours, battling icy sea breezes and waterlogged bogs. The hems of his clothing were soaked and heavy, weighing him down and brushing against his skin. Thoughts of roaring fires danced through his head.

The sky began to lighten as they wound along base of the hill. A horse and cart rattled along the single, cobbled street of a sleepy village, the driver nodding a greeting as they passed. Behind closed doors, families would be awakening, readying themselves for a day ahead. If they were lucky, the children would be going to school.

As the night began to give way to day so the villages gave way to small towns until they finally found themselves walking the outskirts of Svenfur. Fingers of sunlight inched through the buildings, bringing promises of a glorious morning and chasing away the icicles of cold. Exhaustion racked Cedo's body, his joints aching and head heavy. The streets became wider, filled with the beginnings of the day. Carts, both horse-drawn and mechanical, stopped and started, dropping off and collecting all manner of goods. Smoke and steam filled the air from the multitude of walkers, trams, and powered carts, their clanking screeching through the air.

Cedo watched the bustling streets, watched the people coming and going. He searched their faces for signs of suspicion or recognition. Yet none of them so much as looked at Billy and himself. Every pair of eyes was firmly facing forwards, focusing on the direction they were going. Relief began to find its way through his aching body and he allowed the corners of his mouth to twist upwards. They truly were free. No one knew who they were. More importantly, no one cared.

The wind lifted his hair and, with a sigh of happiness, Cedo turned his face toward the sky. Beside them, waves crashed across the shingle, a joyful melody he had longed to hear. In the distance sat the pier, its lights extinguished until dusk. To be beside the sea was to be at home, the long lost home he thought he would never see again. Rolling his shoulders, he stretched his arms upwards, catching gusts of wind as they sailed past. The horrors of the previous months disappeared, blown out to sea.

Billy chuckled. "You're 'appy. Not that I can blame you."

Twisting on the balls of his feet, Cedo faced him, the smile still on his lips. Billy smiled, the sea air bringing a touch of color to his cheeks. Feeling his heart soar, Cedo draped his arms around his lover's neck. Strong hands gripped his hips, the wind whipping their hair around them.

"Couple more miles, that's it, Cedo. Couple more miles then I'll 'old an' kiss you."

Arching against Billy's hands, Cedo laughed and tossed his head back, taking in the spring-blue sky. It was beautiful. Below ground he had dreamed of the Downs and the sea, carefully picking over his memories. It had been a sight he had thought he would never see again.

Sliding from Billy, Cedo slipped a hand from beneath the cloak and took his lover's hand. Quietly they walked along the seafront and he took in the sights and smells, allowing them to creep into his mind and reawaken all that had fallen into a slumber. It was a welcome awakening and a smile played on his lips.

As they moved toward Sea View, they came across makeshift wooden fencing closing off one of the roads. Posters attached to the fencing proclaimed that a station for the new underground railway would soon be opening and would greatly improve the lives of all of Svenfur's citizens.

Cedo sighed and lowered his head, gazing at the cobbles. The railway was Erus' idea, a gift to the city. It had shown Cedo that the supposedly soulless man did think of others. They had turned their backs on him as he prepared to protect their country. Not just the country, but all who lived on her fair shores. He slowed and stopped, gazing out to sea.

"Beautiful, ain't it?" Billy whispered.

Cedo nodded and gripped his lover's hand tighter. Now that he had returned to the seafront he did not want to leave. Did not want to return to Erus' house. The freedom smelled as divine as a fresh summer's morning.

"Do you think we should return?" Cedo asked. "He has been gracious to allow us to leave, but I do wonder."

"To Erus?"

Keeping his eyes on the sea, Cedo nodded. Beside him, he heard Billy sigh.

"We 'ave to. I 'eard what 'e said to you. An' as much as I might not like 'im, right now might not be the best time to piss 'im off. Not if you want to keep a roof over your 'ead. I 'ave a feelin' that if you annoy 'im 'e'll make your life a livin' 'ell. Not just in Svenfur, not just in the Great Kingdom, but right across the world."

Once again, Billy was right. Glancing once more to the sea, Cedo allowed himself to be led away.

CHAPTER 3

Cockler's Walk was a long street of leaning houses. While the walls tilted to one side, the gables tipped over the narrow street, making it feel dark and claustrophobic. The cobbles were wet and stained with puddles of sewage. Refuse was piled along the walls, left to rot. The stench threatened to choke Cedo. It was not the perfect image of the city that the Patron was laying out with the new railway. It was an area that had been forgotten, deliberately it seemed.

Cedo brought a hand to his mouth as he stepped over the puddles that littered the street. He did not know how anyone could live in such dank and dreary conditions. Despite that, the front of each house was spotless, the steps clean and blackened. The residents were obviously proud of their homes, even if the city government was not.

Billy stopped them before a crooked house. The white walls looked freshly painted and the gables almost gleamed in the fragments of sun. He knocked and stepped back, a smile creasing his face. A moment later, the door flung open to reveal a burly, red-faced woman bearing down on them. Narrowed eyes flicked back and forth, sweeping over them.

"William Burton, just where in Inferno's name do you think you've been?" Her voice matched her body, husky and deep. "I've been worried sick about you."

Cedo looked to Billy, watching as his mate's grin widened and he stepped forward to embrace her. She laughed, her arms pulling him tightly to her.

"It's a long story, Ma. A really long story. If you let us in, I'll tell you all about it."

She pulled away and motioned them in. "Aye, you do that."

The interior of the house was as dark as the street. A roaring fire occupied the small kitchen, a dark wooden table and chairs taking up most of the room. Above them hung a tiny oil lamp, waiting patiently for nightfall, and a small dresser took up the back wall. The mantle above the fire was covered with the detritus of a working family: hair brushes and combs, a clock, a small pot of rouge, hair pins, a length of ribbon and, amid it all, a small photographic plate of a smiling Billy. It was most definitely a house filled with women. From the stories Billy had told him, Cedo was not surprised.

Seated at the table, he watched as Ma Burton—for she had given him no other name—settled the kettle above the fire. Billy sat opposite him, a weary look in his eyes.

She straightened up and stared right at them. "You going to introduce me to your friend or do I 'ave to guess the poor lad's name?"

"Sorry." Billy yawned and stretched his arms above him. "Ma, this is Cedo Reilly. Cedo, this, obviously, is me Ma."

The uneasiness at being in the home of another melted away and Cedo stifled a chuckle. Dressed in a long gray dress, which had obviously seen better years, and a brilliantly white apron, Billy's Ma bustled around the table. She set a teapot and cups before them, and a small plate of cakes appeared from the sideboard.

"You could 'ave given me warning that you were comin'. I could have cleaned up."

"Ma." Billy stood and placed a hand on her arm, slowing her for a moment. "The place is bloody…"

"William Burton!" His mother spun on him, eyes blazing in the light of the fire. "You watch your mouth, 'specially around company."

Grinning, Billy sighed. "The 'ouse is spotless. Always is. Besides, couldn't 'ave let you know I was comin'. Not where we've been."

"So where 'ave you been, then?" She waved at Billy, motioning him to sit before taking the kettle from the fire and filling the pot. Replacing the lid, she sat at the head of the table, watching them intently.

Raising his chin, a wicked look played on Billy's face. "The Dynasty."

His mother's eyes snapped to him, a mixture of disbelief and horror flashing over. "William Burton, if you're lyin' to your own mother…"

Reaching into his coat, Billy removed the picture cards and spread them on the table. Slowly she picked over them, holding them up to the fire. A quiet "Bloody Inferno…" hissed from between her lips.

She peered over the top of one from Paris. "What took you there? Work?"

Billy shrugged. "You could say that."

She placed the small pile of cards on the table and turned her attention to Cedo. "So, Master Reilly, what brings a nice lad like you to my house?"

Cedo smiled weakly and he looked the ample woman in the eye. With a mass of blonde hair piled on her head and a friendly face, he could see from whom Billy had inherited his looks. Despite her energy, her age was showing, flecks of gray hair streaking across her head and wrinkles around her eyes and mouth.

"I work for Erus Veetu," he began before looking to his hands. "Work is the wrong word, I believe."

Staring at the well-used table, he tried to find the words to describe what he was. How did their relationship look to the outside world? How would others take it? His heart still ached for his Master, a dull, throbbing ache that nothing could dash away.

Finally, he lifted his head. "Owned," he whispered. "Erus owns me like one would own a pet."

Cedo studied the woman before him, but the impartial look never fell from her face as she sipped from her cup. Tracing his finger around the rim of the dainty cup before him, Cedo stared into the depths of his tea.

"I thought Veetu was dead? Executed for killin' his own?" he heard her say.

Dread clenched his stomach, and he looked from Ma Burton to Billy and back again. No one knew that Erus was alive. No one knew that he had been sold into slavery by a government who wanted a war. Licking his lips, Cedo looked her straight in the eye.

"His death was faked. He is alive."

"Master Reilly, I don't like bein' lied to. It ain't nice. I saw the photo plates myself an' he looked like he was dyin' in that chamber." Laying her hands on the table, Ma Burton leaned forward and eyed him with suspicion.

"Ma," Billy interjected. "He's not lyin'. Cedo ain't got a bad bone in 'is body. Veetu's very much alive an' well."

Her hands unclenched and she appeared to relax, her attention returning to Cedo. "So 'ow did you wind up in the grips of somethin' like Veetu? That man is nothin' but trouble, an' I know all about that. Takin' our young'uns, healthy ones at that, an' doin' despicable things to 'em. He ain't human, far from it."

Cedo nodded. There were so many perceptions of the man he loved, all of them negative, yet he had no power to change them. Erus had created the image that people saw, and only he could change it.

Billy's Ma nudged his cup closer to him. "You haven't touched your tea, love. Better get to it before it gets cold."

They spent the day with Billy's mother, talking of Billy's sudden disappearance and their time in the Dynasty. She was more than welcoming despite Cedo's association with Erus. Billy's sisters returned from work, greeting their brother and introducing themselves to Cedo before they began the evening chores. The Burtons' house truly was a home, a place filled with love and acceptance.

As night fell, the kitchen was cleaned of pans and crockery. A lumpy straw mat and a thin, fraying blanket became a bed for Billy and himself. Lying before the fire, his lover's fingers peeled the shirt from Cedo's breast, lips finding his collarbone and gliding along it. Hands resting on the back of his lover's head, Cedo shuddered as Billy's wandering tongue made its way to his neck, finding the tiny spots which made him gasp. Teeth nipped and sucked just above the collarbone, no doubt leaving raging red marks. Not that he cared, or at least tried not to.

"Billy..."

Kisses danced along his breastbone and relaxed blue eyes looked into Cedo's. Trying to steady his breath, Cedo smiled and reached out to stroke his lover's tussled hair. It hung around Billy's face in soft, billowing waves, making him look like some celestial being. Lying still, they held one another's gazes, Cedo trying to read his mate's thoughts. Soft shadows thrown by the fire hung over them, the warmth washing over his skin. Despite their new home, Cedo felt far happier than in recent months. Their job was over and they could finally spend time enjoying each other.

"Thank you," he finally whispered.

"For what?" Another sea-breeze soft kiss was placed on Cedo's porcelain skin.

"For bringing me here. For loving me even if I have been horrendously stupid. You are my world and the key to my heart."

Still Billy smiled and kissed Cedo's chest once more. "You've got such a way with words. I love 'earin' you speak. An' the same goes for you. But you need to start talkin' more." His fingers tapped Cedo's chest. "I suspect there's much 'idden in 'ere that you want to talk about. It's what makes you do stupid things. What makes you flip your lid an' do other things. You did it when we were in the Dynasty an' I thought you were goin' to get yourself killed. I watch over you. That's what I'm 'ere for, an' I don't want to be the one to find your body 'cause you've done somethin' stupid. But that's only part of it." Billy lowered his head. "I don't want to lose you 'cause I love you. Love you with everythin' I've got. Never felt this way about anyone. Love you with every bone in my bein'." He shook his head. "I'm such a stupid fool."

"Why are you a fool?"

Billy's body shook as he chuckled. "'Cause I shouldn't be sayin' things like that. I'm supposed to be the strong, silent one."

Smiling, Cedo ran his fingers through Billy's hair, enjoying the moment. "There is no one to hear you, so you can say whatever you so please."

"I love you."

The kisses resumed, Billy inching the linen from Cedo's body as if he were unwrapping the finest jewels. Beneath the feather-soft lips, Cedo melted into the simple straw mat.

Above them, the clock struck midnight. But he did not hear it. Arching his back, he spread his legs and welcomed his lover home.

Bowls of thick porridge thudded to the table, the small kitchen suddenly feeling very cramped. The three sisters—Rosa, May, and Dawn—kept glancing at him with small smiles. Cedo wondered what they knew about Erus, Billy, and himself. Ma Burton had not so much as batted an eyelid when he had spoken of Erus and he suspected she would do much the same if he and Billy confessed to their relationship. She did not appear to be a malicious woman and her kindness was obviously mirrored in her children.

"Now, I'm not 'aving you goin' back to that Veetu." She placed a mug of tea before Cedo and he glanced up at her with a smile. "It'll be cramped but you can stay 'ere. We'll get by, we always do. I can't imagine what livin' with that man is like." Taking her place at the head of the table, Ma Burton curiously looked at them. "Are you goin' to tell me what took you to the Dynasty? Can't imagine theater work takes you there."

Silence fell over them, the scraping of bowls the only noise. Picking up a spoon, Cedo took several mouthfuls while he mulled over an answer. The silence grew heavier, pressing against his skull.

"At the very least I have to return," he finally replied, watching as one of Ma Burton's eyebrows arched upward. He could already feel the guilt of being overdue eating away at him. "And we went to find Erus. The Patron faked Erus' death; no one knows and he is still believed to be dead. The Patron had been offered money for Erus and he took it, selling him to a man named James. James has this burning desire to invade us, as he believes he is

43

being wronged by not being allowed trade links with us. Erus was designing his weapons. We brought him back and now James is on his way. But it seems that the Patron has denied Erus the business of creating our defenses."

"Bet it ain't stopped him."

Drinking from the earthen mug, Cedo shook his head. "It has not. He was working on plans when we left."

Leaning back in her chair, Ma Burton rubbed a finger beneath her nose. She looked around, quietly studying her four blond children. She appeared to be thinking, and Cedo wondered what was running through her mind. Her food went forgotten, and all of them watched the home's matriarch.

"You're a brave lad, I'll give you that," she said, eyes returning to him. "But I'm wondering; where's your own Ma in all of this? Why ain't she up in arms about you running around the world? 'Andsome young lad like yourself. You're in short supply in this city. Must be 'undreds of nice young ladies lining up to marry you." She waved a hand, as if dismissing the questions. "Ignore me. Ramblings of a mother. I'm just curious, that's all."

Cedo felt his heart wrench, an icy cold feeling of horror and sadness chilling it.

"I do not know where she is," he softly replied. "My father left us for another woman, and my mother disappeared a good few years ago, now."

Gazing at the table, he idly clicked the silver ring against the wood, memories playing painfully over in his mind. Reassuring fingers slid over his, another ringed thumb resting against his own, and he looked up to smile at Billy.

"I'm sorry, lad," Ma Burton's voice was quiet. "That seems to 'appen a lot. What was her name?"

"Isobel. Isobel Reilly. We took her maiden name after my father left."

Ma Burton rapped her fingers against the table, nails rattling like a train over tracks. Briefly it reminded him of Erus and his displays of impatience. However, Ma Burton seemed to use the tiny distraction for entirely different purposes.

"Let me put me ear to the ground. See what I can find out."

A flame flickered to life in his soul and his eyes shot up, staring at her as intently as the sun burned. She grinned.

"Trust me, Cedo, the newspapers ain't got nothin' on the grapevine 'round 'ere. If anyone knows anything about your Ma, it'll be someone round these parts that'll know it."

Unable to stop grinning, he whispered, "Thank you, ma'am."

She shook her head, her smile still in place. "A pleasure, me lad. Just remember to pass on the kindness when your time comes, okay?"

The breakfast dishes were cleared away, washed in a simple stone sink with water drawn from a pump in the street. Billy's sisters finished readying themselves for the day, huddled around a small mirror as they gossiped and set their hair before melting off to wherever they worked. Sitting at the table, Cedo gazed at the silver ring. How his life had changed. While he found the three young women attractive, he did not feel a connection to them. Not like the connection he felt to the man who was diligently stacking the clean crockery. It was a feeling he could not explain, one that resonated on many different levels. It was as if his soul had been sending out a beacon that only a handful of people could hear. And Billy had been the one to reply.

Resting his chin in his hand, Cedo watched Billy. His mate was right; there were so many things he was keeping hidden, things that were preventing him from being the person he was supposed to be. Only now did he realize that his past was contributing to who he was. It was dictating how he responded. It was causing him to flee at the first sign of danger and to cling to the people who showed him affection. The chair scraped against the flagstones as he stood.

"Billy, we need to return."

Returning crockery to the small sideboard, Billy straightened up and frowned. "Why bother? We're late anyway. May as well enjoy the freedom a little longer."

Cedo sighed and ran a hand through his hair. The dread was a cold weight around his neck, gripping the necklace and pulling. "You know he will hurt me more than he will hurt you?"

"Come on," Billy softly said. "We'll go for a walk by the sea. Get some air to your 'ead. 'Ow does that sound?"

Staring at the table, he nodded. "That sounds like a fine idea."

Billy's hand gently clapped his back. "We'll leave in a while."

The door to the rear of the house opened and Ma Burton returned, face flushed and an empty pail dangling from her hands.

"I've put the word out there," she said between deep breaths. "We'll see what comes back to us." She turned to Billy, her face curling into one of menace and anger. "Did I tell you your bloody father turned up the other night?"

Billy leaned against the table and shook his head. "What did 'e want?" His voice fell an octave. "'E didn't 'arm the girls, did 'e?"

The pail clattered into a corner and she swept up the drying clothes, tossing them over the back of a chair. She pulled out another chair and dropped her ample frame into it, her face dark.

"No, thankfully he didn't. He came in, blind drunk as

usual, an' rambled on that his life is a pile of horse dirt since I put him out. Told him he should have expected it for what he did to us. For putting his girls on the street to feed his filthy habits and for taking money from that bloody Veetu man for your life. You know we saw none of that?"

Across the table, Billy nodded, head hanging, hiding his eyes. His mother shook her head, face still red from anger.

"He took the lot and smoked and drank it away. Never gave us any. But he's gone and we're all the better for it."

Billy pushed himself away from the table and wrapped an arm around his mother's shoulder.

"So why did 'e turn up?"

His mother leaned into his touch, resting her head against his elbow. Silently Cedo watched them and wondered what it must be like to live in a family where their lives were constantly disrupted. At least his father had had the decency to leave them and never look back.

"Just to see what he's missin', I think." She chuckled and stood, shaking off her son's arm. "Why don't you two get out an' enjoy the sun. You both look like you've been livin' underground."

Cedo gave her a strained smile and Billy snickered. Taking his coat from the hook behind the door, Cedo wrapped it around himself before offering Billy his. Billy waved over his shoulder.

"See ya in a while, Ma. You get a bit of rest now that the 'ouse is empty."

Cedo heard her chuckle. "Chance'll be a fine thing."

A glorious spring sun hung in the sky, a gentle breeze keeping the city's sooty fog from hanging over the sea.

Wispy white clouds danced across the clear blue sky.

Cedo slipped off his socks and the tight, pinching shoes. Crafted from the finest black leather, they had been designed for being seen, not walking great distances. Now the leather had faded, dulled and scuffed by their trek across the Downs.

Baring one's flesh was not the done thing in public, but Cedo was beyond caring. The sun was warm and it was a long time since he had last felt so relaxed. Besides, society's rules, whether written or not, rarely applied in Svenfur. It was a city of the free spirited and he intended to let his spirits fly free once more.

Bathing machines, some drawn by horses and others by a simple chain-link sea railway, slid into the surf. Serious swimmers and day-trippers alike alighted into the breaking waves. They all looked so carefree, so happy and gay. He longed to join them, longed to feel the sea against his skin.

Beside him, Billy was stretched out on the shingle beach, eyes closed and savoring the sun, a serene smile on his lips.

"'S great out 'ere. Missed this."

Turning his face back to the sun, Cedo murmured in agreement. "It is a long time since we have last seen our city."

The breeze lifted his hair and he closed his eyes, a smile playing on his lips. Being back where he belonged filled him with happiness. Already his legs were aching to take a walk along the pier. He longed to return to his old haunting ground, to the place where he had spent so many hours. Longed to see if he could once more attract a crowd.

"What do you want to do after we've finished 'ere?"

He gazed back at Billy. "A walk along the pier would not go amiss."

Billy chuckled and twisted on the stones to look up at Cedo. "What I meant is, what do you want to do once the war's finished? The possibilities are endless."

Looking back to the sea, Cedo swept hair from his face. There really was no reason to stay in Svenfur. He was sure that his mother was no longer in the realm of the mortal. The sense that she was alive had long since melted to nothing, fading away like smoke from a fire.

"What about your family? What will become of them?"

Shingle crunched and Billy sat up. "They've survived worse. Besides, they're used to me comin' an' goin'. As long as I send 'em a note from time to time an' some money, they're 'appy. What about you? 'Ow do you feel about goin'?"

A fear, the polar opposite of the sun's warmth, rolled over him. How did he feel? Did he really want to dash away the final connections to the city he had been brought up in? And what of Erus? Would his Master wish to remain in the city or move on to pastures new? That was if any of them survived the war. Yet there were still things that tied him to the city, unseen hands which held him tight, refusing to loosen. It was as if there were a constant shadow standing at his shoulder, chiding him, daring him to step out of the city's boundaries. A chill stroked his spine and Cedo wrapped his arms around his knees, eyes forever focused on the sea.

"I should like to leave," he finally, and softly, replied. "There feels as if there is nothing left here for me. My stories are dead, and I suspect that my mother is too."

Billy's fingers touched his shoulder, warm against his cold skin. "'Old up. I thought you said she was alive?"

Waves rose and fell, crashing against the shore in white, squally crashes, foam biting at the shingle and dragging it away.

Billy drew him closer, fingers tightening around Cedo's shoulder. "You never answered my question."

Tilting his head, he gazed into eyes as blue as the sky above them, eyes which were tainted with worry.

"I do not believe her to be alive any longer."

"An' you want to give up lookin'?"

His heart dipped and he stared into Billy's eyes, wondering what he knew. "Okay, I shall not give up. Perhaps your mother really will unearth something."

Billy's face changed, lighting with a smile as his hand came to caress his face. Lulled by the fingers against his skin, Cedo closed his eyes and shifted against the touch.

"Course she'll unearth somethin'. Knows everythin', she does."

The pier was coming to life as they stepped onto its boards. Strings of colored lights swayed in the breeze, steam generators clattering away. They mingled with gaily dressed locals and tourists, weaving their way to the once familiar spot.

"You have never been here, have you?"

Billy shook his head, hair turned a rainbow of green, red, and blue by the lights.

"Not with you anyway. 'Eard about you from some of the others." A shadowy grin lit his face and Cedo felt his heart skip.

He stepped around a young couple with a baby carriage before rejoining his friend. Hands pushed into his pockets and picking a relaxed gait, Billy gave him a toothy grin.

"Oh aye, used to 'ear stories of this boy who told tales at the end of the pier. Said you mesmerized 'em. Got the shock of me life when you turned up at the theater.

'Skinny,' I said, 'with blond 'air. Looks like 'e fell out of the dressin' up box?' 'Aye,' they said, 'that's 'im.'"

A grin tugged at Cedo's lips and he stopped, pulling himself to sit on the railings. Joy and excitement warmed Cedo, coursing through his veins and making him dizzy. Billy moved toward him, hands resting at Cedo's hips to keep him from the hungry waves below. A dreamy glaze fell over his eyes, the grin falling to a small smile.

"First time I saw you, I knew I 'ad to 'ave you. Not just once, but forever." His voice had become gentle, almost stolen by the wind.

Taking a breath, Cedo released his grip on the railings and draped his arms around Billy's neck. The lights picked out his relaxed reflection in Billy's eyes and he leaned closer, pressing his nose to his lover's. In return, Billy pressed himself closer, arms tightly holding Cedo from a sea that would only too willingly claim him.

Cedo soaked up the atmosphere, the music, the voices, the smells, and the sounds to seep under his skin. Allowing it to whisk him to another world, he slid his mouth to Billy's, losing himself in the beauty of his lover.

The sun was beginning to inch toward the sea as they made their way through quickly darkening streets. Gaslights flickered to life. Now the lamplighters, freed of their long, flame-tipped poles, unlocked a small door and pressed the switch beyond it. Cedo wondered if they missed their nightly ritual of carrying the light the through the streets.

Fog trailed through the streets, winding around their ankles and deadening their view. The sounds of the city were dulled, trapping them in a world of their own.

An afternoon on the pier had been just what Cedo had

needed. They had walked the boards and straddled the railings beside his old haunt at the end of the pier. Seated on a bench, they had watched the world go by, soaking up the sounds, sights, and smells of something Cedo had feared he would forget. It had been the perfect tonic to all that had happened.

As they turned down an alley, a sound, much like that of masonry being chiseled, caught Cedo's attention. Holding up a hand, he stopped, heart pounding, and slowly turned.

At the mouth of the alley stood a single gaslight, two arms stretched from one of the poles. On one sat a small, hunched figure.

A chill wrapped around him, borne on the cold fog. Beneath its fingers, Cedo's skin crawled and he stepped closer, staring up at whatever sat beside the flickering lamp.

"Whenever did they start putting gargoyles on lampposts?" he asked.

"They 'aven't, as far as I know." Billy's voice echoed from the walls.

He could not take his eyes off it, studying the stony features in the glow of the flame. Tentacles of fog danced around it, hiding it before sliding away to reveal the creature. It was an evil-looking beast, no doubt designed to scare away more than the evil spirits of the Darker Quarter.

"So wherever did this one come from?"

"Look, Cedo, I don't know. Let's just go, okay? This place is givin' me the jitters."

It took several seconds for Cedo to drag his eyes away, but not before he noticed the creature's oddly glassy eyes.

They walked in relative silence, picking their way through the murky night. The pleasure of the day was being replaced with the fear of what was to come. Again he had defied his Master, had broken the rules laid down for him. Cedo knew that he would pay and he desperately tried to press the thought to the back of his mind. Fingers of cold touched Cedo's neck and he turned with a start. Each time there was nothing behind him. Each time his mind began to roam, debating what the mist of the night held. Creatures from the depths of the sea? Beings from other realms? Or the scorned figure of his Master?

Finally they stepped across the threshold of Billy's house, welcoming lamps flickering from the walls. His sisters were gathered around the table while his mother paced, a worried look on her face. As the door clicked shut, she spun around, her body seeming to sag with relief.

"Thank the gods you're both 'ome! Come in, sit down."

Drawing out a chair, Cedo sat, watching as she fetched cups and tea. The table was littered with the debris of a pieceworker: fabric, buttons, and spools of cotton piled in the center. An unfinished garment hung from a simple mannequin, one arm dangling as if it had been torn off. Something appeared to be bothering Ma Burton, her face lined with worry. Finally, after she had set the tea before them, she fumbled in the pockets of her apron and pulled out a crumpled sheet of paper.

"The both of you need to see this."

Taking it from her, Cedo smoothed it across the table, balking as his eyes traced the words. Gasping, Cedo regained his swimming vision and read the handbill.

CHAPTER 4

AN ANNOUNCEMENT FROM VEETU INDUSTRIES

Recently our honorable, and much prized, press officer has vanished without a trace. Cedo Reilly first came to the company in the summer of last year and his impeccable work is much missed. His height is approximately five feet and nine inches, and he has hazel eyes and long, blond hair.

A reward of 500 guilders is being offered for the safe return of Cedo Reilly.

Should you possess any information to the whereabouts of our beloved press officer, please visit the offices of Veetu Industries, 109 - 112 Lambeth Road.

Clutching the table, Cedo felt the sickness roll through him. Blood roared through his ears, a thundering silence deafening him. Across the table Billy and his mother stood, their mouths moving, concern on their faces. But he heard nothing.

Feeling weak, Cedo laid his head against the paper, his stomach churning and bile stinging his throat. He wanted to vomit, wanted to rid his system of the poison that was his Master. Now there was money resting on his shoulders. Money that someone in the poorest district of the city would kill to have.

"Cedo." A hand came to rest on his shoulder.

Drunkenly he looked over his shoulder, Billy fading in and out of his vision. Cedo shook his head. There were no thoughts. No ideas. Just a dull ache in his skull.

"They saw you come." Struggling to move, he looked to Ma Burton.

Her face was unusually serene, a complete change from the worry that had lined it only moments earlier. Her hands were in the pockets of her apron, her shoulders slightly hunched as she looked at them.

"They're nosy beggars around 'ere. They'll 'ave seen you come an' go all day, an' the second you step out that door every eye will be on you." She gazed toward the door. "Blasted wolves, all of 'em. They can smell you. An' I bet that each of them is marchin' straight to that office."

Lifting his head, Cedo looked between Billy and his mother, waiting for an answer. Quietly, he remarked, "We need to leave. Get back to the house."

At least if they turned up of their own accord the punishment may be lessened. Billy's hand tightened around his shoulder. Closing his eyes, Cedo savored the warm fingers that held him. Fingers that gently moved back and forth, reassuring him that no harm would come to them.

"Aye, we do. But first, we need to talk. Need to think of somethin' to tell him. Some reason we're late."

"Whatever we tell him, there will be pain. But if we go back now, and turn up without him having to come and fetch us, then hopefully it will not be so bad. What do you propose we tell him?"

Pulling up a chair, Billy sat beside him. "There's a number of things we could tell 'im. If you're that worried, I suggest we work it out while we're walkin'."

Cedo nodded and made to get to his feet. Beneath him,

his legs felt weak and leaden. Suddenly a heavy knock rattled the front door and his eyes snapped to it. He felt the blood drain from his face, his skin becoming clammy. Ma Burton held up a hand.

"You two get to the back door. If it's 'im, I'll wave an' you can make a run for it."

Feeling ill, Cedo pushed himself away from the table and to the door. Billy followed him. Along the hallway he heard the front door drawn open.

"Mrs. Burton, have you seen William recently?"

Erus.

Ma Burton snorted. "I ain't seen him since you took him. He's dead, why would I 'ave seen him?"

Taking a deep breath, Cedo quickly opened the door and stepped out into an alley. Lines were strung between the houses, rows of washing dangling from them. The rows of terraced houses looked exactly the same, all built from the same red bricks, all listing dangerously. Between the lines of clothes, he could make out a few airships idling through the skies and he wondered what had become of theirs. Did it still lie useless in the grounds? Or had some unseen hands made any trace of their existence vanish?

Behind him, Cedo heard the door close, and Billy stopped beside him. There was a strained smile on the blond man's face, his normally relaxed features showing the anxiety of what was upon them. Leaving the safety of the house, they quietly began to make their way along the passage, footsteps echoing from the walls of the buildings. Ahead of them, it opened onto a rectangle of gray light and freedom. Cedo felt his heart soar. They were on their way, making for a new life far from the city and the demons that lived within it.

A long black cowl splayed from the creature's shoulders as it stepped into the mouth of the alley. Its tall body was entirely encased in black leather. A black mask covered its mouth and nose, metal tubes bursting from the sides and to some unseen apparatus on its back. Dark glasses hid its eyes and a tall hat hid its hair.

It was a being of nightmares, a specter from the penny dreadfuls, and it turned Cedo to stone. All he could do was watch as it approached them, cornering them in the narrow street, its leather-clad fingers creaking as they flexed. Slowly it strode up to him, the golden tubes of its mask contracting as it drank in whatever it fed on.

Behind him a voice shouted, the sound quivering on the edge of the spell that held him. It was only when a hand landed on his shoulder that the dark magic snapped and he swung around to face Billy.

"Come on! We 'ave to go!" Billy gripped him, pulling him away from the deadly grasp of the being. "Now!"

The exit of the alley closed on them, open and inviting, a sliver of gray sunlight. His chest tightened and his breathing became labored, red flashes exploding behind his eyes. Only Billy's hand on his arm kept him going. Behind them, Cedo could hear the heavy march of the nightmare, each step bringing it a little closer. Cedo screamed as they sped from the alley and onto the open road. Swinging to the right, they pounded along the muddy street. Not one of the pedestrians gave them a second glance, merely stepping out of the path. He cared not for his clothes. Cared not for the material possessions he owned. All he cared for was getting Billy away from this life.

"Run!" he choked. "Do not stop!"

They ran through the grimy street, dirt thrown up in their wake.

It emerged as if melting from the brickwork, another creature encased and masked in black. Cedo had no time to divert, no time to stop or swing around. An outstretched hand caught him by the collar and tossed him to the ground. What was left of his breath was knocked from him as he slammed to the cobbles. Panic throttled and blinded him, descending into a veil of red. Somewhere, he heard his voice screaming, urging Billy to run. It was a cry that was silenced as he was hauled to his feet, a leather hand clamping across his mouth.

Hauled along the street, Cedo struggled and growled, unable to free himself. Terror knotted in his stomach, a cold rock of unmoving emotion. A black carriage with darkened windows drew alongside them, the driver hurriedly opening the door a second before Cedo was thrown through it.

Landing against the opposite door, he barely had time to draw breath before the being heaved itself in and slammed its fist into the roof. With a jerk, the carriage lunged forward.

The creature's head snapped to look at him, eyes hidden behind bug-like glasses. Cedo slunk along the floor and pressed himself to the opposite door. There was something about the creature that he could not place, something familiar.

Hands tore at the mask, pushing it down. The top hat was tossed to one side, red hair cascading around the being's shoulders.

Cedo should not have been shocked, yet it still came in rolling waves of revulsion. Erus dumped the breathing apparatus at his feet, the tubes of the mask coiling around it. His Master did not so much as acknowledge him. Instead, Erus laid his head against the window and silently watched as the city rolled by. Lying against the door, Cedo panted, desperately attempting to gather himself. Should he crawl to the seat and beg for forgiveness? Or remain where he was, submissive and silent?

Anger flowed from his Master, manifesting itself in tight shoulders and clenched jaw. His hands lay in his lap, curling into fists. Cedo knew his Master was holding himself together, but only just. Images of what was to come—pain, blood, terror—flashed through his mind and he whimpered in response. He did not want to return to that place, did not want to feel what was to come. No matter what he did or said, it was still coming and no one could stop it. He had wronged his Master and the time to pay was upon him. Would it change him? Would he remain faithful this time instead of turning tail whenever he felt wronged?

They traveled in silence, and Cedo buried his face in his hands, refusing to look at Erus. Instead he turned his thoughts to Billy. What had become of him? Had he escaped? With a leaden dread filling him, Cedo tried to turn his mind to the happier times they had spent together. From stolen kisses on the beach to gentle caresses before the fire, from touching words to understanding silence. His heart beat just a little faster at the thought of his lover.

And turned to stone at the sight of his Master.

Erus refused to acknowledge or even glance at him. Cedo knew he had wronged the flame-haired man and hurt him far more than he could imagine.

Lowering his head, he laid his forehead against his hands, trying to stem the hurt that wracked him. He was, he realized, adored far more than he could ever imagine. And he just tossed it away with little thought for the feelings of those around him. He truly was despicable.

The hansom drew up in front of the house, and Erus stepped from it without a word. Head lowered, Cedo silently followed, fear growing around him. He had a chance to turn and run but didn't take it. Everything that was coming, he deserved.

Leaving the breathing apparatus at the foot of the stairs, Erus swung to the right and into his study. Dropping into his chair, Erus rubbed his temples and stared at the desk. Standing before him, Cedo clasped his hands behind his back and silently whispered prayers to himself.

"You want to know what makes me tick, don't you?" Erus finally said. "It's why you keep running away, because the lack of knowledge makes you insecure. You believe me to be nothing but a cruel, heartless beast. You see yourself as the only one who can break the spell."

Cedo did not move, the terror stilling him. Eyes fixated on his Master, he watched and waited, the glorious moments of his mind playing over and over. The words he had heard Erus speak in the realms beyond their world remained with him, feeding him hope. Hope that Erus would look beyond the physical.

"You know the basics of my life: abandonment, pain, humiliation, death. It never changes, and that is all you need to know. What you do not know is that I was courted by every government on the planet. People higher than the governments, those the citizens do not need to know about, showered me with all that I needed. And, in return, they wanted one thing.

"Security.

"They wanted the knowledge that their country would be protected. I provided it. Veetu Industries provides military armory to all of the Great Eight.

"But it runs far deeper than mere protection. Far, far deeper, and much of it I am not at liberty to divulge. There are times when I pray that I will be able to tell you, but it is far more than my life is worth. The things I have seen and the people I have met make my blood run cold. What I was provoked to do by our own government is nothing compared to what the figures in the shadows have done.

"I'm sure you can understand that I need someone

who is strong to remain by my side. Someone who will not press me when I am unable to speak. Someone who will support me. Long ago I thought that person may have been you. Now, I am not so sure."

Steadfastly, Cedo held his Master's gaze, yet he still felt his heart drop.

Erus gazed at the floor, suddenly looking fragile.

"You said I treated you like a toy" he continued. "Perhaps I did. Or perhaps you decided not to delve beneath the exterior. I do not know, and perhaps I never will. You have been good to me, have seen me through some dark periods. But with the enormity of war upon us, I need someone of strength to remain by my side. That, or I need to be alone. I cannot run the supply chain if my mind is constantly turning to you. And hope I want you to be the strength I so desire."

Stepping around the desk, Cedo tentatively laid his head against Erus' and draped his arms around his Master's shoulders. Flame hair felt soft against his cheek, his Master's scent as enthralling as the first time they had met. Erus did not brush him away, did not even move. Just kept gazing at the floor. Eventually, he lifted a hand and ran it over Cedo's head before letting it slip to the small of his back.

"I can be that strength," Cedo softly whispered. "I am so sorry for bringing this upon you."

"I know you can, and I shall speak to the Council," Erus murmured.

Cedo felt his heart lurch. "Which Council is this?"

His Master never looked at him as he spoke. "The Council oversees relationships between Masters and their companions. I apologize now for whatever punishment they see fit to use."

Eventually Francis appeared and collected Cedo from the study. Neither of them spoke as they walked through the house. Sun streamed through windows and, somewhere in the house, clocks began to strike the hour. On the floor, lining the walkways, were stacks of paper, books and boxes. They seemed random and haphazard, the books well thumbed and the boxes overflowing with odds and ends. They did not end at the stairs, the first few steps stacked with piles of paper, all threatening to cause a small avalanche of printed material.

Francis led him to his room. Not the one he shared with Erus, but the one in which he had spent a single, blissful night with Billy. There were no traces of his friend. It was as if Billy had never existed, a mere ghost that flickered through his imagination.

Quietly, Francis dragged the tin bath into the room and filled it. Despite his return from disgrace, Erus was still showing him who ruled the house. There would be no comfortable bathing for him. Taking the initiative, Cedo stripped the ruined clothes from his form and gratefully sank into the welcoming water. His stench was foul, an acrid mix of fear and body odor. It was a relief to finally rinse it from his skin.

"Has there been any word of Billy?"

Pausing before the dresser, Francis looked to him. "I'm afraid not. I can only assume that he escaped."

"Oh." Turning his attention back to his ablutions, Cedo tried to push the thought from his mind.

He had told Billy to escape but had assumed he would return. If Billy truly had lost himself in the shadows of the city then Cedo needed to let him be. Somewhere, he was safe, hidden from hands that wanted to harm him. Yet the pangs of pain and loss were still there, a heart that ached to be beside his love for one more moment. To be there just long enough to tell Billy how much he was loved.

Whether he would see Billy again, Cedo did not know.

He certainly hoped he would, but with the agitated anticipation of war hanging over them, he suspected harsher times were upon them.

For it crept through the house, a silent killer waiting to pounce. It was there, curled in the corners and drifting down the stairs: an air of tension bringing unspoken promises of what was to come. Cedo did not know if the rest of the country knew what was coming. Did they know that soon machines would rise from the waters? Did they know that someone who hated them with unbridled passion was heading for their shores? Or, like Erus' miraculous return to life, was it being kept a secret, handed from mouth to mouth of the higher echelons?

"You need to hurry," Francis softly said. "The Council will be here soon, and I gather you don't want to keep them waiting."

CHAPTER 5

Dressed in his finest blue suit, Cedo sat beside Erus, nervously facing the men who sat across from them. The Council, Cedo discovered, was a group of men charged with overseeing the relationships between Masters and Mistresses and their companions. When a relationship was forged, a copy of the contract, along with weekly records, was sent to them. If, at any point, they feared for the safety of either party, then they would step in and take appropriate measures.

The five elderly gentlemen sat around the table of the hurriedly cleared dining room, dressed in expensive suits, pens resting on blocks of paper. Already Cedo could feel that his palms were slick with sweat, nervousness eating away at him.

The chief overseer of the Council lifted his eyes and looked at them. His face was stern, hands clasped on the table before him.

"Erus," he began, "you contacted us with regards to annulling the contract with your companion. You cited a number of reasons, all of which we agreed upon. Yet you now want to cancel this annulment. Pray, why have you altered your decision?"

Cedo had never seen his Master filled with such embarrassment. Erus had his hair pulled back into a thick braid, giving Cedo had a clear view of his face. The

Rae Gee

redhead's eyes flicked between his clasped hands and the men opposite. All his strength and poise, everything Cedo knew him for, had drained to nothing.

"I acted in haste and anger, traits for which I am sadly known. I now regret what I said, and I would like to offer my humblest apologies."

The man's dark eyes remained locked with Erus'. "Yet, in your letter to us, you said that these misdemeanors had gone on for many months and that you were having problems educating your companion to your ways. Why now have you changed your mind?"

Looking to his Master, Cedo felt guilt weigh him down. He had disobeyed Erus many, many times and deserved to be cast away. Yet Erus was willing to give him another chance.

Erus sighed and looked to his hands before lifting his head. "Because, as much as I hate to admit it, I was wrong. I believe I deliberately chose Cedo because of these traits within him. I wanted someone who was not going to agree with everything I said or did. I wanted someone to challenge me, someone who would hold my interest far longer than a more disciplined companion would give me."

The man did not respond, sitting statue-like as his fellow officers made notes.

The man's fingers tapped against the untouched paper. "If this is the case, then why did you register a companion?"

For a moment, Erus was silent, eyes focused on the small gathering. Cedo dared not move, focusing instead on what was happening. A knot of fear tangled in his stomach and he tightened his hands in his lap, nails digging into his palms.

"There are a number of reasons." Erus' voice was regaining its power, its deep, rich sound carrying around the room. "I wanted someone who would give in to the complete exchange of power, something which Cedo has performed fantastically. While he does question it, and me, he allows me to control every aspect of his life. Secondly, I wanted some protection, not just for myself but also for him." He leaned forward, resting his elbows on the table. "Gentlemen, I'm sure you can appreciate that there are many different types of companion relationships."

The man took a deep breath, the air rattling through his nose. Erus' words were a comfort and made Cedo's heart sing with joy. Beneath the table, Cedo wiped his hands against his trousers and slid his fingers over Erus' thigh. Only Erus' muscles responded, twitching before relaxing. The words that had been spoken meant much to Cedo, proved that Erus wanted him to remain.

"Because of the circumstances you listed," the man said, "we are required to punish your companion."

A chill descended over Cedo. Not just from the lack of use of his name but also the threat of punishment. One of the Council reached beneath the table and laid a large, long case before the overseer. Shivers began to take over Cedo, rippling over his skin, the dread growing. He felt sick, his vision swimming as the case was unlocked. Erus' hand came to rest on his arm and he flinched, hurriedly turning to Erus.

His Master leaned close. "Whatever happens, just keep your eyes on me. I shall be here for you."

The contents of the case were carefully laid on the table; two pairs of wide leather cuffs both joined by a bar, several lengths of chain and a slender cane. Cedo felt his throat contract as each piece was revealed. The overseer stared at him over the open case, ignoring the hands that emptied it.

"Companion, stand and remove your clothing." The overseer's voice held no emotion.

Shaking, Cedo stood and carefully undressed. Each item felt like a dead weight as it came away from his figure.

"Stand at the head of the table," the man ordered.

Flushing at his nudity, he did as he was bid. The four officers rose and collected the cuffs. Feeling himself weaken, Cedo struggled to remain standing as the cuffs were tightly locked around his wrists and ankles, his legs and arms spread wide.

A cloth was spread over the immaculate table and the chains were attached, first to the leg bar and then to the arms. An officer stood to either side of him, each holding a length of chain. Finally a thick, rubber bit was forced between his teeth, making him cough and choke as the straps were buckled behind his head.

The overseer stood, his face still and stony. He held out a hand and the cane was delicately laid across his palm. Fear struck Cedo, his body shaking. He whined around the bit, his teeth sinking into it. Everything was so cold, so impersonal.

"Companion," the man began, "you have been accused of defying your Master. The Council finds you guilty on the following charges: insubordination, abandonment, neglect, and disobedience of orders. Each charge carries a sentence of five lashes. Your signature on your contract gives your consent for this to happen."

Cedo felt his knees give way, the men catching him before he could fall. Slowly they inched him to the table, his feet barely shuffling against the floor. The chains were pulled taut across the table, his torso stretched over it, leaving him scared and exposed. Shivering, he laid his head against the fabric, eyes on Erus.

His Master looked worried, face lined. He stood and leaned across the table to run a hand through Cedo's hair. That single movement sent a spark of warmth through him, a tender breath of comfort. Erus leaned closer, laying his head before Cedo. In the green eyes, Cedo could see his reflection, could see the panic and fear that worried his face and the bit that so cruelly pulled his mouth apart.

"I'm sorry." Erus continued his caresses. "I'm sorry for failing you."

Cedo wished he could smile, wished he could break his arms free and return the gentle touches. Wished he could refute Erus' words.

"Erus, step away." It was the overseer, now out of his view. Knowing what was coming, Cedo tensed, his body shaking with the strain and the pain of his position.

His Master stepped away, standing in his line of sight, hands resting on the back of a chair. Worry still defiled his face.

The first strike cut into Cedo's thighs like fire. He howled around the gag before his jaw clenched tight. The chains pulled tight, holding him still, anticipating what was to come.

There was a pause before the second one struck, striking his buttocks and sending another jolt of searing pain through him. Beneath the lashes, Cedo shook, hands and jaw clenched shut, face hot as he tried to withhold the cries and sobs of pain. Already his eyes were stinging and he desperately blinked away the tears.

Over and again the cane snapped against his skin, each lash leaving a line of raw pain. Each lash sent his body into spasms, jerking against the table, the chains rattling as he was held tight. There was no relief, his body aching from the pummeling. The taut, bent position did little to help, his body slamming into the unforgiving table with each strike. Unlike Erus's beatings, the Council took their time, drawing it out and letting the agony simmer before adding another layer of pain. They wanted to see him cry, wanted to see him buckle and break. But he would stay strong, would keep the tears at bay and not allow them the pleasure of breaking him. If anyone would have the pleasure of such a chore then it would be Erus, not the cold and clinical ruling Council members.

It was Francis who collected Cedo from the dining room. It was Francis who tended to his wounds, bathing and dressing them before dressing him in a nightshirt. It was Francis who sat beside Cedo as he lay on the bed, aching and sore.

His skin was broken, flayed away from his buttocks, leaving exposed and bloody wounds. He had howled as Francis had bathed them, carefully applying soothing ointment before covering them.

Through the window he could see the sky beginning to change, shadows lengthening as night made her slow descent on the world. Cedo wondered if, somewhere in the city, Billy was also watching the sky. He pondered the likelihood of himself being in the blond man's thoughts. Most likely not. Billy was a free spirit, born to live on the edge of society, coming and going as he pleased. He was not designed for a life of servitude and consortship. He was in a better place, wherever he was.

Other thoughts flitted through his mind: his mother, Misty's whereabouts, the coming conflict and a small, yet pressing, hunger.

"He'll want to see you in a while." Francis moved to sit beside Cedo's head, one hand resting on the pillow.

"Has he said anything?"

Francis frowned. "About what?"

His body ached as he lay on his side, pain causing muscles to contract. "About anything."

Lifting his head, Francis stared at the far wall and

sighed. "He has worked tirelessly and, from what I can gather, has spent time at the factories. Your disappearance sent him into quite a panic, one which he covered by locking himself away."

Guilt stung through Cedo. Had his abandonment triggered the waterfall of words? Had it caused the about-face with the Council and the apology? As Erus had said, he had refused to scratch the exterior, instead choosing to give up when the road became too hard. The time to stand strong was upon him. The time for him to complete his transformation was now. He would rise against the machines and stand beside his Master. He could not fail him again.

"What in—"

Lifting his head, Cedo stared past Francis and to the window. There on the ledge, staring in at them, was a creature he had first encountered in the Dynasty's forests. Clothed in the shadows of the night, its huge, luminous oval eyes watched them.

Fear snapped along his spine, and Cedo found that, just as in the forests, he was paralyzed. Unable to move, he just stared at it, unable to fathom what was before his eyes.

There was the sound of wood moving and the sash window began to lift. Without a care for the pain he was already enduring, Cedo flung himself from the bed and slammed the window shut. Beyond the glass, the eerily lit eyes narrowed and, beneath his fingers, the wood shuddered as it tried to move. Panic held him there, his fingers digging into the window frame as he struggled to hold it shut. Whatever was beyond the glass was far stronger than he had anticipated.

Behind him there was the sound of someone scrabbling around yet he dared not look. Suddenly Francis appeared beside him, a poker brandished in his hands. The being's eyes snapped wide as Cedo threw the window open and the iron rod was thrust into its shadowy torso. The creature made no sound as it fell. The only noise was that of its body hitting the shrubbery below.

Slamming the window shut, Cedo wrestled the heavy curtain closed and sank to the floor.

"What the blazes was that?"

Shaking his head, Cedo stared at the carpet. He should have been wracked with the pain of his earlier beating, yet after facing that nightmare, it had faded to nothing. He should have seen the fibers of the floor. Instead, all he saw was the forests, the darkness, and the strange beings that had infested them.

"It came from the forests of the Dynasty," he murmured. "I saw one in the trees, clinging to the branches and just... watching us. Perhaps it is the same one."

The memories, harsh and jarring, continued to come. Their arrest, the rape, the haunted forests, the strange flying crafts. They sickened him, chilling him with fear and sending acid burning his guts. Cedo wanted to vomit but his body refused to respond, staying motionless beside the wall.

"Unfortunately, I cannot answer your questions. Following my incarceration, I know little of what James created. What I do know is that he's vicious. Cruel and unforgiving. Some of the things he has created are beyond comprehension, and I only hope Mr. Veetu is ready to counteract them."

The cycle refused to break, the images repeating themselves. Cedo felt cold, as if an ice wind were howling through the room. He wanted to speak but the words were no more, locked away somewhere inside his mind. He wanted to tell of all he had seen, all he had felt. Yet it felt as if the memories were locked away, inaccessible to anyone but himself, never to be spoken of again.

It was a hand shaking him that snapped him from the nightmare hallucinations. Francis knelt before him, face impassive.

"It's time," he softly said. "Mr. Veetu requires your presence."

Struggling to his feet, Cedo made for the door, his body still crying with the pain of the beating. The chill remained with him, turning him cool and clammy as he made for his Master's room. A single gas lamp lit the hallway, throwing long, suspicious shadows before his feet. The house seemed to be in hibernation, awaiting the moment when it would be called back into service. Waiting to be filled with life, life that could be given and taken at a whim. Pulling the thin shirt to his frame, Cedo knocked and waited.

He knew what lay beyond the door, and a mixture of excitement and guilt coursed through him. It had been many moons since he had last felt his Master's touch and Cedo craved the feeling of the strong fingers against his skin. Despite his downfall, Erus still possessed an air of power and strength. His posture spoke of a man who knew the intricacies of the universe.

However, his Master had gifted Cedo with another to whom he was loyal. Even though Billy had disappeared into the clutches of the city, he was still very much a part of Cedo's thoughts. Until he heard otherwise, Cedo assumed they were still betrothed to one another until death took them on their next journey.

"Come!"

Stepping into the room, Cedo quietly closed the door behind himself. The room was bathed in the soft light of candles, their warmth negating the need for a fire. The drapes had been tied back from the bed, and his Master sat at the foot of it, head lowered and hands clasped in his lap. He still looked forlorn.

Cedo looked at him, studying the hunched form swathed in a white nightshirt that appeared several sizes too large. Stepping toward the bed, he knelt before his Master and clasped his hands around Erus'.

Finally, he whispered, "I am sorry."

"Whatever for?" Erus asked.

"For being such a terrible companion. For constantly disobeying you and never thinking of your comfort. For not listening to the still, small voice inside of you. For everything."

Silence fell over them and neither moved, their eyes on their clasped hands.

"Your apology means a great deal to me, Cedo. But you know that I chose you for your passion and your voice. I chose you to become the voice of this great nation in its darkest hour. And that is what's bothering me. Sit."

Getting up, Cedo sat beside his Master, trying to ignore the flash of red pain that flared through him. Cedo studied Erus, trying to read his innermost thoughts.

"The time is upon us, Cedo. A time for great strength and courage. Yet still I worry."

"Worry about what, Master?"

"About whether we are ready to face our enemy, to stare into their souls and know that they want all that we hold dear."

"Are we not prepared?"

Erus shrugged, the nightshirt sliding to reveal one pale shoulder. "I do not know. I have to yet to really delve into the intricacies of it all. The Patron, and also, I believe, the Prime Minister, are debating what excuse to give for my sudden, and strange, reappearance. It cannot be contained forever, especially as the control quarters for some of the defenses are beneath this house."

Cedo shivered, the memories of the silent rooms returning. Soon those rooms would become active, filled with the country's military secrets.

"Do you fear it?" Cedo softly pressed.

"The war upon our shores or the possibility that I may throttle the life from the General of the Air Division? No, I fear neither. Nor do I fear the added responsibility which this brings."

"Do you fear anything?"

Erus fell silent before slowly lifting his head. His green eyes, as cold and as hard as emeralds, pierced Cedo's soul. "That we shall fail. That is all that I fear."

Cedo stared at his Master's face and all the knowledge that it held. He knew things that Cedo did not want to know. He had seen things that would flummox the most skilled of writers.

Getting to his feet, Cedo pushed the thoughts to the back of his mind. Night was upon them, and he refused to sleep alone. Billy was gone, lost somewhere in the depths of the city. The pain of the loss still rang through Cedo's soul. Stroking his fingers along Erus' jaw, he tilted the weary eyes to his own. His Master gave no resistance as Cedo leaned in to taste his long-awaited kiss. Instead, they hung there, angels in the night, lips barely touching. With his heart hammering, Cedo stepped forward and gently pressed his Master to the bed.

Erus did not struggle. Instead, he allowed Cedo to hover over him, lips and fingers gently exploring his body. Cedo slid his hands along his Master's back, drawing the nightshirt up. Pulling back, Cedo allowed his Master to draw it over his head. The fingers swept along his spine, drawing him back to their embrace.

"I have missed this," Erus murmured. "Have missed all that you do. You may not be able to fathom it, but it is true."

Goaded by his Master's words, Cedo pressed his lips to Erus' shoulder, feeling a long-forgotten passion begin to rise. It took over him, rolling across his skin and making him squirm beneath its teasing touches. Memories of the donjon melted away, the hurt fading into the air. Erus' hands clasped the back of his head, holding him close, his Master's soft breath touching his cheek.

"Allow me." Carefully Erus moved him to the bed, positioning him as if he were the most delicate of objects. Pillows were placed around him, supporting his beaten and aching body. "Do not move."

Cedo's Master stepped away and returned a moment later, long strips of silk wound through his fingers. Barely daring to breathe, Cedo closed his eyes. His body was gently positioned, wrists tied above his head, legs tugged apart and ankles secured to the bedposts. The smooth fabric whispered over his skin, leaving goose-pimples in its wake. Finally a piece was draped over his eyes and Erus' lips touched his ear.

"Relax. Do not think of what tomorrow brings. Just live for this moment."

Erus' lips and fingers stroked Cedo's skin, making him shudder and moan. They slid from his throat and to his chest, his Master's tongue deftly working his nipples to hardness. To feel and not see brought new sensations, the tiny touches far stronger, far more sensuous. Cedo's cock was hard against his belly while his attention drifted to the tingling trails left by wandering lips.

Erus kissed his stomach, his tongue sliding to Cedo's groin. Groaning, Cedo bucked his hips, the bonds frustrating and exciting him in equal measures. His pleasure was in the hands of another, something he had not felt for many months. The burning ache of his caning faded away, leaving behind the bliss which Erus saw fit to lay upon him.

Beside him, the bed moved, Erus' hands and lips leaving his skin. Erus drew a fingernail along the sensitive curve of his foot, causing Cedo to flinch and moan.

From somewhere in the room, Erus chuckled. "Give me a moment and I shall give you the world."

It was a phrase Cedo had often heard his Master use. It was a phrase that seemed to have no meaning to it until he dug into the depths of his soul and mind. It was only then that he realized how much Erus had given him. How much he had been through to keep Cedo at his side. How often he had returned the wayward storyteller to his life and home.

The bed undulated and tendrils of smooth fabric wrapped around his cock, sending bolts of pleasure through him. The feeling grew, prickling his skin as the material tightened and teased. Arching from the bed, he cried to his Master, begged for release.

As quickly as it had appeared, the material whispered away, leaving him naked and cold. With it, the pleasure also ebbed away, becoming a slow burning fire in his belly.

"Patience, dear boy. Patience. You shall get what you desire but you need to wait."

Breathing heavily, Cedo groaned and tugged at the bonds, his vision blinded by the veil of red silk. His body screamed and smarted, the ebb rising and falling with every tiny touch. It flowed over his body like water, tantalizing every inch of his flesh, pushing him closer to that delightful moment before fading away like a dying star.

With it came his Master's lips, soft, caressing kisses and a hand cupping his jaw. In his mind's eye, Cedo could see Erus, could see the carefully constructed persona crumbling before the promise of a blissful existence. He could feel himself drowning in Erus' heady scent, a rich mixture of jasmine, chalk dust, and masculinity. It surrounded him and tugged him close, pulling him into the world of his Master.

Silk-draped fingers returned to his cock, slowly stroking.

"Please?" he whispered.

Erus paused before his hand slipped away. Then there was nothing. No lips, no touches. Eventually even the reassuring weight slipped from the bed, a wisp of a memory fading into the night. Howling with indignation, Cedo fought the bonds only for them to slide and tighten and hold him firmly in place. Even the sounds of his Master had faded to nothing.

"Master?"

Nothing.

Sighing, Cedo tried to relax, left only with his thoughts and the aching arousal. Images of how it would end meandered through his mind.

Time appeared to stand still. Cedo's thoughts remained, thoughts of furious rutting and passionate words. The pain slowly eased to delicious pleasure, the pleasure of anticipation and the promise of what was to come.

Something, the barest of touches against his toes, broke the spell, and Cedo heard himself call to Erus. The weight returned beside him, the smooth fabric once more kissing his shivering flesh. Emotions flared, raging through his blood like midsummer sun. Coiling through his blood and singeing his flesh, it called to him to reach that blessed moment of union.

Cedo writhed and howled and begged, yet the sultry touches came and went. He did not know how long it lasted before warm breath touched his cheek, and a deep, familiar voice asked, "Ready?"

Nodding, Cedo felt a welcome weight settle against his legs and the veil of red was lifted from his eyes. Erus' face was flushed, eyes wide, the depths of his soul on show. It would only ever be Cedo who saw what lay behind the great walls.

Brushing strands of hair from Cedo's face, Erus placed a gentle kiss on his lips and carefully eased himself into his lover. Gasping, Cedo closed his eyes as the blessed pleasure reached a peak. How many nights had he dreamed of this moment? How many guilty minutes had he spent lusting after his Master while Billy lay beside him?

Hands glided along his flanks, over his stomach and chest and to his face, holding him still as they began to gently rock. Desperately he wanted to return the touches, wanted to let his own hands drift over Erus' skin, wanted to feel his Master's taut flesh and pull those delicious lips to his own.

Instead he moved with his Master, pleasure blurring his senses. For so long he had been held captive in the bed, eased to the point of release before it had faded away. Over and over, for what felt like days. Now he was held in the arms of his first love, the one who had stolen him from the sea and placed stars in his eyes. The one he had chased across borders and mountains to bring safely home.

Bucking his hips, Cedo encouraged Erus to finish the blissful night, to sway faster and carry them both away on a heady cloud. Hands slid beneath his shoulders, pulling him close as Erus buried his face in Cedo's shoulder, lips pressing kisses to Cedo's throat, voice whispering words of adoration. Never had he known his Master to love him in quite such a sensual way and Cedo hoped it would be the beginning of something great.

The feelings grew and enveloped him. Beneath gentle fingers, he writhed and softly moaned. The night Cedo had spent so long dreaming about was rapidly coming to an end, but he did not care. There would be many more in its wake, many more nights to fall into the arms of his Master.

Sliding over his stomach, Erus wrapped a hand around Cedo's cock. A howl ripped from the storyteller's lips and he cried to his Master.

Erus' lips remained at his ear, teeth tugging at his lobe. "Come, Cedo."

With a whimper, Cedo came, his hot seed splattered over his stomach. The orgasm pounded through him, far more powerful than any he had experienced before. The blood roared through his head, deafening him. Through the haze of bliss, he heard Erus call his name, felt his thrusts become deeper and quicker until he spent himself deep inside of Cedo. The heat of sex clung to them like early morning mist, the musky scent heavy in the air.

Finally, Erus slid from him and to the bed. The bonds disappeared, whispering away before the sheets were pulled around them. Lying beside him, Erus brushed stray strands of hair from Cedo's face. A smile played on his Master's lips.

"I have thought about this moment often," Erus said softly. "Whenever it fell quiet in the Dynasty I would think of you and me."

Gazing into his Master's eyes, Cedo felt at a loss for words. It was strange to hear Erus speak in such tones, to hear him praise the boy from the streets.

"What else did you think of?"

Brushing a handful of fire-orange hair over his shoulder, Erus gazed at the ceiling, at the branches that swirled above them. "Many things. You, I, Billy. Whether the country was safe. Whether I should remain with James. How I felt for him, whether I loved or hated him. How I could keep us safe. How we would fight them once they arrived. Those and many other things went through my head every single moment I was down there. Mostly I hoped I would survive long enough to find out whether Francis' message had reached you."

Stroking his Master's face, Cedo smiled before his heart fell. "I must go and look for Billy tomorrow."

Erus nodded, and Cedo realized that his Master's carefully constructed barriers had not returned. Yet, at the mere mention of his plans to look for Billy, they begin to rise, Erus once more falling behind them.

Erus snapped his fingers, the lights dying at the sound.

"Sleep," he murmured, "and we shall solve everything in the morning."

CHAPTER 6

True to his words in the donjon, when Cedo awoke, he found Erus sleeping beside him. With the weight of the coming months hanging over them, they had risen, bathed and dressed, leaving the bed a rumpled mess to be dealt with later. His body still bore the pain of the previous day, and Erus was only too happy to redress the wounds, a needle sliding beneath his skin to deliver relief through his veins. He had argued against the life-lengthening serum, but Cedo gratefully received the clear anesthetic. The house was still silent, devoid of the life it once contained. Still there was no word of the staff, whether they were alive or dead.

Curled in a corner of the dining room, Cedo read while Erus worked. Misty, now curled on his lap, had walked in, sat at Erus' feet and mewled. Looking at her like she was a creature from another planet, Erus had given her the barest of scratches before returning to his work.

Papers were scattered across the table and whispered curses occasionally punctuated the air. The blackboards were filled with markings and equations, strange scrawls which Cedo could not even comprehend. From across the hall there came the metallic thunk heralding the arrival of a pneumatic message.

"Cedo." Resting a finger on the page, he glanced up to see Erus flick a hand toward the door. "Will you fetch that, please?"

It was that moment, that single wordthat made Cedo feel as if the world was changing. Teetering on its axis, threatening to swing one way or the other. A single word was all that held it in the balance. Placing the book to one side and easing Misty from his lap, he walked to the study. Like the dining room, it was a hovel filled with papers, the once bare bookshelves piled with whatever dregs of knowledge Erus could salvage. Flipping open the postal service's lid, Cedo retrieved the tube, Erus' address neatly placed in the little window.

He returned to his Master's side, and Erus plucked the tube from his fingers before unscrewing the lid. Erus unfurled the message and silently read over it. Forehead furrowing, he tapped a finger against his teeth and held the message out to Cedo.

Coming war has been confirmed, it began. *King requests your presence to chair meeting of the War Cabinet. Need to discuss tactics and armaments. Will return all documents to you and spin story to your survival. Airship will collect you at 0900 hours, 7th July.*

Jules.

Two days, that was all they had. Two days to put everything in order and secure the country. Cedo's heart turned to stone and he dropped the note to the paper-strewn table.

"Billy..."

Erus sighed and Cedo looked to his Master. The flame-haired man had a slide-rule in his hands and strands of hair clung to his forehead.

"You have twenty-four hours to find him. After that time, you must return home, whether you have him or not, and trust that he will return of his own accord."

Cedo walked Witheybrooke's High Street, his pockets laden with guilders. At the top, under the arches of the coaching inn, stood the hansom cabs, ready for hire. It was the first time he had ever truly seen the village. The High Street was lined with shops, several public houses, the coaching inn, the post office and a small branch of the Great Kingdom bank. Through narrow alleyways he spotted streets of houses and clusters of trees.

The hansom horses were resting, heads lowered. A cab driver stared down at him, the brim of his wide hat shielding his face from the sun.

"Svenfur, please," Cedo said. "Cockler's Walk."

The driver nodded and leaned down to open the door. With his stomach in knots, Cedo climbed into the cab. Cockler's Walk seemed the obvious place to start. Whether Billy would be there was another question.

The hansom cab halted at the mouth of Cockler's Walk. Paying the driver, Cedo looked along the narrow row of houses. Women scrubbed their doorsteps, gossiping as they preened their small patch of the kingdom. Water was pouring from a hand pump on the corner, barefooted children paddling in the overflow. The warmth of the sun had given rise to the fetid stench of poverty, of filthy water and an area with little access to the sewage system.

Spying Ma Burton kneeling before her door, Cedo approached and crouched beside her. She flinched and placed a hand over her heart, as if she sensed his presence.

"You'll be sendin' me back to the demon weed, you will." A smile spread over her round face. "It's good to see you, Cedo. Miss you after your run-in with Veetu."

Steadying himself against the wall, Cedo smiled, the woman's warmth spreading through him.

"If you're lookin' for our William, your best bet is The King's Feathers on Christchurch Road. He's been doin' a bit of buildin' work there, gettin' some money together to pay his fare back to you."

This confirmation that Billy had not forgotten about him warmed Cedo. She smiled and dropped the scrubbing brush back into the pail. Sitting on the step, she patted the bare stone beside her. Seating himself, Cedo listened as she spoke.

"Smitten he is. Absolutely smitten. I'm so happy he's happy. Really, I am. He deserves to be with someone who loves him just as much. I do worry, though."

"Worry about what exactly?"

Ma Burton stared off into the distance, a faraway look on her face. "Him. You. I worry for the both of you, livin' beneath the roof of that Veetu fiend. He ain't good for either of ya."

His own eyes drifted away, following the shadows of airships that danced along the street. There was no response for Ma Burton's words, and if there was, he did not want to hurt the feelings of the affable woman.

"We look after one another," he finally replied softly.

"Aye, I'm sure you do, but it doesn't stop an old woman from worryin'."

Cedo chuckled. "You are not old."

Ma Burton laughed and patted his knee. "You certainly know how to charm 'em, Cedo. Now come an' have somethin' to fill that belly of yours before you start huntin'."

The King's Feathers was not the most regal of places. In Cedo's eyes it needed demolishing rather than repairing. Yet in the ghetto area of Sea View, it obviously served its purpose as a watering hole for the down and outs, for those with nowhere else to go.

Stepping into the fetid, smoky public house, he ignored the wandering eyes and walked to the bar. It was an establishment that appeared to serve just two kinds of drink: gut-rotting whiskey and cheap beer. He supposed there was nothing more that the inhabitants of such a place needed.

A metal monkey sat on the bar, gangly limbs folded into its lap. Beady glass eyes focused on Cedo, and the automaton creature gave a metallic hiss. Cedo just smiled and leaned against the bar. There appeared to be no one taking charge. A pile of dirty glasses was stacked beside a bowl of greasy water. At the opposite end of the bar lay a pile of coins, a sign, to Cedo at least, that anyone who stepped into the rancid building could just help themselves.

Leaning an elbow on the beer-slicked bar, he surveyed the faces of the patrons, who stared back at him. "Who is in charge here?"

There was a snort from the crowd and a burly man, one eye crudely sewn shut and tattoos on his forearms, rose to his feet. The man swayed, a three-fingered hand clutching an empty glass as if it were the one thing that would save his life. Whereas Cedo would have normally balked at such a sight, now he just surveyed the man with a quiet contempt. Life was changing, the balance was shifting and soon, if Erus was to be believed, he would be the voice of a nation at war.

"Where you from, toff?" The man sneered, his roughly stitched face contorting into something even uglier.

Fixing his eyes on the man's single one, he sighed. "None of your business. I am—"

"I asked you a question."

Pursing his lips, Cedo stared at the man. A slow boiling

rage throbbed through his veins. Staring the man straight in the eye, he said, "Why are you so interested in where I am from? Envious?"

There was a roar of laughter from the assembled crowd of misfits, and the man glared at him. He took a step toward Cedo, swaying between the tables, mouth moving with silent curses. Keeping his back to the bar, Cedo inched back toward the door, eyes never straying from the anger filled face of the man.

"You shouldn't be 'ere, toff. We don't like your kind here."

Chuckling, Cedo slid his fingers against something. Glancing over his shoulder, he wrapped his fingers around the neck of a bottle.

"That is okay, because no one likes you either."

There was another guffaw of laughter from the bar. The man looked over his shoulder and shouted something unintelligible. Swiping the bottle from the bar, Cedo sidestepped the man and brought the heavy glass down against his skull. Fragments of glass spun through the air, some remaining embedded in the man's skin. The burly being slumped against the bar, blood streaming from his bald head. But there was no time to think, no time to worry about him. The bar's patrons were all on their feet, the smell of a fight ripe in their nostrils. They came at him like a pack of rabid wolves. Leaping onto a table, he sent glasses flying as he made for the door, springing from table to chair to table to floor. Behind him, voices bayed for his blood, calling for the head of the man who had wounded one of their own.

Fleeing into the narrow streets, Cedo ran. He did not look back, not until the drunken screams had faded into the everyday sounds of the city. Leaning against a wall, he drew in deep breaths, his lungs aching with a fiery pain. Pulling out the pocket watch Erus had given him, Cedo flipped open the ornate lid and checked the time.

4:15pm.

With nightfall still several hours away, he dared a second glance at the pub. From the exterior there were no signs of work and there was not a cat's chance in Inferno that he was going to step back inside. So hiding in the lengthening shadows of an abattoir, he waited.

People came and went. None were Billy and as dusk fell, so did his hopes. His mate had obviously finished and moved on, picking up a few more guilders' worth of work elsewhere.

Moving from the arches of the slaughterhouse, Cedo walked away, glancing over his shoulder as he did. There, perched atop a gas lamp, was one of the strange gargoyles, its eyes fixed on him as if it were watching. With a shiver scraping his spine, he made his way back to Ma Burton's.

Sitting at the table in the small kitchen, he watched Billy's mother bustle around. Eventually she placed a mug of tea and a bowl of thick, rich smelling stew before him.

"I ain't got the foggiest where he's at, then." Ma Burton huffed around the kitchen, tending to her daughters before seating herself at the head of the table. "Damn wayward son. I'll have him if he leaves you here high an' dry."

Managing a small smile, Cedo picked up his spoon and looked to the clock above the fire.

7.59pm.

At Ma Burton's insistence, he had gone to the theaters, asking if his lover was working for them. All had replied negatively and, worn down by exhaustion and heartache, Cedo had found himself back at the door of 59 Cockler's Walk. Still, sixteen hours remained and during any one of those, Billy could step through the door.

Yet Cedo did not want to get his hopes up. Did not want to feel the cold hand of rejection if his lover did not return. He could not fathom where Billy had disappeared to. Whether he had taken on a late night job, or had made a few new friends, Cedo did not know. He was not going to begrudge Billy friends. If Billy had not been there during the beginnings of his relationship with Erus, Cedo knew he would have given up and faded away. Billy had taken him and built him up when he most needed it.

Dipping into his meal, Cedo mulled over the coming days. He had never been to London, yet had heard much about it. Like Svenfur, it was a city of dreams. A place where the lost were found and the found lost themselves among the gin houses, theaters, and murky streets. It was a place of excitement, and a place of darkness and clandestine meetings.

"He better turn up tonight." The thoughts shattered and he looked at Ma Burton. She had a stern look on her face, a Sea View woman with whom none wanted to mess. "If he don't, there'll be trouble."

"What kind of trouble?" he dared to ask.

"The kind where I give him a good clip 'round the ear for lettin' his dinner go cold an' keepin' his gentleman waitin'."

Chuckling, Cedo allowed himself to relax. He had not realized how tired he was, how weary his body felt.

"I've been looking for that information you asked for. On your Ma."

At the mention of his mother, Cedo sat upright, the exhaustion fading to nothing.

"And?"

Ma Burton shrugged. "Nothin' as of yet. But there might be a couple of people who can help. Goin' to see if they'll go diggin' through the archives at town hall for me. See if they can find anythin'. Best place to look."

She smiled and nodded toward his meal. "Better eat that before it gets cold. Unlike my wayward son."

Lying on the thin straw mattress, Cedo watched the hands of the pocket watch in the dying light of the fire. Minutes passed, lost forever to the sands of time. Still there was nothing except for the sounds of a street waiting for the dawning of a new day.

Cedo's final moments with Erus before his departure played over in his mind. Something had changed within his Master, tiny flakes of his normally cold exterior chipping away forever. Erus had not referred to Billy as Cedo's toy and, while there had been no warmth in his voice, there appeared to be an understanding that Billy was important to Cedo.

There was also no denying his own love for Erus and this time, rather than run, he would return and stand by his Master through all that was to come. No longer would he desert Erus at the first sign of trouble. No, this time he would stand tall, have courage, and remain by Erus' side through it all. He did not approve of the war, but he understood why it would have to be fought. They had done all they could to prevent it and failed. Sometimes there was no stopping the determined.

Another sweep of the second hand. Another moment lost. Another step closer to what was to come.

CHAPTER 7

The clock chimed the hour and Cedo woke with a start. Panic gripped him, and he clambered to his feet.

7am.

No one had appeared during the night, nor had anyone woken him. Rolling up the blanket and mattress, Cedo stowed them back in the small cupboard beside the fireplace. There was no time to waste and the little that remained was racing away.

Behind him, the stairs creaked and the plump figure of Ma Burton appeared. "You may as well wait, lad. If you go racing out that door, you're liable to miss each other."

She sounded forlorn and they both stared silently at the dead embers of the fire. It was how Cedo felt; dead, empty. But he had to trust that sooner or later his lover would return.

"When he gets here, I'll send him back to you. Mark my words. An' before I do I'll find out what he's been up to."

Cedo smiled. Ma Burton was certainly a lovable woman, and he was glad to not only have made the acquaintance of her son but of the rest of the family. Whereas his had seen fit to abandon him, the Burtons had, despite some of the less appealing parts of his life, taken him in, and for that he was grateful. It felt nice to be embraced by the arms of a true family, if only for a while.

As the clock struck ten, Cedo left with a heavy heart. Ma Burton refused to take money for lodgings and food, protesting that any friend of Billy's was welcome within her walls. Before Cedo left, she promised to get Billy to send a pneumatic postal message to him. Willingly embracing her, Cedo left and made for the seafront. He scanned the streets as he walked, jostled by the rush of tourists and tradesmen, hoping to catch a glimpse of Billy.

It was to no avail and Cedo found himself standing alone beside the sea. Looking out over it, he wondered what was to come in the weeks before them, wondered what had happened to his friend. Today, the sea air did nothing for him. It neither invigorated nor excited him. Cedo had thought it would help to see the pier and the crash of the waves. Instead it made him feel even more alone.

Cedo hailed a hansom and settled back into its cushions, eyes still watching as the city sped past.

For once, the door to the Witheybrooke house stood open, the solid locks deactivated. Beyond it, the house was as silent as when he had left, the gentle tick of the clocks the only sign that someone was dwelling within the walls.

Pushing open the door to the dining room, Cedo felt a renewed sadness wash over him. Seated at the table, his Master looked exhausted. Rolls of paper were piled on the floor and a mass of pneumatic postal tubes lay on the table. Erus scribbled on a small slip of paper, slid it into the tiny window on one of the tubes and dropped in a roll of paper. Repeatedly he performed the task, the pile on his left growing while the pile on his right dwindled.

Despite the age-halting serum, his Master suddenly looked old. Cedo could see the lines beside his eyes that, while not deep, were there in the harsh light of day. Gently he ran a hand down Erus' hair, unsurprised when the ashen figure jumped. Silently they stared at one another, Cedo studying the millennia of knowledge and isolation which swam through Erus' eyes. It pained Cedo to see the lost years, fleeting time which had faded away. There was so much within his Master that he wanted to learn, yet it was a vault to which he did not know the combination. The moment he learned it, it would change.

With a sigh, Erus laid his head against Cedo's stomach, arms draping around his waist and holding him close. Wrapping his arms around his Master's neck, and his own weariness forgotten, Cedo held him. A silence, tinged with the weight of an impending war, hung over them. Gently he stroked Erus' head, hoping that somehow he would lull and soothe whatever snapped at his lover's soul.

They stayed together for several long moments, Cedo savoring the closeness. Finally, he pressed a kiss to Erus' temple and moved away.

"Francis is in the kitchen." His Master's voice was flat and hoarse and he never lifted his eyes from the table. "I would like it very much if you could fetch me something to eat and drink. Then prepare for our departure. We shall be in London for several days."

"As you wish, Master."

Cedo bent and gave Erus the barest of kisses. Pride began to swell through him, filling the aching cavities of the previous hours, pride that he would stand beside the

man who would help protect their country from all that
was to come.

With Misty following his every movement from the
safety of the dresser, Cedo flung clothes into trunks, not
caring how they fell. By leaving, he felt as though he were
betraying the one bestowed upon him, tossing Billy to the
wind as if he were the previous day's news.

Wrenching a suit from its hanger, Cedo glared at it and
growled. He did not want to go, but etiquette told him
that Erus would refuse to be seen alone. It was a world
away from the days when Erus had left Cedo locked in his
room with little more than his thoughts, banished from
everything he did. Now he was to stand proudly beside
his Master, supporting him through all that was to come.

Heaving the trunks shut, he sat upon one and stared
at Misty. Cedo wondered if she knew the secrets of the
world. Secrets passed down from the cats who had once
been worshiped as gods. She blinked, yawned, and settled
down.

"He'll return."

Cedo jumped at the voice and turned toward the door.
Francis stood in the open doorway, a bowl clasped in his
hands. He walked into the room and handed it to Cedo.
A stew of some kind filled he vessel, its thick, meaty scent
tickling his nostrils. Taking up the spoon, he began to eat,
his starved belly suddenly making itself known.

"Billy is the loyal kind, and I doubt he'll be away for
long."

Resting the spoon against the bowl, he looked up to
Francis. "How can you be sure?"

"You need to have more faith, Cedo. I've seen his kind
many a time. The horrors of the Dynasty push people

in two directions, either toward death and brutality or toward each other. Billy isn't the kind to stay away for too long. He's proved his loyalty to you time and again. Right now, all you can do is go with Erus and give Billy the time he needs."

Something wet pressed against his hand and he looked down to see Misty rubbing her head against his arm. He retrieved a piece of meat from his bowl and held it out to her. She gave it a cautious sniff before swallowing it whole.

"Can't be too bad." Francis chuckled.

"What exactly is it?" Another piece of meat disappeared from his fingers, the edges of sharp teeth brushing his fingers.

"Pigeon."

Cedo almost choked. "Pigeon?"

"Yes." Francis stretched his arms before him, joints clicking. "Your Master needed to relieve a little of his stress. He took it out on the local population. It appears that the guards were lazy when taking their evidence and missed Erus' not-so-small stash of weapons in the bunker. Besides, you ate far worse in the Dynasty."

Looking at the bowl with trepidation, Cedo carefully ate, his stomach and brain fighting against one another.

"My father was like Billy." Francis' voice had become low, tinted with melancholy. "He went away to work for the president, to find out what was happening within our country. He was away for months at a time, forever seeking the truth. My mother spent many a night awake, wondering where he was and whether he would return. Finally he did return, but he was a changed man, filled with the hardships of what he had seen. Yet he never took it out on us. I was determined that I would carry on and finish his work." He chuckled. "Look where it got me."

"Will you ever see your family again?"

"I hope so. I hope to return to the Dynasty one day, once all of this is over. I'm confident that the Dynasty will be freed from the president's tyrannical reign. Three hundred years is quite long enough. It's time for him to go."

Placing the empty bowl on the dresser, Cedo turned his attention back to Francis. "Do you think you will ever see such a time?"

Francis looked to the floor, hands knotted in his lap. "In my lifetime? I certainly hope so. But we don't know what the future holds. In a year's time, none of us may be here. Or we may have freed the world from those who chose to enslave her."

"What do you believe the world needs?"

There was a long pause and Francis eventually looked up. "Love. The world needs a great deal of love. Which is why I'm hoping that this war is swift and merciful. Only then can we begin the journey of rebuilding her."

Four spiked bolts shot from the base of the gondola and buried themselves in the ground. Slowly the great ship began to drop, pulling itself along the taut wires. Wheels dropped from beneath it to meet the ground.

Around them the garden had been cleared of the debris they had encountered on their homecoming. Its replacement was several large digging machines, smoke pumping from stacks as their metal teeth ate into the soil. The ground shook beneath Cedo's feet as the large tracks rumbled across the grass, depositing earth into the backs of large hoppers to be disposed of.

The ship settled on the grass, its red and gold royal livery glowing in the warm summer sun. Several trunks were stacked beside Cedo, some containing their belongings, the others carrying items he had never seen. The airship's door opened and a set of steps unfolded, coming to rest a few feet from him. Black-clothed figures emerged, their faces obscured by strange breathing apparatus and dark glasses, rifles resting in their arms. Strings of ammunition ran from the guns over the men's shoulders. They positioned themselves around the ship, their blackened eyes watching all around them. Following them were two men dressed in matching red and gold uniforms who, without so much as a wayward glance, collected the luggage and stowed it in the ship. Completely alone, Cedo stared at the craft, taking in the large, golden envelope and the sweeping gondola. Guns were folded at the helm and the large picture windows appeared to be blacked out.

Sweeping past Cedo, Erus boarded the ship. Despite the warmth, Erus was swathed in black, his hair a stark contrast against his clothes. It seemed as though he was in mourning, Cedo suspected for all he was being forced to endure.

Following in his Master's footsteps, Cedo boarded the ship.

A patchwork of fields and towns passed beneath the ship, all dappled with the summer sun. Shortly after takeoff, silver, fin-like sails had unfurled from the side of the ship. They were, Cedo had been told, to catch the rays of the sun and harness their energy. The sun's power excited his Master in a way Cedo had never seen. Erus seemed to step out of the shell of mourning as he explained the properties of the unseen magic.

The airship was a flying palace, the interior spacious and filled with the trappings of the wealthy. Deep, leather chairs surrounded mahogany tables and waiters dressed in gold and red served them food and drinks. Chandeliers lined the ceiling and the walls were decked in a gold-hued wood, the long windows allowing a perfect view of all below. Other than the staff, they were the only ones aboard the ship.

Erus brushed against his arm and gestured to the window. "You can follow the railways from here," the redhead softly stated. "Some of our grandest lines and termini reside in the city of London. It is where Svenfur has taken so much of its inspiration from."

Cedo smiled, the small fragments of information warming him. Never had he heard Erus speak with such fervor, other than about his own work. To listen to him speak about the landmarks of their country made him happy, a side of Erus he had longed to see.

"Hopefully," Erus continued, "we shall get time to see some of the sights of the city. Tower Bridge is a wonder to behold, and as for St. Paul's cathedral, well, you must see it in person to believe in its beauty. It is well and good seeing it in the books and periodicals, but one must stand beneath its dome to truly absorb its majesty."

Sinking back into his seat, Cedo watched the world below. Watched the barely visible gray lines of the railways and the towns they happened upon. Wrapping an arm around his waist, Erus rested his chin against Cedo's shoulder and took in the view. Gratefully, Cedo leaned into the gentle touch, enjoying the peace and tranquility.

"London is a city like no other." Erus' words brushed his ear, warm and filled with passion. "You may be in love with Svenfur, but you will be crying for more once you have experienced an evening in London's embrace. Compared to Svenfur, she is a lady, a wonder of the night, a place who can show you a thousand sights in a matter of moments. She will overload your senses and leave you craving more."

Below them, the towns began to change, the outskirts beginning to merge into one. The dappled green of the fields slowly melted away, leaving a mass of buildings behind. Soon the buildings disappeared, the clear air becoming a swirling smog of gray. They were joined by other flying crafts, all of them making for the capital. Most were airships, but there were also several of the bi-wing crafts Cedo had seen in the testing facility on the Downs. They were smaller than the airships, single or twin passenger crafts with compartments that were open to the elements. He could not imagine that they were comfortable to fly in, especially if the weather took a turn for the worse.

As the airship began to drop, the solar sails folded away, the sun disappearing into the smog. Below them, London appeared, its vastness stretching toward to the horizon. Tall, tripedal machines soared from between the buildings, cylindrical heads moving back and forth, powerful lights scanning the skies. Large, concave metal dishes extended from flexible arms, moving with the strange looking heads. They were strange and intimidating, a stark reminder of what was to come.

"Whatever are they?" Cedo asked.

"Sky Searchers. They are one of the first lines of defense against an attack on the capital, looking and listening for the enemy."

"Have they always been here?"

Erus gently stroked Cedo's hip. "No. They were installed several years ago, when the Dynasty began to fight within its own borders. We always knew that the war would one day come to our own shores; we just did not know when."

There was a Sky Searcher on every street, imbedded among the buildings, forever looking upward, anyone who walked among them dwarfed by the giant machines.

"Are they yours?"

He felt his Master nod. "Indeed they are. Within the coming weeks the latest model will be installed along the coast. As well as being able to spot an imminent attack, they will also be able to disable any enemy attack crafts."

"How do you identify the enemy?"

Erus chuckled. "Easily. They're normally the ones coming at us at a great rate of knots."

Smiling, Cedo watched London drift below them. So many landmarks he had only heard about and many that he had yet to discover.

"In all seriousness, there are many ways to identify the enemy," Erus continued. "Their engines are different, giving off a different tone to our own. Our people on the ground, in France and Prussia and the Dynasty, will be able to tell us when they are approaching. Their crafts have different markings. Most of all, we have to be alert at all hours. We listen, we watch, and we wait."

A cool terror settled over Cedo, the terror of the unknown, the terror of what was to come and the death it would bring. Would they survive? Undoubtedly it would change all of them. How was another question.

Shifting in the deep leather seat, he looked at Erus. For the first time since their return, he could study his Master's face, to see the lines that the elixir had yet to hide.

"What happened to you below ground?" he softly asked.

For a long moment, Erus stared at him, eyes glazing and unblinking as if the horrors of the past refused to die.

"If I told you, you wouldn't believe me. You would think I was lying, trying to hide the truth from you."

Placing a hand on Erus', Cedo pressed on. "Tell me. I shall believe you."

His Master's emerald eyes blinked and refocused.

Something stilled within the red-haired man, time momentarily pausing.

Then he began, "You remember his army, the one of copies? He asked my advice on them, brought the ruined and dying men to see me. They had pipes coming from their organs, wires strapped to exposed brains. Some had clockwork hearts to keep them alive for longer. I worked as quickly as I could so as to minimize their pain. No one deserves to suffer like those poor innocents did. They were selected for what they were: the strong, the fast, the intelligent. Their nuclein were intertwined into one. How he made the copies, and made them so quickly, I do not know. All I know is that he brought the first finished one, number zero-zero-one, to me and left it with me for programming. That was when I taught it words from the dead language. James will break that code but we can only pray it takes him longer than I expect."

"And the machines? You said that you modified them. Did he release you from the prison?"

Erus shook his head and sighed, strands of hair dancing before his eyes. "It had to be done. He allowed me to leave and see his arsenal. There were guards, but they were stupid. None knew what I was really doing. I promised to improve the machines and, while I did, my own personal modifications outweigh any improvements."

Emotions rattled his Master's voice, darkness welling from the very place he kept it locked away. Slowly the real Erus was making himself known, a man who craved justice and righteousness. No longer was he the cold-hearted killer who had plucked Cedo from the pier.

"Why do you stay with me?" The question was so pitiful, spoken so quietly, that it caught Cedo off guard.

Pausing, Cedo stared at his Master, searched the depths of his eyes, of a soul bared for the first time in an age. Taking Erus' hand, he gently stroked the strong fingers, feeling the veins that lined the skin. Cedo could feel the emotion begin to choke him.

"Because I believe," he softly began, "I see someone who is not just a monster. I see someone who can change the world for the better. I see someone who is capable of greatness, someone who has already achieved the impossible. I see past the monster that others see. It is something I have always tried to do and have finally mastered."

Erus slumped in his grasp, head lowered. His shoulders rose and fell, rogue strands of hair from his thick braid barely hiding the emotion which crossed his face.

"Never." His voice was hoarse and strained. "Never has anyone said such things about me."

Leaning close, Cedo pressed a kiss to his Master's temple. "Now they have, and I want you to know that those words will never change. Yes, it took me a long time to realize why I remained with you, but when I realized why, everything became as clear as day. I love you, Master, and I always shall, as long as we may live. No longer will I run. No longer will I hide. I will stand beside you with pride because I know you are not the man they paint you to be. In fact, I often wonder if you did not become the man the newspapers wrote about just to prove a point to them. I feel that, for many years, you remained hidden from them, behind these barriers, just getting on with what you believed you needed to do."

Erus said nothing, his eyes downcast, chest gently rising and falling. Cedo ached for his Master, ached for all he had been through, for all he had had to hide from the world. The world had demanded a monster and they had received one. What truly lay beneath Erus' thorny exterior was anybody's guess, but Cedo knew he was slowly discovering it.

"Do you fear love, Master?"

Erus remained silent, head still lowered.

"Yes."

The answer did not surprise Cedo. Instead, he felt as though something were opening, a flower blooming in a summer's field. Cedo knew that he had to tread carefully or his Master's walls would rise again.

His voice was gentle. "Why?"

"Because to love, to feel, leaves you open for so many opportunistic attacks. People come to know your weak spots and exploit them for their own gain."

"I shall never do that."

He saw the corners of his Master's mouth lift in a smile, yet Erus remained downcast, eyes focusing on the swirling pattern of the table.

"I know, Cedo. I know you shall never do such a thing. At times it feels as though you have, but this is a lesson, and it takes people time to learn about one another. Your profession of love means so much to me. It shows just how far we have come."

Below them, the capital drifted by. They were making for their meeting with the King. The Queen had succumbed to an assassin many years before and her loyal husband had spent the following years in mourning.

The airship dropped through the smog, the thick cloud enveloping them for a few moments. When they emerged, they were hovering over a giant dome of glass and steel. It completely encased the palace and, as they descended, several panels slid away, allowing them to land on the neatly manicured lawns.

CHAPTER 8

Seated in a bunker deep below the palace, Cedo allowed himself to take in the scene before him. A long table ran along the center of the room, blocks of paper placed at each seat, a speaking tube and pneumatic postal door at the head of the table. Maps lined the walls, and a series of clocks, each showing a different time. At the far end was a large metal door.

Erus sat beside him, facing the King's empty chair. Cedo leaned close and whispered, "I thought that the King was sick?"

Erus did not lift his head from studying his hands. "Do not believe all that you read in the newspapers. They are fantastic when it comes making others appear feeble."

"Yet everyone was speaking of it, some malady brought back from the shores of Kamerun."

Sweeping stray strands of hair from his face, Erus looked to him, a smirk on his lips. "We may not have been able to save the Queen from the assassin's bullet, but the same cannot be said for His Royal Highness. But tell that to press and you shall be locked in a madhouse."

Cedo grinned; he had no intention of ever telling another living soul. All that his Master told him was kept in the strictest of confidence.

The bunker was cool, a near silent hiss of air sweeping from vents high in the wall. Glass-shielded lights hung from the ceiling, throwing pools of white light into the room. The palace, he had been told, had its own generator, keeping the building powered through even the darkest of days. Automaton creatures scuttled from doors in the floor, the metal flaps locking in their wake, their slender legs clicking against the stone floor. They scurried around, preparing the room. They placed water jugs and glasses on the table, while others climbed the walls and checked the air vents with long, jointed tentacles. London, it seemed, was far more advanced than Svenfur. Cedo had heard it said that the capital was at least ten years ahead of the rest of the country and twenty years ahead of the rest of the continent. Yet the Orient soared ahead of them, and Cedo longed to see the advances that were being made in the Far East. If England could create flying fortresses and electrified sea defenders, then he could not fathom what was coming from the Far East.

The large door swung open, and the King's majordomo entered. Dressed in the red and gold livery of the royal household, he stepped to one side, allowing a group of identically dressed men to walk by him. Clothed in black and white suits and carrying sheaves of paper, the men stood behind the seats of the table. Erus touched Cedo's elbow and silently, they stood.

The King's chief steward stood to attention. "Gentlemen, the King."

Dressed in a black mourning suit, the King entered and nodded to the gathered men. Seating himself, he waited until everyone had settled before his piercing eyes turned toward the lower end of the table.

"Mr. Veetu, I am so glad that you could join us, and pleased to see that you returned from the Dynasty relatively unscathed." King Albert gave the room a tense smile. "So, what is our plan of attack for when these fiends reach our shores? I assume that you have seen inside their arsenal?"

Taking a sheaf of papers from the leather-bound tube, Erus nodded. "I have indeed seen their arsenal and some of it is strikingly fearsome. However, despite the president's suspicion of me, I was able to get him to grant me access to his weaponry."

"And?"

A frightful sneer twisted Erus' face. "Let us just say that some slight modifications were made to them."

The King grinned, an expression that was equally as shocking as Erus'. "Good man! I trust it has brought us time?"

"Some." Erus stood and walked to the map-lined wall. "If his own engineers find the mistakes, then it will take time for them to be repaired. If not—"

The King's face became stony, his pale eyes following Erus. A chill crept up Cedo's neck and he instinctively moved in his chair.

"If not?"

Pausing, Erus looked to the King. "If not, then they will destroy themselves before they arrive."

"But this could mean enemy troops and weapons threatening our allies."

"It could," Erus replied. "However, most of the modified machines are walkers. They are too heavy to be moved by James' air-machines. There are one thousand five hundred miles between Akimov-Gunkanjima and the border, by which time they will have shaken themselves apart."

Cedo watched as Erus gestured to the map of Europe. The air was heavy with the expectation of fear, their meeting in the bunker far below the palace a solemn affair. Never did he think he would live through such a time of crisis.

Yet Cedo realized just how much luck was favoring him. He was in a place of protection, with a man who was willing to keep him close. Thousands of others, he knew, would not be offered such luxury. They would have to fend for themselves while all Inferno broke loose. It was a weight that would lay across his shoulders for all eternity.

"The plan is three-pronged," Erus began. "Firstly, our coastal regions will be protected by lightning pylons. It will mean keeping our waters clear of any shipping."

The King frowned, one finger tapping against the table. "What exactly do these pylons do?"

"Each is powered by a turbine which produces an electrical charge. Once enemy ships are spotted, the turbines are started and an electrical charge will be passed between the pylons. The current, combined with the salt water of the sea and metal, will be lethal to any human which dares pass through it."

"But what of supplies?" one of the suited men asked. "How do we get those in and out of the country?"

Erus chuckled. "Don't think that hasn't been thought through. We have many weapons in our arsenal which James will never possess. One is the flying fortress. From this monolithic craft, we can deploy airships and smaller flying craft. Protected by the fortresses, they will be able to fly supplies into the country and out to the troops."

There was the near-silent scratching of pens against paper.

"And pray, where will these supplies come from?" another of the men asked.

"Our allies are all ready to help, as we are to assist them," the King replied. "We should have them within the week."

The King paused and appeared to ponder the discussion, his cold eyes focused on Cedo. He asked, "What of our plan of attack? What can you bring to the table?"

"As I said, the attack is three-pronged," Erus began.

"Firstly, as discussed, we have our naval attack. Should the pylons fail, our battleships will be waiting in port. Second are our newly formed air defenses. Lastly, we have our land army."

Steely blue eyes left Cedo and followed Erus, tracking him as he strode. "Tell me about the air defenses," the King said.

"Our air defenses range from smaller fighter craft to flying fortresses, as well as airships which can be loaded with bombs. They are currently finishing development and testing."

"And the land army consists of?"

"We have our ground troops, who will be equipped with hand-held weapons. They will have everything from rifles through to the high-energy blunderbuss. We will also have walking machines. Some are operated by a single man, like walking suits of armor loaded with belt-fed guns. Others will be crewed by several men and will either be walkers or tanks. We have an array of guns that include land, rail, and weapons to take down any flying craft. Oh, and the cavalry."

Cedo could hear the smile in his Master's voice and he turned his attention from the King. Erus leaned beside the map of Europe, the smile still on his face.

"The cavalry?" the King asked.

Erus spoke again, "Yes, except we're substituting the horses with mechanical, armor-plated ones. Each one stands sixty hands tall and carries twin cannons, and is operated from the interior by a team of two men: a rider, so to speak, and gunner. They can be used for straight-up combat or for drawing guns into place. Like a normal horse, they can travel at up to twenty miles per hour. Our mounted mecha-horses can reach speeds of up to thirty miles per hour and are as nimble as a thoroughbred. They are equipped with a single cannon and an armored rider.

The King's face broke into a malicious grin. "Perfect."

"Of course," Erus continued, "we do have more. I shall show you the designs in a moment. I would like to finish by telling you of our greatest secret. I trust that your Highness has heard about the forays into wireless technology?"

"Indeed I have."

It was Erus' turn to grin. "I have managed to refine it and make it capable of carrying human speech. Our boys will no longer have to rely on the signalers or other means of inadequate communication. Each of the machines will be equipped with wireless carrier and receiver units. It means that we in the bunkers will also be able to communicate with them. Of course, everything shall have to be coded but that is not a problem. Already the greatest minds in the country are working on a secure code."

"I hear that you were also dabbling in this new-fangled moving photography. How is that coming along? Will we be able to use that?"

Erus held the King's gaze. "I hope it will be ready. The gargoyles around Svenfur have been extremely effective."

"And they move, do they not?" the King asked.

"Indeed they do."

It was all Cedo heard as a low buzzing filled his ears. His vision began to swim as the memories flickered through his mind.

The falling granite as he had read Billy's map. The crumbling brickwork and sand accompanied by scrabbling in the tunnels beneath the city just moments before he had stumbled upon Veetu Industries' underground lair. The gargoyle sitting on the lamppost, watching as he and Billy walked.

Suddenly it all began to make sense, the pieces of the puzzle falling into place. Erus had been watching him all along. He had known where his consort was at every moment. The cold chill of realization settled over him and he watched the rest of the meeting play out, his Master's hands sweeping over great maps and plans.

Yet nothing could have prepared him for that moment.

Still seated at the long table, Cedo watched as plates of food began to arrive. Heads of pigs, their mouths stuffed with apples, and entire roasted birds were placed before them. Decanters of wine, glasses, and crockery were passed out by a troop of butlers. Some were human, some were automatons, but all were dressed in the red and gold livery and all were silent. Even the workings of the machines could not be heard.

The meeting had dragged on late into the afternoon. Every little detail had been pored over and debated. There would, he had been told, be many more meetings of the same. The thought tired him and he turned his mind to Erus. How did one survive on such little sleep? Was there something else, a wonder drug perhaps, behind his Master's constant animation? But the wonderment did little to null the realization of his being watched.

Leaning close to Erus, he quietly asked, "Did you use the gargoyles to watch me?"

Placing his fork beside his plate, Erus inclined his head. "Of course I did."

"But why?"

"Because I am beholden to protect you. The streets, as you well know, are not a pleasant place. I did not want to truly lose you forever."

"You knew where I was, even when I fled?"

Erus nodded. "Of course."

Betrayal cut through him, raw and chilling. Cedo pushed his plate away and gazed at the table. There were no true freedoms any longer, privacy becoming a thing of the past.

"Why does it anger you so?" His Master's voice was soft, not raising the attention of their fellow diners.

"Because people should be allowed to go about their lives as they damn well please," he hissed in reply.

"And if your life isn't your own?"

His head snapped up, eyes focusing on Erus' face. Inquisitiveness flickered through green eyes as if he had no concept of what was wrong, of the morals behind what he had been doing.

"Not every person in this country is owned by you."

Erus just stared at him, eyes cold. "I don't own anyone. The government, however, has other ideas."

Narrowing his eyes, Cedo whispered, "How do you mean?"

Erus stared straight ahead, his voice low. "In times such as now, people panic. It is best for the government to step in and make the citizens believe that all is well."

"And when the war lands on our shores?"

"Oh, they will know well in advance. They will have been given the strength and unity propaganda."

Relaxing into his chair, Cedo kept watching his Master, absorbing his words. He did not believe in war, did not believe that nations should fight over things as trivial as trade routes. But it had been going on since the dawn of time and he was just a single person in a world of many. Despite his disagreements, he knew that it would be best if he played his part and supported his nation.

"What do you believe our chances are of winning this war are?"

Erus fell silent for a moment. "I believe we are the stronger side. As has been said, James' army is constantly weakening. He does not know with whom to pick his fights, so he takes on all comers. He refuses to have advisers on such matters. In fact, he refuses to have advisers for anything, killing those who try to help. He's also a thief, stealing the ideas of others and using them for himself."

"Which is how he came to have your turbines?"

"Precisely. Those were destined to be placed along the border between Prussia and the Dynasty and act as an electrical barrier to stop him crossing. Obviously he stole them and has been using them to power his city."

Cedo's meal was cooling but he did not care. The secrets between governments and countries were far more interesting. "Does he replicate them?"

Eris nodded. "Most definitely. But his standards have never been as high as ours. While we take our time and do our research, he prefers to do a rush job. Rush jobs, as we know, equal inferior products."

Turning back to his meal, Cedo mulled over their conversation. Two superpowers, throwing their weight at each other just to see which would come off the stronger. Their country had seen nothing like it for many years.

"Who knows about your projects?" he finally asked.

"It is on a need to know basis. Of the highest secrecy. What you have heard here is only a fraction of what we have. Like an iceberg, there is much, much more hidden beneath the surface."

Government secrets, the power to hide them and keep them hidden. Cedo wondered what else went on behind closed doors. What else was locked away in vaults and minds? It was the same curiosity that had led him to the tunnels beneath Svenfur, following a trail of crumbs to uncover a deadly secret. Now he had to do it again, following Erus and linking the pieces of the war together. None of which would make it into his future broadcasts.

Fingers swept over his shoulder and he looked to Erus. His Master smiled, eyes suddenly warm as if all thoughts of what was to come had melted away.

"Tonight we shall go to the Inferno Club. A chance to relax after today."

"The Inferno Club?"

A devilish glint raced across Erus' face. "You shall see. Trust me, you shall enjoy it."

They traveled, not by road or by air, but via a series of interlocked tunnels. Horseless carriages trundled them from the palace across the city and to a secret location. Relaxing into the deep, velveteen seats, the darkness of the carriage surrounding him, Cedo let go of his earlier anger. Instead his confidence began to reign. Erus sat across from him and, in the shadows, Cedo heard him twitch and adjust his suit. They were off to somewhere special and, wherever it was, it was exciting his Master. Or making him nervous.

The carriages deposited them in a tunnel, a great pair of doors before them. Gas lamps stretched from the walls, illuminating the motifs of cavorting couples etched into the wood. The doors creaked open and they were ushered through and into the capital's most secretive club.

Carved from the bedrock of London, the Inferno Club stretched as far as Cedo could see. Flame-lit chandeliers hung from the high ceiling and candles dotted the small tables. Bars serving every kind of drink, and several narcotics if the menu was to be believed, sat beside lavishly set stages. They wandered amid drapes and hangings, stepping from one open space to another, each one staging music or performance arts. People mingled, clothed in all or nothing. Some hid faces behind elaborate masks, while others openly leered. The air was filled with an unforgiving heat, and the scent of jasmine from overhead burners was so strong it could almost be tasted. A series of tables lined one wall, a variety of goods displayed for sale. Several tables were covered with a variety of weapons, none of which Cedo had ever seen. Touching Erus' elbow, he nodded toward them.

Erus chuckled. "I suspect several of mine have been modified. Bastards."

Cedo felt no fear as people looked at him, their eyes, masked or not, sweeping over him. Instead, the confidence remained, burning through him. Tossing his hair over his shoulder, he straightened his back and stared back.

"Would you care for a drink?"

Never had Erus broached such a question with him. Cedo raised an eyebrow.

His Master grinned. "We will be here for a while, so we may as well enjoy the delights."

"In that case, I shall have a gin."

Erus' eyes darkened, the grin twisting to a sneer. He leaned closer, fingers brushing Cedo's elbow. "Manners."

Feeling the hunger wash over him, Cedo gave a husky chuckle. "Please."

"Better. Take a seat. I won't be a moment."

Slumping into one of the chairs, Cedo watched the hubbub of people. Most appeared well-to-do, their clothes and jewelry pointing to money. Some walked around on hands and knees, chains around their necks. At least one gentleman had mechanical hind legs, a modern day centaur. On the nearest stage, a woman was bent over a high-backed chair, her bare bottom being lashed by a woman in military uniform.

"Perfect."

CHAPTER 9

Cedo followed the voice and looked up. Standing before him was a man dressed in the white laboratory coat of a scientist. Black hair touched the man's shoulders and black, unnerving eyes stared at him. The man grinned, displaying teeth filed to razor-sharp points.

Cedo arched an eyebrow. "And you are?"

"They call me the Physician." The man's voice was almost a hiss, changed by the shape of his teeth.

"Do they now?"

The man's grin widened, turning his narrow face into a wolf-like mask. "Yes."

Crossing his ankles, Cedo leaned forward. The man unsettled him but he refused to let it show. "And you are a physician of?"

The Physician continued to grin as he admired one hand and its long fingernails, all filed to points. "Pleasure."

"Really, now? I did not think it was possible to gain a license in such an area. Or do they give them to just anyone these days?" The words fell from his mouth before he could think, each dripping with sarcasm. Yet Cedo felt no guilt for his words, a raw energy nipping at his heels.

The dark eyes snapped back to him, and the man gave a guttural growl. Dropping into the seat beside Cedo, he glared.

"What I create will have you screaming for mercy," he hissed. "Never again will you feel such pleasure unless it comes from my creations. Whenever I release something, they line the streets to buy it."

Tearing his eyes away, Cedo instead stared at the stage. The two women had been replaced by exotic dancers dressed in little more than feathers.

"I wish to use you in an experiment," the Physician purred.

"Do you? And if I refuse?"

"Then I'll take you by force."

Throwing back his head, Cedo laughed. "I wish you the very best of luck. I shall not be leaving this spot."

Growling, the Physician rose to his feet, lithe body towering over Cedo. A flicker of fear shot through him as he gazed into the all-black eyes.

"Do not trifle with me. You have no idea who I am," snarled the dark-haired man.

Cedo started to stand, but before he could, there was the snapping of fingers. The Physician's head snapped up and his lips peeled back into a snarl from his teeth.

A woman clothed in a long, flowing dress placed her hand on the Physician's shoulder and pulled him back.

"This one does not belong to you and never will." Her eyes never left the Physician's face, yet he never turned to look at her. "He arrives and leaves as a companion. If you must test your so-called toys on someone, let it be one of the playthings."

Sandaled feet peeked from beneath the dress as she held the man at arm's length. The Physician hissed, a low, dangerous sound, and spat at the woman's feet before slinking into the shadows of the club. The woman stared down at him before gesturing for him to stand. "Cedo Reilly, I believe. Companion of Erus Veetu."

Cedo nodded. "One and the same, ma'am."

She stepped around the table. "Your Master has requested that I look over you to make sure that you are medically fit to be within the club. So if you'll follow me we can begin."

Cedo did as he was bid and allowed her to lead him through the club and into a spotlessly clean room. Gone was the odor and heat of the expansive space, the music and conversation cut off as she closed the door. The room was painted white and had all the trappings of a small hospital. Leaning against the desk, she looked him up and down.

"My name is Lady Seren. I'm the real physician here. As a new companion entering the Inferno Club, you are required to undergo a health inspection before you can enter any of our free areas. Should you require medical attention during the evening then I shall be on hand."

From what he had seen, Cedo had an idea what the free areas were: places where the occupants of the club could be themselves, free of the constraints of the above-ground world. It was freedom of the highest kind.

Seren was swift, her touches cool and impersonal as she searched him for imperfection and illness. He watched her with a strange fascination, shivering as her fingers wandered over him, prying, pinching and prodding. In time, she stepped away and strode to the sink.

"You may dress. You have a clean bill of health. Go and enjoy the rest of the evening."

Seren said no more. Cedo redressed and silently left the clinical room. The sight of his Master on the opposite side of the door, face a painting of shadows, gave Cedo a turn. Erus chuckled, the low light dancing across his face, a glass proffered to Cedo.

"Drink, relax, and then we shall have fun."

Something darted through his Master's eyes. Whether it was the flicker of the candles, lust, or something else,

Cedo could not tell. Taking a seat beside Erus, Cedo turned his attention toward the stage before them. A pair of duelists faced one another, their bodies and faces covered in thick, protective clothing. They clasped strange-looking weapons, fashioned on the blunderbuss, yet with pipes, flared muzzles and other adornments. Some seemed to have a purpose while others were purely ornamental, brass filaments winding around the barrel and stock. The tension rose as the two faced one another, their weapons clearly aiming for the heart. At a precise, unseen signal, both fired. Yet, instead of slugs of melt, pulses of light emitted from the muzzles of the guns, slamming into each of the duelists. Both stumbled and fell, lying motionless. Cedo felt his heart race and he began to stand. A hand at his wrist stopped him, easing him back to his chair. After a moment, both of the opponents stood, brushed themselves down and readied for another round.

Sipping his drink, Cedo watched in morbid fascination as the rival fighters went for round after round. In between bouts, they would study their guns, making minor alterations, before once again facing off.

A glass thudded against the table before them and a hand touched his elbow. Beside him, Erus stood.

"Come. I want to take you somewhere."

Emptying his glass, Cedo watched the duel for a moment longer before standing. They walked amid the throngs of people, all of whom subtly ignored one another. Cedo found himself gazing at the costumes people were clad in. One woman was dressed entirely in white, a pair of sparkling horns twisting from her forehead, face hidden behind an expressionless snow-white mask. A man had a headdress of feathers, his body clad within a tightly strung corset, his waist as narrow as a twig.

Cedo began to suspect where Erus was leading him and a grin twisted his lips. A hunger began to twist deep in his soul. It had been a long time since they had done such deeds and the club seemed like the perfect haven for them to surface once more.

"Veetu! Just the man."

The voice caused them to stall and Cedo turned to see a tall, well-built man with steel-gray hair. A red, jeweled mask covered the right side of his face. The naked left side showed a dark eye and a thin mouth, a narrow, curled mustache sitting above his lips.

"Stoker!" Erus took the offered hand and shook it. "Good to see you."

"Indeed. It's been too long. I trust you're well?" The man—Stoker—dropped his hand, his gaze focused on Erus.

"Very. And yourself?"

The two men stood close, shouting over the din of their surroundings.

"Mustn't complain," Stoker replied. "Business is good, what with the fracas in the East. I don't think I've shipped this many supplies in a long time. And it's only going to get better."

His Master chuckled. "Indeed."

"Anyway, I was hoping I'd see you tonight. I've gotten myself involved in the automaton boxing championships. Built the ruddy thing myself and I was wondering if you'd do me the honor of being the controller? Oh, I can do it myself, but it would be far more fun to have the master at the controls."

Erus inclined his head a little. "It would be a pleasure. But are you sure that's allowed under ABC rules?"

Stoker grinned and shrugged. "Just as long as I let them know before noon. It's like nominating a jockey for a horse."

"In that case, I accept." Erus held out his hand and the two men shook, sealing the deal.

"Tomorrow, 9pm, Regent's Park. I'll see you there."

"Until tomorrow."

Stoker melted back into the crowds and Erus turned to him, a radiant smile on his face. "Tomorrow shall be fun. Now we have even more reason to celebrate."

The room was lit by candles, shadows sloping along the carpeted floor. A large, canopied bed dominated one wall while a long, padded bench sat before it. Leather straps hung from its legs, waiting for whomever would become a part of it. A dresser held an assortment of lotions, the bottles sparkling in the light. Beside the dresser stood a wooden rack of assorted canes and whips.

Cedo felt his heart beat faster, a warm flush rising to his cheeks. Behind him the door clicked shut and he heard the lock turn. Silently, Erus collected a brush and length of ribbon from the dresser before moving to stand behind Cedo.

The brush gently touched Cedo's hair, metal prongs tugging at strands. Slowly he relaxed as his hair was brushed and parted, lengths tugged and twisted before the end was secured and the braid was laid against his back.

"I want you to undress and lie face down on the bench, legs on either side." Erus' voice was husky and deep, dripping with the promise of forbidden pleasure.

Erus' hands touched Cedo's shoulders and slid down his arms. His Master's warm breath brushed his throat. The redhead's fingers wrapped around Cedo's waist, Erus' lips touched his jaw, sending shivers of excitement through him. Oh, how he had dreamed of this. Dreamed of being beaten by his Master's hand, of feeling the burn ache through his skin before roughly being taken. Already the wounds from the previous punishment had faded, a miracle of the new medications Erus had been concocting.

Cedo turned and faced Erus. Erus watched him as Cedo picked at the buttons of his heavy coat, carefully plucking them undone before letting it slip to the floor. Looking into his Master's eyes, Cedo felt the lust and assurance bloom through him. This man, the one he called Master, was watching and admiring him, silently pleading for him to bend to Erus' will.

Slipping the waistcoat from his shoulders, Cedo held it by the tips of his fingers before tossing it away. The shirt followed, the cotton whispering over his skin, warm air wrapping around him. Across the room, the shadows whispered around his legs, he could see Erus sigh, chest rising and falling, eyes intently watching.

He unbuckled the boots and nimbly stepped from them. Kicking them to one side, Cedo removed his trousers and undergarments. They became a part of the pile, discarded and forgotten for the moment. He stared at Erus for a while, taking in the lusty look on his Master's face. It made Cedo's heart swell with pride. He, and only he, could do this, could hold his Master's attention. He turned to the bench and laid himself along it, placing his feet and hands against the floor. Erus secured the straps around his wrists and ankles.

The leather was cool against Cedo's skin, his body already beginning to react to the prospect of what was going to come. The cane struck the supple flesh of his buttocks, and Cedo groaned, teeth bared as pain flared through him. Slowly the sting faded, becoming the luscious burn he remembered. Impatiently he waited.

Behind him, Erus grunted and the cane once more bit into his skin. The heat flared from his haunches, blinding him with shades of red and teasing his trapped cock. Over and again there came the pause and the strike,

Cedo groaning with each one, fingers wrapping around the bench's wooden legs. The pain would spike before the tantalizing ache would blossom. Shuddering, he tried to rub himself against the smooth leather, desperate for release. Instead, he was trapped, the straps holding him tight.

The tip of the cane stroked along the sensitive skin of Cedo's inner thigh, touching his strained balls before probing his entrance. Whining, he tried to raise, to push himself closer to the pleasure he so desired. The cane fell away, leaving him alone and wanting more. With his head on one side, Cedo panted softly, eyes focused on the wall. He could not see his Master, could barely hear him as he moved around, feet soft against the carpet.

Something soft touched his rear, tendrils touching his skin, swirling over him before disappearing. The soft touches came and went. Cedo groaned and pressed himself against the leather, the need for release ever growing.

Finally the silky tails disappeared, leaving nothing but air to touch his sensually sore skin. For what felt like a disproportionate length of time, Cedo lay, eyes on the wall, his cock aching for attention. He whined and tried to shift against his bonds, the lined straps rubbing against his skin. He wanted freedom, to move and do whatever his Master bid of him next. What that was could only be imagined, but even mere thoughts of it sent bolts of lust through Cedo.

Fingers nimbly unbuckled the straps. "Get on the bed." His Master's voice was gruff. "Face down, rear in the air."

Cedo's legs felt weak and he struggled to stand. Massaging his wrists and ankles, he moved to the bed. Kneeling upon it, he lowered his head, resting it against the swells of pillows. His cock swelled, blood rushing to his shaft, and Cedo fought the urge to wrap his hand around it and stroke. The position he was in made him feel deliciously exposed and sensual, a sight to behold for the man behind him. Still he could not see Erus and, with the thought of the additional pain and punishment overwhelming him, Cedo glanced over his shoulder.

Erus stepped from his breeches, his cock bouncing free. Collecting a jar from the dresser, the redhead swept a cream along his hard shaft. Panting, Cedo buried his head back against the bed, anticipation smarting through him. Behind him, the bed dipped and hands gripped his hips before sliding over his punished buttocks, a raw fire flaring through Cedo.

"Please," Cedo softly pleaded.

Fingers traced the marks the cane had left behind, causing Cedo to twitch and moan. "Please, what?"

His hands balled into the bed linen, perspiration sliding over his skin. "Please take me."

"Oh, I will." Kisses were placed on his exposed buttocks, his Master's tongue tracing the thin lines. The gentle touches sent shivers through Cedo and he pushed against the warm, wet mouth, quietly demanding more.

Instead, Erus pulled away and slapped Cedo's flesh. Groaning, Cedo shivered, his body beginning to sag.

"I will," Erus softly repeated. "But first I want to admire you. You look so alluring kneeling here, ready to be roughly fucked. Is that what you desire?"

Cedo felt his breath hitch and catch in his throat. "Yes," he whined.

He felt Erus press against him, his cock rubbing against Cedo's offered rear.

"You sound so delicious when you beg."

Cedo could feel it building within him, a pressure that needed to be released. Pressing himself back against his Master, he begged and pleaded. Erus' hands glided over Cedo's skin, leaving goosepimples in their wake.

Erus eased himself in painfully slow. Their collective sighs filled the air, and Cedo sank his chest to the bed. It had been a long time since they had had such contact and it felt delightful. His Master held him as they shuddered, savoring the moment.

"I have missed this." Erus kissed the base of his spine.

Lifting his head, Cedo nodded. "As have I."

His Master began to slowly thrust and Cedo felt himself melt into the bed. His body became limp, and he groaned softly, hands grasping at the bed linen. Pushing himself back, he silently demanded more, silently pleaded to reach euphoria. Erus did not disappoint, his hands gripping Cedo as he pushed in deeper.

Their voices grew, each beseeching the other as their movements grew more frantic. Stretching an arm beneath himself, Cedo gripped his strained erection, sighing with relief at the contact. He stroked in time to his Master's assault. The need balled inside of him, tightening his muscles and sending flutters of heat across his skin.

Gripping his cock, Cedo growled as he came, strings of semen coating his hand and the bed. Behind him, Cedo heard Erus grunt, strong hands tightening around his hips as he pushed in one last time, filling Cedo with a liquid warmth. Panting, they remained kneeling until Cedo's legs could not take it anymore and he slid from his Master's grasp. Rolling to his back, he grinned at the man above him. He knew that, after the confines of the Dynasty's donjon, these first couplings would not last more than a few moments, yet neither of them seemed to care.

Erus took deep breaths, his eyes dark and skin touched with a deep pink tint. A smile eventually tugged at his lips, and Cedo reached up, draping his arms around Erus' shoulders. Growling, he pulled his Master down and sealed their lips in a searing kiss.

Like wisps of fog, they melted back into the club. Time stood still, revealing neither night nor day as people wandered amid the tables and stages. Settling into a deep velvet chair, Cedo draped one leg across the other and turned his attention toward the stage. People were gathered before it, arms outstretched. A single person stood upon the stage, body encased entirely in black and eyes hidden behind an elaborate mask. Antlers curled from the front of his or her head, sweeping up and over the forehead, while tubes thrust from the sides, tumbling behind the figure. A number of tiny lights danced over the mask and along the horns, the person's identity completely hidden. Before the performer, a flat, opaque glass surface stretched across the stage. The masked creature's hands waved above it, filling the air with a tangle of sounds. It was like nothing Cedo had ever seen or heard, strange sounds seemingly produced from thin air. Yet they were all recognizable: drums and stringed instruments, wind instruments and piano sounds, all mixed together to create a queer, yet intoxicating, symphony. Cedo could feel his foot begin to tap, the rhythms speaking to his soul. They seeped into his blood and sparked through his mind. Rising to his feet, he smiled down at Erus and offered a hand.

"Dance with me?"

Smiling, Erus shook his head and shrank further into his seat. Reaching out, Cedo took one of his Master's hands and pulled him to his feet. Erus staggered and tried to pull away. Instead, Cedo pulled him close, staring up into shocked eyes. Clasping Erus' hand, he wrapped the other around his Master's waist.

Pressing his lips to Erus' ear, he whispered, "I said, dance with me."

Drawing them away from the safety of the table, Cedo walked them to the open space before the stage.

The invisible symphony grew louder, the music washing over them in pulsing waves. Keeping Erus close, Cedo swayed in time to the beats, joining those who had already discovered its magic. Beneath his fingers, he felt his Master become tense, struggling against the situation. Stroking the small of his back, Cedo whispered and soothed, tempting him to give in. Erus' face was pale in the candlelight, perspiration dotting his forehead. He shook his head and tugged at Cedo, silently urging them back to the shadows. Cedo refused to back down, refused to allow the feelings to die. Holding onto his Master, he continued to move, continued to sway, allowing every note to control him.

Slowly, Erus began to relax. His shoulders rolled back and his eyes became hooded. Smiling, Cedo tempted him closer, drawing him into the newly discovered world. Around them, people danced alone or in groups, their bodies controlled by what they heard. Arms were held aloft, hands trying to catch the magic that flowed from the stage. Astride the stage, the masked creature threw its head back, mouth opening in a silent scream, the light reflecting from sharp, gold teeth.

Sliding his hand along Erus' back, Cedo gently clasped the back of his head and drew their lips together in a passionate, heated kiss. No one could be bothered to point or to jeer, all lost in their own hazy world. For they were in a place where no one cared, a place where anyone could be whoever, or whatever, they so pleased.

Cedo could remember little of the return journey to the palace. Curled in the horseless carriage, he laid his head against his Master's shoulder, an arm nestled around his waist. The music still beat through him, rich in his blood, the hairs on his arms quivering to attention. It had been an evening of delicious, forbidden pleasure, one that would live on in his mind for longer than memory of the journey to London. He hoped it would remain even as death rained down on them.

Beside him, Erus relaxed, his fingers caressing the nape of Cedo's neck. Cedo smiled and murmured. It felt good to have his Master in such a way, to feel his body free of any tension.

CHAPTER 10

Their room for the night was the largest suite of the Savoy hotel. No expense had been spared on ensuring their comfort, yet exhaustion left them with little energy to enjoy it. Cedo stripped away the layers of his clothing and exchanged them for his nightshirt. Brushing his fingers over a metal wall panel, he lowered the gas jets and slipped beneath the sheets. Erus was already snoring softly, red hair stark against the pure white linen.

Resting a hand on his Master's hip, Cedo gazed at Erus' shadowy form. A pang of guilt gnawed at him as the memory of Billy crept into his weary mind. He had not thought of Billy since they had landed in London, quickly becoming engrossed by all he had seen and heard. Staring at the canopy above the bed, he deliberated on the whereabouts of his lover, the ache growing.

Eventually, he slipped from the bed and, draping a coat around his shoulders, he stepped out onto the balcony. Beneath him, London still bustled, the embankment before the River Thames alive with people walking through the night. A few carriages clattered through the streets and several boats made their way along the dark, murky river. Pressing himself to the railings, Cedo took in the sharp night air, closing his eyes as a breeze lifted the hair from his face.

Looking up, he gazed at Waterloo Bridge, at the lights which shone along it. Across the Thames stood one of the Sky Searchers. From his vantage point on the balcony, Cedo could see just how tall they were, towering above even the tallest building, their lights constantly sweeping back and forth, forever turned toward the heavens. Even the building beside it, one of the new types of tower that stretched a hundred or more stories high, was dwarfed by the silent protector.

With the ache for Billy still in his heart, Cedo's mind turned toward what was to come. Who knew of the impending war? Did the average person who walked the street know? Or was that knowledge confined to those in positions of power?

A dull, pulsing sound floated through the darkness. Looking beyond the Sky Searcher, Cedo strained to see. Something was there, invisible against the night sky. Its sound throbbed toward him, deep and menacing and, as he focused, Cedo saw it.

A large platform moved through the sky, barely picked out by the lights below. Cedo could just see eight large propellers, one on each corner and one on each edge. They swung back and forth, constantly correcting the great craft. As it drifted by, Cedo could make out the guns that were loaded along the edges of the platform, all of them quietly shifting, focusing on objects he could not see. Of course, with the smokeless obtainium the flying crafts were able to be lighter, quicker and more undetectable than before.

With a sense of unease settling over him, Cedo returned to the suite, shutting the doors on the nightmare vision of the skies. Whatever it was, it could only be destined for the war.

Morning dawned, the heavy smog hanging over the city. Because of it, the street lights remained on, their flames albeit turned lower. The murk that drooped over the city threatened to plunge toward the city and encompass all who lived within her at any moment.

A carriage had been sent for them, despite Erus' protestations that he wished to use the Metropolitan District Railway. It was, he had told Cedo, the forerunner to Svenfur's own subterranean railway, except that theirs had many improvements on the London one. Svenfur would soon change completely to the cleaner, and far quicker, electricity-driven locomotives. The current corporation, Erus had continued, had no desire to change, instead spreading as far and as wide as they could. Svenfur, he had declared, would lead the world when it came to underground railroads.

As with the previous day, they entered the bunker. The men were already seated around the table, hands folded over blocks of paper and cigars smoldering in ashtrays. They took their seats at the opposite end of the table and awaited the arrival of the King. No one moved and no one spoke, all lost in their thoughts.

Cedo looked at each of the black-suited men in turn. National security had decreed that he could not bring his notebook into the bunker, lest he write down something that could one day fall into enemy hands. It had saddened Cedo, but he had understood the reasoning. He was left with his thoughts: thoughts of darkness, of horror, and of his missing mate.

The King arrived. The gathered company rose and were motioned to sit. Drawing a sheaf of papers toward him, the King surveyed the room.

"Underground protection for the higher echelons. What ideas do you all possess?"

The men looked at one another and, finally, Erus rose.

"Your Highness, if you'll allow me to speak, I have several ideas."

The day passed by slowly, as if time had taken its leave. Even the clocks on the wall appeared to have halted. Cedo stared at them, willing them to move. He wanted to leave the stone coffin and, for a while, go above ground and forget all that lived in his mind. He feared the worst for Billy, feared that the blond man was dead, dropped into the ocean by an enemy.

Or by someone related to the house of Veetu.

A rawness swept over him and he glared at his Master. Erus was in full flow, speaking to the gathered men, outlining how they could rapidly assemble a linked network of underground shelters. Cedo knew that, despite his acceptance of Billy, Erus still held animosity toward the man who had tried to steal Cedo away from him. Even though his Master had said little regarding Billy, Cedo could feel it floating from him whenever they did speak of him. It sat there, like a leaden weight in his Master's heart, another wall to close him off from the world.

Cedo wondered if it would ever go, or if it would remain, an unspoken jealousy that would make an appearance whenever his Master was angry. Deep down, he hoped that the animosity would leave and that they could live together in harmony, for however long that may be.

Regent's Park was alive with people. Crowds filled every available space as two burly men escorted them toward the Inner Circle. Vendors called their wares—potent beer, greasy foods, and tiny, tin automaton toys. Others hawked bets, while some sold illegal remedies. Men, women and children swarmed through the night-laden park, all hoping for a glimpse of the evening's challengers. The night was humid and dusty, the close-knit buildings of the city containing the heat from the sun. Running a finger around his collar, Cedo loosened his cravat. A bath would most definitely be in order upon their return to the hotel.

Above the din, Cedo heard the referee reel off the details of the upcoming bout. Pushing through the crowds, they stepped into the cleared space of the Inner Circle. At some time in the past, Erus had explained, the Inner Circle had been a garden. Now it was a huge clearing used for the Automaton Boxing Championships. A tall, chain-link fence surrounded the circular amphitheater, towering over the spectators. Within it stood a pair of stages, facing one another from opposite sides of the theater and between them, lit by powerful lights, stood the two automatons.

From his vantage point, Cedo could see that the stages held banks of levers, buttons, dials and gauges. Thick cables trailed across the sandy floor, linking each automaton to a stage.

"Wait here." Erus grinned at him, the harsh lights picking out a twinkle in his eyes. "Trust me. You will enjoy it far more from out here than in there."

Erus walked away, ducking through an entrance and into the ring, making for the referee. He was dwarfed by the automatons.

The great iron men were a sight to behold, soaring several stories high, and Cedo found his eyes drawn to them. He suspected that all around him others were doing the same, admiring the massive marvels of engineering.

They were humanoid, standing tall and straight on two legs. Giant metal hands were balled into fists by their sides and fires blazed in their bellies, smoke pouring from stacks on their shoulders. Gears, pistons and mechanics were on show amid the metal plate armor, all taut and primed. While essentially the same, each had minute differences: different colored metals, gears placed in other places. Stoker's was painted a mixture of red and gold and had his name painted down one metal bicep. The other, painted all black, bore the name *Audley*.

A woman dressed in a smart maroon suit, her brown hair piled on her head, strode across the arena and sat behind the second console.

"Ladies and gentlemen!" the referee bawled. "Boys and girls! Welcome to the Automaton Boxing Championships!"

The crowd roared, all surging to the chain fence. Cedo felt penned in as they pressed close and the excitement grew, an electricity in the air. He could not help but get caught by the feelings, clinging to the fence. Around him the crowd swelled as the rules of the fight were listed:

The fight was to be a fair and upstanding fight in an area of one thousand square meters, or thereabouts.

No wrestling was permitted.

There were to be three rounds, each lasting three minutes, with a minute break between bouts.

If either automaton falls, it must return to an upright position in less than one minute. The other automaton is to become completely still and, when the fallen automaton has returned to an upright position, the bout may continue if the three minutes are not up. Should an automaton fail to return to an upright position within the allotted time, then the referee has the power to award favor to the opposing automaton.

An automaton that remains unmoving shall be considered down.

No seconds or other persons to be permitted into the ring during the rounds.

Should the contest be stopped for any unavoidable reason, the referee is to name the time and place for finishing the contest so that the match may be won and lost.

Each automaton will be inspected by an independent adjudicator before each contest. Should an automaton be found to be harboring illegal modification then the contest will be called in favor of the opposing automaton.

An automaton on one knee is considered down and if struck is entitled to the stakes.

No modifications are allowed. This includes all and any kind of weaponry. The definition of weaponry is listed in the Automaton Boxing Championship handbook.

Automaton owners are allowed to nominate a controller other than themselves as long as the nomination is made before mid-day on the day of the contest.

Around Cedo, the energy grew, the sound of the crowd becoming a roar, all demanding that the contest begin. The referee stood on a podium between the two automatons, striding back and forth as he riled up the crowds.

"Tonight's contenders are two of the best in their ranks. Stoker has not lost a bout in the past nine months. This evening he faces the current reigning ABC champion, Audley! If Stoker wins, he will take the title. If Audley succeeds then it will be her second year as champion. This evening, Stoker's automaton will be controlled by Erus Veetu, while Audley has opted to drive her own."

The sound of the crowd rose, and Cedo found himself roaring with them.

"Lady and gentleman, start your automatons!"

The energy reached a fever pitch as the referee stepped from his podium, a small group of men moving in to remove it. Around them, the deafening sound of engines took over, the gears and pistons growling as the automatons began to move. Sparks flew from their bellies, landing in the sand and extinguishing. The choking smell of burning flooded the air.

From above the noise, the referee's voice called, "Round one!"

A bell chimed twice, and the two automatons lumbered forward, arms raising as they aimed blows at one another. Fists landed home, deep, metallic sounds rumbling around the amphitheater. People screamed and shouted, climbing around each other to get a better view. Pressed to the fence, Cedo joined them, all thoughts of the past few days melting to nothing. Ordinarily he would have found himself repulsed by such events. But these were not humans, no one was going to get hurt, and the only thing that would be spilled was the wounded pride of the loser.

Erus' machine rocked back and forth, and Cedo held his breath as it threatened to tumble. Righting itself, it moved toward the other automaton, fists jabbing at its head. Audley's machine quickly retaliated, bringing its heavy arms up to protect itself before throwing a punch at Erus.

Looking toward his Master, Cedo watched as he kicked the chair away and stood behind the console. Erus pulled at levers and worked wheels as he earnestly kept his automaton balanced.

Round one came to an end with both machines still standing. Men raced to level the sand before the referee called the start of round two. From where he stood, Cedo could see across the amphitheater, could see the crush of people. Some climbed the fence to get a better view, while some were carried on the shoulders of others. Children were lifted aloft to see the great machines. All around him was the stench of smoke, fire, people and heavy food. There was something primal about the gathering, something tribal, and it galvanized him, running through his blood.

The machines powered up, lumbering up to one another. They jabbed and blocked, bobbing out of the way of flying fists. An uppercut caused Erus' machine to stumble, sending it crashing to the ground. A flurry of sand rose around it, the crowd gasping and booing. For a moment, it looked almost as if the great automaton was breathing, trying to catch its breath. Slowly it began to struggle back to its feet. It rose, hands placed against the floor to aid it. Gripping the metal fence, Cedo looked to Erus. The look of fury was evident even from across the sandy expanse. From the corner of his eyes, he saw Audley, rejoicing, her hands in the air, loose strands of hair swirling around her head. A countdown began, the referee calling the seconds that remained before the bout was called to the opposing team.

With just seconds to go, the automaton's engine roared and it straightened up. The crowd cheered in response. It moved forward, throwing punches at its rival. The other automaton could not keep up and it stumbled and fell. Metal sheered off from its limbs, crashing into the fencing and sending people running for cover. As the dust settled, the audience returned, watching as it struggled to regain its purchase. But it seemed all was lost; falling onto its side had left it with few methods to climb back upward. Once more, the referee began to count, the numbers falling away. Around him, Cedo heard the crowd hold their breath and he felt the excitement growing.

Glancing toward the opposite stage, Cedo watched as the woman battled with her downed machine. She yanked at levers and appeared to cry obscenities into the night. Yet the automaton still lay in the sand, limbs flailing and fluid spraying as it tried to right itself.

Along with the referee, the crowd began to count. "Five! Four! Three! Two! One!"

The crowd thundered as the referee lifted Erus' arm. "Ladies and gentlemen, your new champion is Stoker!"

The sound grew louder, rolling around the dark park. From the shadows, Cedo saw Stoker dash across the ring and onto the stage. He shook Erus' hand before collecting the trophy and raising it above his head. The hysteria only grew, and Cedo felt wrapped up in it, excited by it, left wanting more. Around them, the darkness and the threat of war was forgotten, pushed away for a few, ecstatic moments.

In the ring, the men shook hands once more before leaving the stage. Pushing through the hordes, Cedo made for the exit, wanting to greet them as they left.

Laughing and looking relaxed, Erus forced himself through the crush with Stoker at his side. His eyes lit up when he saw Cedo.

"What did you think?"

Cedo grinned, the excitement of the night rolling through him. "Most enjoyable. I did not think I would like such an event, but it was rather entertaining."

Around them, people filed away, talking and laughing. Some stopped to clap Stoker and Erus on the shoulder or shake their hands.

"Glad you enjoyed it." Erus' smile widened. "Might make an automaton controller out of you."

Laughing, Cedo shook his head. "Somehow I highly doubt that. After your display this evening, you would no doubt put me to shame."

Both Erus and Stoker laughed. "You'd probably do quite well," Stoker interjected. "What with living with Erus and all. I am sure he can teach you the tricks of the trade."

"The only thing wrong with that contest," Erus began,

"was the opponent. I thought Audley had passed away." A dark look shadowed his Master's face. "That woman has been after my business for a bloody long time. I suspect that she rejoiced when she heard I had been executed. Thought she would be able to get the lion's share of the work."

Cedo looked at the men, confused. "I do not understand."

"Audley," Stoker explained, "is the head of Audley Innovations. She's of the notion that she can produce far superior weaponry. The fact of the matter is, she cannot. It's why she has been reduced to making the nuts and bolts that go inside of them. She has a real chip on her shoulder over it. And tonight we well and truly showed her where her place in the pecking order is."

Both men guffawed, hands grasping for the other's shoulders.

"I did not think women were allowed to have their own businesses? Gainful employment, yes. But to be in the seat of power for a company, then no."

Stoker looked to Cedo, one hand still resting on Erus' shoulder. "Times are changing. Women are now looking to become more a part of society than merely housewives. Some days I think it is a good change. Other times, not so much."

Silence fell over them and people jostled to pass them. Some stopped and congratulated the two men, clapping them on the shoulders and shaking their hands. Cedo stared at the trodden grass between his feet. It had been strange seeing a woman behind the controls of such a giant machine. Yet he was glad that times were changing, that women were becoming more a part of their world instead of hiding away in the factories, homes, and mills of the country.

Finally he turned to his Master and asked, "How did

you get involved with automaton boxing?"

Pushing his top hat back onto his head, Erus turned to him, eyes glistening with tears of laughter. "Oh, several years ago. Stoker came to me, asking me if I could build such a machine. Of course I said yes. The rest, as they say, is history. Being a controller is jolly good fun, even if it is only for an evening. I could most definitely do that more often."

Stoker looked to them both. "Would you both care for a drink? I'm feeling mighty parched after that."

"That would certainly be appreciated." Gently Erus guided Cedo forward.

Mingling with the crowds, they made their way toward the park's gates. Still people chattered and laughed, reliving the moments of the night. As they were departing, something piqued Cedo's curiosity. The lights from the amphitheater picked out something among the trees and, with his interest growing, he closed in on what he had seen.

However, he soon recoiled in revulsion. What Cedo had first thought were simple shop mannequins were real humans. Dangling from the tree, their necks wrapped in ropes, the right hand of one had been lashed to the left hand of the other. The area stank of death and feces and the light clearly picked out the signs around their necks.

Hanged for buggery.

They were most definitely dead, and Cedo felt bile rise, burning his throat. Grasping Erus' shoulder, he vomited, his stomach churning. His Master turned on him, face darkened by a scowl.

"Whatever is the matter? Surely you have not eaten something that raw."

Wiping his mouth on the sleeve of his jacket, Cedo shook his head and pointed toward the shadowy glade of trees. Erus pulled away and looked toward them. He returned and sighed, linking an arm with Cedo's and steering him away. Slowly they continued to walk, caught up with the slow moving crowds.

"Unfortunately there are still those who believe our kind to be unclean. I believe that this despicable act may be the work of the Black Rod Alliance." Erus sighed. "They do not like anyone they consider 'unclean.' People of different races and religions. People like ourselves. More should be done to regulate such groups but, unfortunately, people have to be allowed their freedom of speech. We cannot live in the dark ages forever."

Stepping out onto Albany Street, Erus hailed a hansom cab. Holding out a hand to help Cedo in. Collapsing into the seat, Cedo rested his head against the window, hating himself for what had happened. He should not have been repulsed by what he had seen. His time with Erus had shown him far worse. Yet still the sadness and the anger rolled through him.

"It should not happen," Cedo muttered.

The door slammed shut and his Master seated himself. "You are right, it shouldn't happen. Unfortunately, it does. Hopefully, in years to come, people will become tolerant not just of us, but of others who are considered a minority."

Peering out of the window, Cedo watched as London rolled by. Around them, traffic was heavy, their progress slow. Even at such a late hour people walked the streets. Some fought, some, like himself, vomited, most likely through excess rather than horror. Some sang and some sold their wares. Rubbish was piled on corners, waiting for the early hours when the automated cleaners would roll through the city and collect it. Despite what he had seen, it was a fascinating city, full of new ideas, all waiting to be put to use. It was a place where, unlike Svenfur, progress was encouraged. Cedo hoped it would last.

CHAPTER 11

Every day was the same as the first, with meeting after meeting held in the faceless subterranean room. The only things that changed were the faces. Generals, manufacturers, suppliers, the Prime Minister and ambassadors of the Great Eight all graced the oppressive room. Silent as a ghost, Cedo sat and listened as they discussed what was to come, how they could reduce the damage, and ultimately win. Copies of the weapons' schematics were made and whisked off via the pneumatic postal service to factories around the country. Work was to begin in earnest and, he heard, the country would be completely fortified within two months. Plenty of time, the men estimated, before James and his army arrived on their shores. The Prime Minister promised that they would begin calling up every eligible young man in the country. Training would be begin within two weeks. Any who did not answer the call would be classed as deserters and imprisoned. The bunker below Erus' house would be utilized, providing a safe haven for the highest ranking Generals of the land, sea, and air armies to oversee the protection of the southern coastal area. It would also serve as the headquarters for the supply of weapons. Erus would oversee the weaponry, keeping the armies supplied and pulling in machines that were in need of repair.

Still, Cedo longed to return to Witheybrooke, desperate

to hear if news of Billy had arrived. He doubted that it had, but still hope lived on. Cedo knew he should not be so reliant on a single person, but how did one explain it?

By night, he and Erus slept in the great suite. The room was larger than the entire ground floor of the Witheybrooke house. Their every need was provided for with a bathtub as big as an ocean, delicately prepared foods, and a bed that would have slept a small army. Automaton butlers came and went, their small fusion powered brains nowhere near powerful enough to comprehend what their glass eyes saw. Despite the luxury of the room, his Master was often too exhausted to romp, preferring to stretch beneath the sheets and fall into a deep slumber. Cedo found himself wandering the rooms of the suite, often leaning on the balcony railings and watching the city below.

As the morning of the tenth day dawned, a knock awoke him. His Master's name was called from the opposite side of the door. Erus stirred and finally slipped from the bed. He opened the door a crack and Cedo strained to hear what was being said. But voices were kept low, clandestine secrets being switched back and forth.

When the door closed, Erus turned to him, a grim look on his face. "Get dressed, as we need to leave within the hour."

London, Cedo discovered, was riddled with tunnels. Not only were there ones for the rail system but also a myriad of secret ones, linking a number of different places. He suspected that they stretched far beyond the city, finding their way to many establishments. He wondered if their house had one.

The horseless carriage took them from the hotel, winding its way beneath London. The gray tunnels were oppressive, their walls lined with tiles and seeming to stretch on for miles. Cedo would have much preferred to have traveled above ground but suspected that the confidentiality of his Master's work called for such travel.

No one else rode in the carriage with them, and silence prevailed. It felt as if there was nothing to say, nothing to speak of or discuss. Wherever they were going was a place of great secrecy, a place where the nightmares that could end the world were created. Heavy metal doors, designed to blend with the tunnels, flew by in a blur until eventually they stopped before one.

Stepping from the cab, the driver walked to the colossal door and opened a panel on the wall. Pressing a series of buttons, he retreated to the carriage and waited.

The sound of a horn began to fill the air. It sounded with a long, constant drone. Heavy locks pulled back, thundering as they retreated, and the door began to ease open. There was no grating of metal; instead, the thick slab swung easily to one side, its monstrous size filling the tunnel. The carriage eased forward, entering the new tunnel, the door hammering shut once they had crossed the threshold. A sound like a metallic clap of thunder filled the confined space.

The carriage rolled along a short corridor and into an open space. It was larger and airier than the passageways. Gas lamps clutched the white tiled walls and people dashed around, coming and going from the many entrances which led from the grand, domed hall. At the heart of the space sat a large, circular desk. A number of people sat behind it, moving papers, talking into speaking tubes, and answering questions.

The carriage bypassed the desk and made for one of the many entrances to the left of it. The passageways had opened up, making it wide enough for people and transportation to easily move side by side. As with the entrance hall, the walls were white and lit by numerous flickering lamps. All the people they passed looked official, dressed in suits or white laboratory coats. Along the passageway were a number of other doors and entrances, all leading away into the great, underground organization.

They took a final left turn and found themselves in a smaller, yet no less grand, hall. A sign hung from the ceiling with *Auditory Department* neatly printed on it. Another desk sat before three entrances. The lady behind the desk looked up, a strange device strapped to the side of her head. It covered one ear, and what appeared to be a small speaking tube covered her mouth.

"Mr. Davenport? Yes, Mr. Veetu is here to see you."

A moment later, an elderly gentleman exited one of the passages and walked up to them, hand held out to Erus.

"So good you could make it, Erus. There's much I want to show you."

Dressed in a fitted suit of tweed and with his silver hair cropped short, Mr. Davenport led them back along the way he had come. Erus walked beside the gentleman, leaving Cedo to attempt to keep up.

"What do you have for me, Donald?" Erus' voice reverberated from the curving, tiled walls.

"There've been some interesting breakthroughs of late that I'm eager to show you. I'm sure you'll approve of them."

Mr Davenport brought them to a halt before a door marked with *Studies Into The Control Of The Mind*. Ushering them through, he led them to another door. Beyond it was a sight that chilled Cedo.

A control console of sorts sat in the main part of the room. Before a large window sat banks of dials, buttons, and knobs. White-coated people sat before it, and beyond the glass was a white-tiled room.

Memories of Erus' underground chambers flooded back, the cruelty and bloodshed within them all too fresh in his mind. Stepping up to the console, Cedo peered into the white room beyond it. Each corner held an amplification device, a black box that stretched from the floor to the ceiling. Each box contained four horns. In the center of the room crouched a person, head hanging, hands clasped over his ears.

A wave of revulsion rolled through Cedo, and he stepped away. In the glass of the window, he saw his pale, disgusted reflection turn and look at the men behind him.

"We've discovered," Mr. Davenport began, "that certain frequencies can alter the way a person thinks. We can implant thoughts and feelings, or encourage them to perform certain deeds. We can even use it to erase the memories of what they have done."

Glaring at Erus, Cedo hissed, "You promised."

A look of confusion crumpled his Master's face. "Promised what, dear boy?"

"That there would be no more experiments. If you have not forgotten, you were tried and executed for such things."

Mr. Davenport guffawed. "Oh, that? Bit of a show trial, wasn't it?"

Closing his eyes, Erus pinched his nose and shook his head. Cedo's anger grew, his jaw tight.

"Indeed it was," Erus softly replied.

The sound of something starting drew his attention back to the control console and the white room beyond it. The whirring sound grew in pitch until it was almost too painful to listen to. One of the white-coated men pushed a button and, in the room beyond the glass, something began to happen.

The crouching person slowly got to his feet. Cedo saw that it was a young man, perhaps not much older than himself. His face was pockmarked with scars and his eyes held the cruel glare of evil. A dial was turned and instantly the boy's look of menace fell to one of complete blankness. His eyes became unfocused and stared off into the distance. Stepping up to the console, Mr. Darlington pulled a speaking tube from amid the array of controls.

"Samuel, this is control speaking. Are you receiving me?"

The boy lifted his right hand and kept it raised until the elderly gentleman spoke again.

"Good. Thank you."

The hand was lowered and the boy continued to stare, seemingly at nothing.

"Samuel, are you ready to receive your directive?"

The boy nodded, just once, all of his movements as slow as that of a sloth. Stepping back, Cedo shivered, the coldness remaining with him. It was repulsive to watch someone's free will taken from them so clinically and so easily.

Placing a hand over the speaking tube, Mr. Davenport turned toward Erus. "What you are about to see may shock you, but I want to assure you that all of our test subjects are criminals that have shown no signs of being able to be rehabilitated."

"There is not much which shocks me these days, Donald. Do what you will."

Cedo's Master had his arms folded across his chest, eyes staring straight through the glass.

Touching his fingers to Erus' elbow, Cedo whispered, "I do not think I can watch."

Erus did not look at him, his voice cool and quiet. "In that case, go and stand in the corridor."

As he was about to leave, Mr. Davenport spoke again,

once more addressing the boy in the room. "Samuel, on the floor to your left is a gun. I want you to pick it up, place the barrel to your temple and pull the trigger."

"No!" Cedo whirled around, all diplomacy leaving him. Snatching the speaking tube from the gentleman's hand, Cedo glared into his eyes. "I will not let this happen. Not again."

"It's too late," Mr. Davenport replied. "The process is already taking hold."

Cedo glanced into the room. Just below the window lay a revolver. The boy wrapped his fingers around the deadly device and lifted it. A door stood to the left of the console and Cedo moved to it. Twisting the handle, he growled as it refused to give way, locked against anyone who wished to step into the room beyond it. His eyes fell on a number pad to one side of the door.

"The combination?!" he bawled.

No one responded and even though he knew that it was a pathetic attempt, he began to press random buttons. From the corner of his eye, Cedo watched as the boy pressed the gun to his temple, his face as blank as before. Heart pounding, Cedo struck his shoulder against the door. The door merely trembled beneath his onslaught. From beyond the door came a muted explosion and Cedo looked up to see the body of the boy slump to the floor.

Holding his tongue, he looked to his Master, the green eyes indifferent as they stared at him.

"Come," Mr. Davenport said softly, "there's more I wish to show you. I know that you're very much in demand and I don't wish to impose on your time."

Erus never said anything as he left the room, arms still folded across his chest. Barely containing his anger, Cedo silently followed, murderous thoughts rolling through his mind.

They left the room and walked along the corridor. No

one spoke, nor did they look at one another. It was as if the death of the boy had affected them all. Cedo doubted that the two men before him would mourn the loss of such a person, for as Mr. Davenport had said, the experiments were carried out on criminals, those who had no future other than to disrupt the smooth running of life.

Mr. Davenport turned the handle of another of the impenetrable doors, this one marked with the words *Classification and Correlation Of War Recordings.* Lights flickered on as they entered, the gas catching and illuminating the space. Before them was a large, cavern-like area, walls sloping up to a rounded ceiling. As with everywhere else within the tunnels, the correlation room was tiled in white. Along one long wall sat an expansive row of pigeonholes, each one identified with letters and numbers. On either side of the small boxes were tunnels, leading off into the distance. Other than several chairs sitting before the wooden shelves, the room was completely empty.

"This is where your recordings will come in," the lab-coated man said. "Each of those pigeonholes corresponds to a county and is connected to the pneumatic postal service. Recordings from all manner of people will arrive here and be safely stored. We may choose to make copies of them and send them on to others. Your broadcasts will most definitely have copies made and we will send them all across the land."

Cedo remained silent. He had nothing to say to either man, and his being drawn into the war by making inspirational speeches now angered him. He wanted nothing to do with what was being planned, wanted to be away somewhere safe and wait for it to end.

"Through the corridors is the area where all the recordings will be stored. How do you plan on broadcasting these recordings?"

From the corner of his eye, Cedo watched his Master nod.

Eventually, he spoke. "As you probably know, we have perfected the use of wireless technology. All of the different regiments will have receiver and transmitter units so that they can relay messages. We are going to build and distribute receiver units to every household in the country. Already the transmitter equipment is being built and installed. It should not take more than a few weeks before everything is in place and we can begin."

"That is an undertaking of great proportions. Erus, are you sure you are capable of it?"

His Master chuckled. "Of course. We're more than equipped to take on such an undertaking."

The silence fell over them once more, a cloying sense of dread carried upon its wings.

Mr. Davenport obviously picked up on the emotions and gave a polite cough. "Well, I believe that is all for in here. Gentlemen, if you'd like to follow me."

They meandered from room to passageway to room, the tunnels going on for as far as they needed. As they neared the end of the excursion, Cedo suspected that they had not seen even a fraction of the labyrinthine complex. What else lay beyond the doors, unwilling to be shown to them? Were others still being murdered in the name of freedom? The questions lay over his shoulders like a metal mantle, cold and heavy, weighing him down.

Finally, they reached the grand hall through which they had entered, where their carriage continued to patiently wait for them. Upon seeing them, the driver tipped his hat and strode back to the horseless beast. Opening the curving cover at the front, he did something until the engine roared to life. It spluttered and choked before eventually catching. The driver moved to the rear of the machine to toss more fuel on the fire.

"That gent has just reminded me," Mr. Davenport said. "I've heard all about your breakthrough in smokeless fuel. Do you know when we'll be getting it?"

Cedo's Master, who had not spoken for a good while, said, "We're already rolling it out. Some of the new flying crafts, especially the gunners, are already being calibrated to use it."

"Splendid. I cannot wait to finally use some of your newest technologies. The world has been so eagerly awaiting them."

Holding out his hand, Erus shook Mr Davenport's. "For now, I'll bid you farewell. Thank you for showing us around. It is greatly appreciated."

Mr. Davenport smiled. "Any time at all, Erus. You know where we are."

Erus grabbed Cedo's elbow, guiding him toward the carriage. Once they were seated and the door was firmly closed, Erus turned to him, eyes ablaze with the eternal fires of damnation.

"How dare you," he hissed, teeth bared.

Instead of cowering away, Cedo sat straight, shoulders pulled back and head held high.

"How dare I, what?" Cedo replied. "Stand up to you? Tell you that what is happening is wrong?"

Erus raised an arm. Still Cedo remained as he was, tall and proud, refusing to bend to the will of the other.

"Go on," he breathed, his own voice low and filled with the hate he felt for the people who drove the horrors. "Beat me because I have defied you. It is what you have done in the past, so why change your ways now?"

Slowly, his Master lowered his arm. "You demeaned me with your words and outburst. Humiliated me before the very people who are doing all they can to help save this country. And for what? Some criminal who would have wound up at the end of a noose anyway? Why shed your precious tears for these people?"

"Because," Cedo hissed, "as both you and I know, this is morally wrong. If the government had not decided that you were worth more to them alive, then you would have died for it. Would sitting in that chamber and losing control of your body before a watching audience for *this*, for killing people for your gain, have been worth it? How do you, and the others who are involved, differ from a common murderer?"

The look that descended over Erus' face was one of pure fury. His tall body tightened, hands curling into fists. "Tell me why I should not punish you right here," he growled.

"Because you know I am right. These experiments were supposed to be stopped, yet they continue. Why?"

"Because the government wanted you, and the rest of the population, to think that they had," Erus retorted. "We have discussed this at length. There are two faces those in power like to show: the one that thinks for the public, and the one that hides in the shadows. You're all being led astray, Cedo, and the sooner you learn this, the better."

Pressing himself back into the seat, Cedo glared at Erus. "Then why do we not tell the public? Why not show them what is happening right beneath their noses?"

His Master's face became dark, hands uncurling. "Do you want to die?"

"No."

"Well then. Besides, no one would believe you. All they want to believe is that the music hall stars will fall in love with them, that they'll make a lifetime's worth of money without ever working, and that they must purchase new clothing every six months. Anything else is superfluous and will be ignored. Do not get me wrong; there are a few who have awakened to what is happening, but their theories have always gone unheeded. Very few listen to them and those who do are considered mad." Erus sighed, eyes turned to gaze out at the tunnel. "And the ones who make the deepest discoveries about the government do not last very long. Trust me, there is absolutely no evidence of these people."

They fell quiet, the only sound the rattling of the carriage through the unending stretches of tunnel. The lights caught swirls of smoke and flashes of embers, appearing and dying in a heartbeat. Animosity still hung over them, curdling the air between them. Cedo did not want to dwell on what might happen. Whatever was to happen, would happen, and there was no changing it. It did not matter how hard he tried, how hard he pushed, life, the war and his Master's temper would trundle on unchanged.

Upon arrival at their hotel suite, they found that the bed had been turned down, the lights had been lit and food had been laid out. The automaton butlers all stood to attention, lined up beside the door. Standing in the heart of the room, Cedo watched as Erus wandered to the desk, collecting a pile of envelopes from the varnished surface. He leafed through them, dismissing them with grunts and mumbled curses. Opening the final one, he drew out a piece of folded paper and perused it before looking at Cedo, face still stony.

"Wash and dress. We leave in an hour."

CHAPTER 12

Seated in one of the horseless carriages, they ambled through the city. The evening air was cloying and dusty with the promise of rain lingering in the heavens. From his vantage point, Cedo watched the city pass by, marveling at the tall buildings, tubes of glowing colored glass spelling out the names of companies, beverages and entertainments clinging to the brickwork. Every street and avenue had at least one building that was lit with the new technology. Railway lines stretched between the tall buildings, raised hundreds of feet from the ground. Through the darkness, trains had rolled along them, the empty tracks swinging to connect to another building and carry another line of carriages on its journey.

They stopped at a theater, unlike those that graced the streets of Svenfur. Standing proudly on Shaftesbury Avenue, the Palace Theater was awash with lights. They twinkled above the entrance, and above the lights, dancing along the canopy, was a chorus of oversized fairies. Electric lights glittered from their costumes, wings fluttering back and forth. Several moved, powered by unseen mechanisms, pirouetting before the theater's intricately decorated frontage.

Dressed in a suit of blue, Cedo followed Erus' black, tail-coated back. The top hat was pushed onto his head, red hair billowing behind him. His cane swung from his hand. Weaving through the gathering crowds, they were greeted at the door by the theater's manager. The young, well-dressed man led them through the horde of people, opening doors and guiding them through until they reached a box. Seating them, he gave a final smile and gestured to a bell on the wall, advising them to ring it should they need anything. Glancing over the edge of the box, Cedo admired the architecture, the beauty of the building lifting his spirits. For the first time in many months, he felt as though he had arrived home, the call of the theater drawing him to its light.

As the door closed, Erus pulled Cedo back to his seat and looked at him. The redhead's lips pulled back into a sneer and he removed the hat, shaking his hair out before placing the garment to one side. Cedo felt his heart pick up pace, hammering against his ribs.

Snapping his fingers, his Master pointed to the red carpeted floor before them. "Kneel."

"Why?" he softly asked. Around them, he could hear the noise of the audience, of people taking their seats, talking, and of the orchestra warming up.

"Do not ask questions." Erus' voice was deep and gritty. "Kneel."

Unwilling to defy his Master further, Cedo slipped from the seat and to the floor.

"Head down, eyes on the floor. Do not move until I instruct you to."

Heat rushed to his cheeks, his hair thankfully hiding his humiliation. He knew that it related to his earlier outburst that, rather than punish him in the privacy of their room, his Master would do it in public. It was unlikely that Cedo would protest in such a place.

With his jaw tight and hands balled into fists, Cedo stared at the floor. His explosion had been justified, the bloodshed supposedly having been halted by the

153

government. Yet it continued, unseen by the citizens of the country. How had Erus expected him to react to such a display? Or had his Master not known what would take place behind the closed doors of the underground complex?

From the auditorium, Cedo heard the audience fall quiet and the orchestra strike its first chords. Voices rose from the stage, projecting their songs to the waiting ears. He longed to see them, longed to see the costumes he knew would be as splendid as the theater. The music was exquisite, a beautiful infusion of notes.

He thought of Billy, wondering whether he was okay, whether he would make a reappearance. Cedo sincerely hoped that he would, that Billy's disappearance had not become permanent. Many thoughts raced through his mind: that Billy could no longer live the life that had been dealt to him. Or that the blond-haired man no longer wished to be in the presence of Erus. Or that Billy was no longer interested in him, preferring the nomadic life to remaining at the side of another for all eternity. The final thought distressed him, a cold arrow of pain shooting into his heart. Surely Billy would do no such thing, not after his proclamations of adoration. Billy was stronger than that, weathering the storm for those he held dear. He would not just leave without so much as a word of explanation.

His body began to ache, shoulders slumping and legs becoming numb. The first act passed in slowness, yet his Master did not let him up, refusing to speak or even acknowledge him. Cedo longed to lift his head but did not dare, knowing that it would result in something far more painful and far less pleasurable than previous nights.

Eventually, Erus tapped his shoulder and Cedo started to struggle to his feet. Yet his Master held him down, forcing him back to his knees. Instead, Erus looked down at him, the twisted sneer still on his lips. Erus plucked at his breeches and freed his cock. Shifting in his seat, his Master made himself comfortable.

"Suck it."

A blush touched Cedo's flesh once more. No one could see them, yet it still felt perverse. Pausing, Cedo waited to see what his Master would do next. Time felt as though it had come to a halt, ceasing to exist. Again, the darkened eyes flicked down to him, Erus baring his teeth.

"Come on. We don't have all night."

Shambling across the carpet, Cedo positioned himself at his Master's feet. Curling his fingers around the base of Erus' cock, Cedo took a deep breath and closed his lips around the engorged flesh.

Darkness had engulfed them when Cedo awoke. The lamps had been extinguished and the heavy curtains were drawn against the terrors of the midnight city. A welcoming weight pressed against his back, Erus' strong arm wrapped around him and holding him close. With sleep evading him, Cedo pondered the evening at the theater, of being made to kneel and pleasure the one who housed him. It was, he was aware, punishment for the humiliation he had brought upon his Master. Although he should not have spoken out of turn, nor accused him, the feeling of wrongdoing had been overwhelming, choking him unless he made his point. The closeness in the bed was, Cedo knew, Erus' way of telling him that all was well, that whatever had happened was now forgotten and that they should look to the future.

From beyond the curtained windows, a rumble of thunder rolled through the air. Shivering, Cedo pressed himself closer to the warmth of his Master as the rains finally came.

Standing beneath the overhang of a shop, Cedo watched the rain fall. The sky above London remained the same slate gray as when they had arrived, the sun doing its best to battle through the perpetual smog.

Erus had not mentioned the previous evening, instead taking Cedo into his arms and blessing him with kisses. The emptiness Cedo had been left with still lingered, and he waited for it to ease.

Above him, a sky train rumbled along its tracks, smoke and sparks tumbling down its sides, the girders groaning beneath the weight of the loaded carriages. Despite the dull day, the streets were awash with people and machines. Omnibuses were powered by great engines, twin smoke stacks chugging grime into the air. Walking machines teetered on the cobbles, carefully picking their way through the snarling traffic. Unlike Svenfur, London appeared to be cultivating a fashion for multi-rider walkers, several people safely slung between the four legs. Deliveries were made by giant trailers pulled not by horses but by the same huge engines that powered the omnibuses. It looked as though London had completely done away with the horse, replacing it entirely with steam.

He searched the crowds, heartache growing as each passing person was not the one he longed to see. People of all colors, creeds, and walks of life bustled along the streets. Factory workers in soot-stained clothes; office workers in their staunch grays and whites; ladies in tightly laced dresses. His eyes settled on a lady in a long, colorful gown. It was loosely fitting, her sandaled feet peeking from beneath the hem as she walked. Cedo's heart skipped a beat and he reached out to her, fingers brushing her wrist.

Startled, she turned and he smiled, giving the physician of the underworld club a small bow.

"Lady Seren, I apologize for interrupting your day."

She looked at him, as if unsure of why she had been stopped.

"I was just wondering if you had perhaps seen someone on your travels around the capital?"

Seren stepped closer, joining him to hide from the rain.

"I have seen a great many people," she said. "Whom do you search for?"

"He is about my age with long, blond hair and blue eyes. Well-built and muscular. He is a laborer and goes by the name of Billy."

No recognition flickered across her face, and Cedo felt an overwhelming sadness still him. His mate no longer cared, no longer wanted to be a part of his life. He had disappeared into the shadows of the world, not even caring that his lover was in London. Cedo could not blame Billy for leaving; confined to the house of Veetu was not a life for a wanderer. Sadly, Cedo twisted the ring on his thumb.

"Perhaps he remains in your home city," Seren said. "It would be the logical place to stay. Return home and see if he returns with you."

"Ah, just the woman!"

Cedo turned to see Erus exit the shop behind him. Several packages were clasped in his hands and he held them out to Cedo. Trying not to appear disgruntled, he took them.

"I trust you were on your way to the palace?" Erus asked.

Seren nodded. "Indeed, I was."

"I've spoken to the King and he's requesting you return

to Svenfur with us to make the necessary arrangements to set up the field hospitals. You'll be working with General Anderson of the Medical Corps."

His Master did not give Seren a chance to respond, instead stepping through the crowds and into the rain. He raised his arm to hail a steam-cab and climbed in, beckoning Cedo and Seren to follow.

The return journey to the palace was uneventful, the city passing in a haze of gray. By day, it seemed far less attractive than it did by night. By night it became a fairytale land of bright lights and excitement. By day it felt heavy and oppressive, the gritty air irritating the inhabitants.

Closing his eyes, Cedo laid his head against the backrest of the seat. He felt tired, the hurriedness of the previous days sapping him dry, and he dreamed of a night of unbroken sleep.

He was startled awake by Erus' lips against his ear. "I have brought you a gift, a token of my affection."

Erus laid a parcel wrapped in red paper and gold ribbon in Cedo's lap. Picking at the ribbon, he eased the paper from the long box and lifted the lid, smiling at the neatly folded crimson material inside. A motif of flowers and leaves was picked out in threads of green and gold.

Taking the jacket from the box, Cedo held it out, admiring the flared sleeves and neatly tucked waist. The greenery of leaves and flowers danced over it, a veritable rainbow compared to the dull, drab city beyond the carriage.

The carriage stopped at the palace's dome and, after a short delay, they were admitted, rolling over the red courtyard and through to the expansive gardens. Cedo admired them, the explosion of color feeding his soul.

On the lawns sat the King's airship, anchored and waiting to carry them home. Exiting the carriage with their new acquaintance, they boarded the airship. Erus ushered Cedo into a seat before settling beside him. Seren sat across from them, eyes flicking back and forth. Set on the table were a number of leather cases, all embossed with the King's coat of arms. All of the cases were closed with locks.

Cedo felt a shudder and heard a pop as the bolts blew themselves free of the earth. Slowly the ship began to rise, the engines engaging as they lifted above the palace and London's stretching skyline. Below them, the city moved silently by. Airships were moored on the pointed tips of buildings, mazes of bridges swinging out to meet them. Slowly they rose, finally breaking through the smog and reaching the cloud layer, London lost below them. Sailing through the sparkling wonderland of clouds, they reached the azure sky, Cedo smiling as the warmth of the sun touched his face. The solar sails unfurled, sunlight sparkling off them as they caught the powerful rays.

Leaning back in his seat, Cedo watched the rolling sea of clouds pass by. More airships joined them, coming and going from the country's seat of power. For a while, he relaxed, the gentle thud of the props and the never-ending roll of clouds lulling him. Excitement began to grow within his soul, the possibility of Billy's return flickering through him. Cedo hoped that even if his mate had yet to return to the house that there would at least be word of him, that a letter or a pneumatic message would have arrived.

Keys rattled and he turned to watch Erus unlock one of the cases. Paper was neatly stacked inside of it, *Top Secret* stamped in red on the brown cover. Without even glancing up, Erus began to leaf through the pages, face grim.

"What are they?" Cedo cautiously asked.

"Files. Information on the enemy, weaknesses,

strengths. What we can do to defeat them. Plans for weapons they want me to work on. Anything that will help us win."

Engrossed in what he was reading, Erus fell silent and Cedo turned his attention back to the view. He could sense Seren looking at him and felt he should make conversation. Yet there appeared to be little to say.

They had left the harsh gray of London behind, and the splendid greenery of the country began to unfold beneath them.

The Witheybrooke house was just as they had left it, empty and quiet. Only the signs of Francis' organization showed that there was someone beneath the roof. There was nothing else. Even Misty appeared to have taken a leave of absence, no doubt sleeping in a sunbeam somewhere.

Erus rifled through a pile of envelopes and pneumatic postal tubes. "Show Seren to one of the guest rooms. I shall send word to the General that she is here."

Cedo did not move, his eyes on the messages that his Master held. "Are there any for me?"

Peering over the envelopes, Erus gazed at him for a moment before he shook his head. Cedo felt his heart drop. Perhaps Billy was dead, another of his loved ones to join the legions of missing.

Despondent and dispirited, he showed Seren to a room beside the one he had hoped he would one day share with Billy. Like his own, it was a simple room as if, despite his wealth, Erus had little use for material possessions. Cedo knew that a lot of money had been dedicated to the expansive bunker, a place he had assumed Erus had begun work on after he had first met James so many decades before. Even then his Master had known that the fate of the world was not a peaceful one.

The bed had already been turned down and a fire laid, as if Francis had known that their arrival was imminent.

From the window of the room, Cedo could just make out the machines that sat in the garden, the debris of the dead animals having been cleaned away. Already work had begun, the vicious metal teeth tearing at the turf, creating something that threatened to engulf the grounds and the surrounding fields.

"We shall have to talk at some other time, when everyone is not so tense." Seren's voice pulled him from the window.

With a terse smile, he nodded. "Indeed we shall. I apologize for my silence over the previous hours."

Seren opened one of her bags and began to lay her clothes upon the bed. "There is no need to apologize. Everyone is very busy, their minds elsewhere. Once all of this has passed there will be more time to acquaint ourselves."

"Indeed." He looked to the door. "I shall bid you farewell. Sleep well, and should you need anything, please do not be afraid to waken one of us."

Seren looked up and smiled. "Thank you. I shall bear that in mind."

Leaving the lady to see to her routine, Cedo entered his own room, hoping for respite from the leaden feeling in his heart. Instead, he found Francis seated beside the fire, Billy's leather book clutched in his hands. The heat of rage began to boil and he longed to snatch it away and force Francis from the room. The bespectacled man was a friend in a world filled with the darkness of foes and not worthy of Cedo's wrath.

"Have you heard word from him?" Cedo softly asked.

Francis shook his head, eyes on the book. "And it's

not that I haven't wished I had either. But we must press on and hope that he returns."

Brushing past him, Cedo pulled himself into the window and stared at the Downs. The air tasted clearer than that of London, free of smog and grime. Somewhere, beyond the Downs, was Billy. Hope had to remain, no matter how faint it was growing.

"We have a new person with us," Cedo said. "Her name is Seren and she will be running the field hospitals."

"Thank you for telling me. There is sufficient food in the pantries and firewood in the store."

Cedo did not look up. "Thank you."

"Would you like me to leave you alone?"

He sighed, breath fogging the glass for a moment. "Please."

The door clicked shut and, for the first time in many days, Cedo found himself alone with nothing more than his thoughts. Glancing to the bed, he saw that the leather book had been left behind. Climbing from the window, he picked it up and opened it. The pages were filled with Billy's erratic handwriting and beautiful sketches. His heart warmed at the sight, never having known that his mate could produce such pieces of beauty. Slowly he turned the pages, studying them. There were sweeping reminders of the mountains and plans of machines, sketches of the barren trees and the horses they had ridden. The final drawing brought tears to Cedo's eyes for, from the page, he himself stared, eyes turned to gaze into the distance. He did not know when Billy had created the portrait or whether it had been done from memory. It did reinforce the notion Billy loved him as much as he loved Billy.

Clasping the book to his heart, he returned to the window.

CHAPTER 13

The day faded to night, and Cedo returned to Erus' room. Lying beside his Master, he gazed at the tree-like ceiling above them, almost hearing the rain of the previous days hammer against its branches. He longed to read, or to write, but the thoughts of another kept him from doing so.

"I know you worry about William." Erus sounded weary. "But you have to let him go for the moment. Wait a few more days and see what will come. No one knows what tomorrow holds."

"That is what everyone has said," he murmured. "I am tired of hearing it. I want answers, and I am unwilling to wait any longer for them."

Moving to Erus' side, Cedo brushed the fiery hair from the older man's face and gazed down into his emerald eyes. So much was changing, every second bringing something new. Even Erus was changing, seeming to warm to him more than before. Had their months together brought about the changes? Or perhaps it had been their incarceration beneath the earth? Cedo felt the doubts he had once held about walking beside Erus fading. Yes, there were still tendrils of uncertainty licking at his mind, but Cedo hoped that they too would one day disappear.

"Why must the experiments continue?" Cedo asked.

Erus slumped beside him, head lowered. "Because

they must. Do not ask me why they do. I believed I had washed my hands of them."

"You could have walked away!"

Resignation appeared to roll over his Master as the redhead nodded. He never looked up at Cedo. "You're right. I could have walked away. I should have been an example and done just that. Unfortunately, even now, certain things are expected of me."

"Like watching luckless humans have their lives so cruelly snuffed out?" he demanded.

Again, Erus nodded. "Yes and, for that, I apologize."

Cedo felt his heart warm at his Master's words. "Do you mean that?"

Erus looked up at him through a veil of red hair, his green eyes filled with remorse. "Yes, yes I do."

The following morning, Cedo was awoken by the sounds of voices and activity. Slipping from the bed, he wearily drew back the curtains and gazed at the garden and the small army of laborers. They were stoking the engines of the machines, smoke and ash filling the already bright morning. Metal teeth began to turn, ready to tear apart their green and pleasant land. It pained him to see it happen. The lush greenery often fed his soul and chased away the toxins of the cloying city.

"Why must they destroy the garden?"

He heard his Master stir before responding, "Come here."

He climbed back onto the bed, allowing Erus to wrap Cedo in his arms and lavish him with kisses.

"They are building an extension to the bunker," he murmured. "Once finished it will house a few essential weapons."

"How many?"

Erus' hands slid down his back, tugging at his nightshirt. "Enough."

"How many?" Cedo heard his voice begin to change to a growl, the need for information overriding the passion of the kisses.

His Master pulled away, eyes blazing in the summer light. "It will house one flying craft, several of the armored horses, and as many guns and ammunition as we can fit into the spare space. Does that satisfy you?"

Cedo felt himself grin, his mouth returning to Erus'. "Of course. *Master*."

Beneath him, he felt Erus hiss, hands possessively drawing him close, once more feeding Cedo gentle kisses. Slowly Cedo responded to them, sensing that Erus only wanted to help chase away the pain that haunted him.

How things had changed. Now the ice king's heart appeared to be thawing. Hands stroked along Cedo's back and the rise of his buttocks, Erus' mouth tender against his own. For several moments, they stayed together, sharing gentle kisses.

Eventually Erus moved away, leaving him with a particularly fiery kiss. "We must rise, as there is much to do. Your presence will be a great help. I could use an extra pair of hands and it will give your mind less time to wander. And do not bother wearing your best clothing; it will only get ruined."

Breakfast was taken in the kitchen, an odd change from the once lavish routine. Francis had laid out a simple affair of meats, bread, and fruit. It was eaten in silence, the three of them, Francis, Seren, and himself, congregated around the central table.

Cedo had long thought that the suit in which he had entered Erus' house had disappeared, too old to be of use. But it had been folded neatly at the bottom of his dresser. Donning it had been strange, the frayed fabric once so familiar to him. Now it was only useful for the filthy work Cedo assumed his Master had prepared for him.

Within the hour, there came a series of heavy knocks at the front door. Following Erus, Cedo darted into the dining room and peered through the window. He was not surprised to see a large horseless carriage sitting before the house. With room for the driver and passengers at the front, the rear part consisted of a long wagon, its windowless sides concealing its secrets.

At the rear, a pair of doors had been opened, men milling around and peering in. The men were dressed in military uniforms and when Cedo heard a booming voice, he understood why.

"Veetu! So good to see you."

He heard his Master mumble, voice concealed by the walls. Walking to the door, Cedo glanced into the hallway.

The front door had been thrown open, and a broad-shouldered man had stepped into the hall. He wore the red uniform of an army General, his tailored jacket decorated with gold tassels and braids. His brown hair was neatly cut and he had muttonchop sideburns. Cowled in black, his hair loose down his back, Erus stood to one side, allowing the man to enter.

"Looks like I've been assigned to you, old boy. Get this bunker of yours ready."

The two men began to walk through the house, Erus looking pale.

"Cedo, come with me, please," he called from the shadows of the stairs.

They walked to the cellar, following the steps down to the war room. Striding across the open space, Erus swung open the door to the bunker.

"Must put some kind of locking device on that," he mumbled.

"I trust you're going to fix a heavier door to it, too," the General stated. "Don't want those damn pigs coming down to get us."

Cedo's Master ignored the man, instead leading them through the interlinking rooms. As they passed through each one, Erus' fingers brushed against the metal panels, activating the gas lamps.

"You do have generators down here, don't you, Veetu?" the General asked.

"Indeed." Erus never looked to those following him. "A few minor adjustments and they shall run on obtainium."

"Good. Pump facilities?"

"Of course." Cedo could hear a hint of anger in his Master's voice, as if the questions challenged his intelligence. "Water is pumped and filtered from an underground well with chambers to store and clean water in the event of a disaster. Air is pulled from the surface and triple-filtered before it reaches the inhabitants."

"You speak of cleaning the water in the event of a disaster," the General asked.

Erus stopped and leaned against the frame of a door. He chuckled. "Yes, clean. We are now able to take the waste water from baths, the kitchen and water closets and expunge it of any impurities. From there, it can be reused."

"And what of food?"

Erus' face changed, a manic glint tinting his eyes and a sneer twisting his face. It was a look Cedo had not seen for many months, and it chilled him.

"Should we run out of food, General Rowe, then you will be at the top of the list for us to eat."

The broad man gave Erus a chilling look before continuing with his stream of thought.

"I've brought everything we shall need, and many items that you have requested. I shall have the lads unload them and bring them down." He turned to leave before halting and glancing over his shoulder, face blank of any expression. "I trust you shall make us welcome?"

"As welcome as you wish to be made, General." The tone of Erus' voice sent a shiver down Cedo's spine. Cold and filled with menace, it was a warning, not just to the General, but to himself. Below ground, they would take no prisoners.

A chain of red-uniformed men stretched through the house and down to the bunker. Unmarked wooden crates were passed hand to hand until they reached their destination. Upon arrival, the lids were pried away and the contents inspected before they were sent to their final resting place.

Cedo bustled back and forth, moving piles of crates around the commodious subterranean world. He had forgotten how expansive it was, the rooms running into one another, seeming to go on for many miles. Dormitories, listening and receiving posts, a command center, a wireless broadcast room—enough to house a small army. Strange, empty rooms with desks and speaking tubes. All were decorated with dark wood paneling, wallpapers of various colors hanging above it. Several rooms had large maps on the walls, while one had a semi-circle of tables, streets maps set into the surfaces. The whole bunker held oppressive feelings of dread.

The cases contained all manner of objects: food, files, papers, supplies. Cedo was given one that had not been opened and asked to leave it in the drawing room beside Erus' living quarters. When he returned to the door of the bunker, he was given another, but Erus stopped him before he could move away.

"If you are taking that to the drawing room, you may as well follow me."

With a curt nod, Cedo fell into step behind his Master.

The fireplace was devoid of any wood, the dark paneling making the room seem darker than it was. Before the fireplace sat a desk with inkwells, a speaking tube, and a row of pigeonholes on its surface. Behind it sat a large chair. Shelves lined the walls, waiting for their delivery of books. The walls above the paneling were bare of any decoration. Everything smelled of still, stagnated air.

Exhaustion gripped Cedo's body and the deep chairs called to him. But, from Erus' earlier mood, Cedo decided to wait until the older man had arrived before he relaxed. Instead, he leaned against the desk, hands curled around the lip of the wood, eyes suspiciously on the closed crate.

Hearing the door open, he watched as his Master walked in, exhaustion lining his face. Crumpling into the desk's chair, he gestured to Cedo.

"Pull up a chair, and bring the crate with you."

Doing as he was bid, Cedo sat beside Erus, the crate at their feet. Taking a letter opener from the desk, Erus twisted it beneath the lip of the lid, the wood splintering until it gave way. A nest of straw lay inside. Cedo's Master reached in and pulled a metal object out onto his lap.

Looking closer, Cedo could make out familiar curves and lines. Erus' hands danced across the metal, and from inside it there came the sound of something coming to life. A whirr filled the air, and a luminous green light flickered from between the plates of metal. Eventually the sound faded away and the light became constant. Erus

169

placed the object on the floor.

Before Cedo's surprised eyes, it came to life, slender limbs stretching and its back falling into a dip. A thin tail flicked back and forth and a mechanical cat sat at Cedo's feet, glowing green eyes fixed on his own. Sleek and distinctly feline, it had the appearance of intelligence, and of a hunter. He did not doubt that its angular paws hid diamond-sharp claws and that its jaws were loaded with deadly teeth.

The mecha-cat was painted entirely black, a stark contrast to Misty's white coat. Green light flashed from beneath its armor plating whenever it moved, giving a small indication of what lay inside. It flicked its tail back and forth, the jointed appendage tapering to a sharp point.

"It is called Consiliatrix," Erus stated. "The most intelligent creation we have to date."

Cedo felt himself raise an eyebrow, unable to draw his eyes away from the creature. "And just why do I have it?"

"Consiliatrix will aid you during the war. There may be times when we are under attack or you become trapped. Consiliatrix has been taught many things and, unlike a living cat, will remain by your side to aid and advise you."

"So why not create it in the image of a dog?" The cat cocked its head, a deep, rasping purr emanating from its chest.

"Because people expect dogs to remain faithful. With Consiliatrix they will not expect such loyalty. People, the enemy in particular, will see it as just a toy. In fact, it's a highly skilled weapon designed to protect and kill. When the time comes, it will be given a voice command. From then on in, it will remain by your side as the toy people believe it is."

The creature cocked its head, its glowing eyes drawing

Cedo in. He found himself kneeling before the small mecha-cat, the bright ebb of its being forever focused on him. Running a hand along its back, Cedo felt as the metal plates move, rising to meet his touch. The unwavering mechanical purr deepened, the beast lowering its head.

"Adviser in the protection of worlds," Cedo whispered.

"Precisely," his Master softly responded.

Time was irrelevant below ground. None of the clocks were yet working, time instead measured in the grime on their fingers and exhaustion in their bones. The crates were methodically cataloged and stowed. Papers, guns, ammunition, food, files—they were all hidden in straw-filled wooden boxes. Above ground, Seren was preparing herself to go with the General to begin the preparations for the field hospitals. Even though Cedo had not spent a lot of time with her, he would miss her presence. He had hoped to learn more of her before war took them over.

Their aching bodies finally forced them above ground and to the arms of warm baths and nourishing food. Exhausted, but needing some time to recover from the exertions of the day, Cedo rested in the window of the dining room, a new and empty notebook lying in his lap. The cats were curled at his feet, Misty having spent a good portion of the evening pushing, prodding, and staring at the mechanical cat. Consiliatrix, though designed to hunt and kill, had allowed himself to be pushed around until Misty was content that he meant no harm to them and invited him to rest with her.

Describing it with a pronoun for a living being was definitely strange, almost uncomfortable. Yet the way the metal creature acted was entirely natural. Despite the cold, hard exterior and the gentle whirring of gears, the mecha-cat acted as though it were alive, an odd combination of metal, wires, and an intelligence Cedo did not understand. The cat glowed at his feet, the plates moving with its mimicked breathing.

His attention moved to the world beyond the window. Darkness was falling, another day dying and bringing them ever closer to the day their world would shatter apart. Wars rarely had a beginning, no mark on the calendar. They just happened, bloody shows of power. Soon, their crafts would take to the skies, surveying the coasts, as well as France and Prussia, looking for signs that an attack was imminent. The fortresses of the coast would soon be manned, and the air would take on a tense electricity.

From the darkness of the street came the sound of footsteps along the narrow, cobbled street of Witheybrooke. Not one, but many. They appeared from the gloom, several abreast, marching down the empty streets and toward the Downs. Young men who, beneath the pitiful light of the street lamps, looked to be barely out of school and service, taken from their homes and masters. Their skin was as white as paper, shadows of death marching toward dastardly early graves.

Cedo felt ill as he watched them, the uniformed army men never looking at their pitifully childlike charges. So much life, being taken from every street in the country to fight for something that had nothing to do with them.

The silent pain twisted to anger, rushing through him. Leaping from the window, he stormed through the house and down to the empty bunker.

The door stood open, lights blazing from the first operations room. The heat of the lamps matched Cedo's own ferocity as he ran from room to room, bawling his Master's name.

Cedo came across him in a fortified munitions room,

guns and ammunition strewn across the floor. One lay in his Master's arms, its bulbous end glowing yellow.

"You," Cedo hissed.

Raising the weapon, Erus laid the long barrel against his shoulder and lifted his eyes to Cedo. "Me?"

"Yes, you. It is your doing that young men are marching to their deaths. Your doing that soon this nation will be a shadow of its former self. Everything that is happening is all because of you."

His Master raised an eyebrow and slowly lowered the gun. Cedo heard it click, the muzzle again glowing bright. "And pray, how is it all my doing? What has brought you to such a dramatic conclusion?" There was a note of hostility in his voice but Cedo refused to acknowledge it. Below ground, the battle lines were being drawn.

"You taunted James, allowed him to see what he could not have. You gave him what he wanted and then tore it all away. You showed him a world without him and now he wants it all. This is your doing and it is time for you to take responsibility!"

He stared at Erus, the silence growing between them. It was a tense, poisonous silence. Cedo felt it crawl over his skin, piercing his flesh. It cried to him to back down but he refused.

Throwing his head back, Erus bawled with laughter, the gun grating along the floor. "You stupid, stupid boy. You think I started this? Go and read your history books. The Dynasty has always ostracized itself from the world, cut off because of its unwillingness to play by the rules. This is just the latest move in a very long game. As well as that, their government wants him dead. They want to unseat him and bring to power someone who does takes the rights of humans more seriously. Not only that, but it is James' way to get into the country and secure himself the trade links he believes he has a right to, the links we

173

refuse to give him because of the way he treats people."

Cedo felt his body stiffen. His words had not seemed to not reach his Master's ears. Cedo had seen, with his own eyes, what had occurred between the two men. The war was clearly little more than a power struggle between them.

"But still—"

"But still, nothing!" Erus roared. He strode up to Cedo and wound a hand in his hair, pulling his head back. Beneath Erus' fingers, Cedo growled, his fury growing.

"You dare to defy me," his Master hissed, bared teeth dangerously close to his eyes. "Dare to question all that I know. You forget, Cedo, that I know far more than you ever will. All you know is what I choose to tell you. Your little jaunt to London was barely the tip of the iceberg."

The strong hand jerked at his hair, piercing pain flaring through his skull. Fighting against it, Cedo glared up into his Master's eyes, silently pushing him to react. It was stalemate, the two men glaring at one another, rage boiling Cedo's blood. He could see it in Erus' eyes, calling Cedo's bluff and mocking him. They knew what was coming and nothing could stop it. The pressure of what was coming finally seared through them.

Cedo's hand made contact with Erus' face, knuckles grazing the high cheekbones. Before Cedo had time to register what he had done, his arm was twisted behind him and he was forced downward, his knees thudding to the cold, hard floor. He did not cry out, instead struggling against the man who held him.

His head was pulled back, eyes forced to gaze at the specter of wrath above him. Obsession: that was what fed his Master's soul. An obsession to be the best, to drive the country forward, to conquer all. The obsession had a hold on Erus like nothing else would, forever bubbling to the surface.

Tears prickled Cedo's eyes as his hair was tugged, a red-hot ache blistering through his wrist. "I will leave you here to give you time to compose your apology," Erus said.

"And if I do not want to apologize? What if I choose to stand beside my opinion?"

Once more, his hair was pulled and he gave a muted yelp, the pain blinding him. "What you have said is not an opinion but an unfounded accusation. I shall leave you to think upon what has happened here. Do not make me punish you."

The hand released him and Cedo slumped, his hands stroking over his head, trying to ease the pain. Behind him, the door slammed shut and he was left, alone in the cold, soulless room. The walls were thick, undecorated brick, the door a slab of metal.

Cedo mulled over the previous moments, stubbornness rife. He did not want to bow down and apologize. Yet the more he mulled over their previous words, the more Cedo realized that he stood in the wrong. He did not know all the facts. All he had spoken had been hearsay, passed along from one person to the other without the barest of facts being checked. The rumors of the war had abounded for years, and Cedo had heard many of them. The guilt he felt for flinging them at Erus, and his Master's subsequent reaction, chilled him.

Rising onto his aching legs, Cedo retraced his steps, walking through the bunker and cellar, climbing the stairs and making for Erus' rooms. Head lowered, he rapped his knuckles against the door. When a reply came, he opened it and stepped inside.

His Master stood before the window, gazing out as he drew a silk bathrobe around his frame. Freshly washed hair, darkened to a burnt orange by the water, fell down his back. Sitting in a chair, Erus picked up a book and began to read.

"Master." His voice felt harsh, his throat dry. "I come to seek forgiveness."

Erus turned his attention from the book and to the man standing before him. A smile pulled at his lips. "Thank you. I appreciate it."

Cedo frowned. "Why are you being so amiable about this?"

The red-haired man placed the book to one side. "Because we all must reach a place in our lives where we become more accepting. Hopefully this will be a turning point for us both."

Cedo felt himself smile. "And I thank you. I really must research more before I say such things."

Erus climbed beneath the covers and leaned against the mountains of pillows. His eyes glimmered in the light of the gas jets, looking at Cedo.

"Stand there and undress. I want to appreciate you."

Gratefully, he stripped away the dusty, cloying clothes and let them fall around him in a growing drift. He could feel his Master's eyes watching him, feel them riding over his flesh. Cedo removed each garment carefully, exposing a little more of what lay beneath. From the bed, he heard Erus give a low growl and a smile broke Cedo's lips. All that had been before was now forgotten, washed away by a few simple actions.

Warm air tickled his skin and Cedo stepped away from his clothes. Kneeling on the bed, he crawled over Erus, hands cupping his face and pressing hungry kisses to his lips. Hands wrapped around his slender waist and pulled him to his Master's lap.

Sinking lower, he surrendered, giving himself over to the man who desired him.

Commotion. Voices. Fists hammering on doors. The house all but shaking, Francis' voice calling his name, feet thundering up stairs and along hallways. Cedo snatched up a sheet and dashed from the bed, draping the cloth around himself. Jerking the door open, he ran for the stairs, Francis still calling to him.

Yet he got no further than the brow of the staircase, his heart stalling. He felt as though time had suddenly stopped as he gazed toward the front door.

CHAPTER 14

Abruptly he found his voice. "Billy!"

He managed to make it to the hallway without falling, Billy meeting him at the foot and sweeping Cedo up into his arms. Cedo could feel tears prickling his eyes as he wrapped his arms around Billy. Burying his face in the waves of sunlight-blond hair, Cedo cried, his heart breaking and healing in a single breath. Beneath him Billy shuddered, soft sobs finding their way to Cedo's ears. Sliding to the floor, Cedo held Billy close, his lips finding Billy's through his tears. Hands stroked along his jaw, making him tremble and moan, and he pressed his mate to the wall, wanting to feel every inch of him.

Finally, Billy pulled away. Instead of joy, his eyes were filled with fear. Sweeping the tears away from his lover's face, Cedo studied him, searching for an answer.

"Whatever is the matter?"

Beneath his fingers, Billy shuddered and shook his head. "I've been called up. To fight in the war. I leave in ten days."

It took only a second for the words to sink in, Cedo's vision becoming blurred, ears filled with a low whining sound.

"No," he murmured. "No. Please, no."

Billy's arms went around him, holding him tight. Cedo wanted to break down but he needed to remain strong, to hold onto his love and offer his support.

With his arms around Billy, Cedo lifted his head and looked toward the stairs. At the brow, clothed all in black and with his hair looking like the flames of Inferno, was Erus. Beside his feet sat the two cats, one snowy white, the other the blackest of night.

"You can stop this," he called to his Master. "You can put an end to our loved ones going to their deaths. And you can start now. I do not care who you have to speak to, you will get this revoked."

Silently Erus stared at them before shaking his head. "I cannot do anything."

"Why not?" Cedo bawled. "You have a hand in this. You have been talking to the King and the Generals. You can speak to them and have Billy's conscription canceled."

A ghost of a smirk breathed over his Master's face before the exhaustion returned. "But that does not mean I have any sway over them. They are customers, as fastidious as any cat. If I do not supply them then another will, and at a far better price. It is I who dances to their tune, not they to mine."

Cedo felt a bolt of tension shiver over his skin, a strange excitement building that was redressed by the cold aura flowing from his Master.

"Still, you could try. For us."

Erus narrowed his eyes. "Are you daring to defy me?"

Every one of Cedo's instincts called at him to say no, all of them fearing the punishment that would be meted out. He wanted to stand up to Erus, yet the memory of the previous evening began to arise. His conscience called to him and, with a deep breath, he backed down.

"No," he replied. "I am not defying you. Merely questioning your standing in this strange circle of power."

Erus' eyes were fixed on him, cold and hard even from the brow of the stairs. "Good. We shall be leaving later.

Go and eat and make yourself ready."

With that, his Master turned in a whirl of clothes and hair, disappearing back to the depths of his quarters.

Despite the warmth from the fire, the kitchen felt as cold as ice. They sat at the table while Francis fixed tea, Misty and Consiliatrix patiently watching the bespectacled man's every movement. Erus was goodness knew where and, at that moment, Cedo did not care. All he cared about was the man beside him.

"Why did you stay away for so long?" he asked softly.

Billy shook his head, eyes on his clasped hands. "I came 'ome one night, ready to come back to you. 'Ad the money to get back 'ere an' everythin'. When I got 'ome, the notice was waitin'. Felt like my world 'ad fallen apart. That were a week ago."

"You could have returned then."

"There was so much goin' through my 'ead. Didn't want to put any pressure on you."

Sighing, Cedo watched Francis place crockery and milk on the table. Laying his hands over Billy's, he pressed a kiss to his friend's temple. "All I have wished for is to see you again. That is it. Every day I have dreamed of you, and now you have returned."

Billy smiled warmly at him, his silence saying all Cedo needed to know.

The machines were all but done, the tearing up of the garden complete. In their wake lay a black chasm of a hole. Men swarmed over it, carrying hods of bricks into the abyss. Large, rotating, cylindrical devices were filled with cement, an unending stream pouring from their nozzles and filling the waiting buckets. Steel plates lay on the shattered grass, waiting to be put into place.

Leaning against the window, Cedo watched his idyllic landscape disappear. In its place lay the ravages of what their country was becoming, slowly disappearing beneath new, larger constructions. What it would house he still did not know. Behind him, Billy slumbered. Misty and Consiliatrix were deep in sleep, curled beside Billy's head.

His attention was broken by a knock at the door and Erus calling to him. Cedo pressed a kiss to his lover's cheek before sweeping from the room and joining his Master, their footsteps echoing through the silent house. He loathed leaving Billy behind, but Cedo knew the other man needed time to recover, to gather his thoughts and enjoy his last few days of freedom. For soon he would be gone, covered in armor and roaming the Downs.

"We're going to one of the factories out on the coast," Erus started. "There's something you need to learn about."

"And that would be?"

"You shall see once we arrive. It is of the utmost secrecy and importance, a piece of equipment which could mean the difference between life and death."

A steam-carriage sat in the road before the house, gentle wisps of steam puffing from its twin funnels.

"Are you going to replace the horses you lost? And with flesh and blood, or metal ones?" He climbed in, settling himself as Erus joined him.

Slamming the door shut, Erus tapped his cane against the roof and the carriage began to wind its way along the street, engine clunking away.

"Indeed, I am. Although I am tempted to replace them with an all-steel stable. Yours was a magnificent beast and I am sure that the scientists and engineers have

greatly improved upon it. Time is of the essence, though."
Taking a watch from his pocket, Erus opened the lid and
gazed at the face before tapping a finger against the glass.
Replacing it, he continued, "I will send them a pneumatic
message when we arrive in Porton."

For a while, Cedo admired the interior of the carriage.
It was much like the horse-drawn ones except for a few,
seemingly slight, differences. Gone were the gas lamps in
each corner, replaced by ones with filament bulbs. The seats
were deep and plush, an assurance on the manufacturer's
part that they would only be used by those who could
afford them. A speaking tube was attached beside one
door, leading, Cedo presumed, to the driver at the back.
Which made him wonder why Erus had used his cane to
signal their readiness. Habits, he assumed, still died hard
even in times of progress.

Erus seemed serene, a change from the previous days
of urgency. He relaxed into the seat, legs crossed at the
ankles, eyes fixed on the passing scenery.

"Penny for them, Master," he softly pressed.

Bewildered eyes turned to Cedo, as though his Master
had been in a far-off land, chasing thoughts of other times,
other people, other places. A slow smile spread over his
lips and he took the top hat from his head.

"Not much, dear Cedo. Just hoping for better times
once this period of darkness has lifted."

"What do you see for us?"

"For us, personally? Or us as a nation?"

Placing a hand against the wall of the carriage, Cedo
steadied himself, moving to sit beside his Master. Erus
placed his hand on Cedo's thigh, drawing him closer.
Cedo gratefully leaned against Erus' strong body.

"Both."

Erus chuckled and rested one foot on the seat Cedo
had vacated.

"For us, I see a future free of all that we are experiencing at this current moment. I see a future where man and machine live side by side, where there is no need for conflict."

Cedo interrupted, "But surely that would put you out of a job."

Tilting his head, Erus smiled. "Indeed, it would. Although countries will still want to maintain an armed force. Besides, you have shown me that there are other ways in this world, that death and destruction is not always what is needed. Should our world become one of peace, we shall survive. Money does not always bring happiness."

A feeling of comfort and warmth spread through Cedo. The cracks in Erus' exterior were beginning to grow, never to be filled again. Placing a hand to his Master's jaw, he gently drew their lips together.

The factory stood on the edge of a cliff, the rolling Downs behind it and the swell of the sea before it. It was, Erus had said, in a prime position to be attacked and so the building had a number of defenses. Guns sat all around it, lining the ground and the roof, all pointed toward the heavens.

Sunlight dazzled from the white roof, partially blinding him, and Cedo lifted a hand to his eyes. The building stretched along the edge of the cliff and curved away up the coast. Its green walls helped it to melt into the surrounding countryside. Touching his back, Erus encouraged him closer and they followed a narrow stone path.

A small door, all but hidden from view and dwarfed by the size of the building, allowed them to enter. Raising an eyebrow, he turned to Erus. "Surely such doors should be locked in times of war?"

Leaning against the open door, his Master turned to him, face glowing with a childlike glee. Erus motioned to a panel beside the door. It was blank, a sheet of nondescript metal with five indents laid into it.

"Place your hand against it."

Warily, he did, and instantly regretted it as a loud siren sounded, echoing off the rolling hills. Below that, there were other noises, clicks and thuds and the pounding of feet. Erus laughed and pushed him away, placing his own hand against the panel. Instantly the siren fell silent. From their left, a man in white lab coat trotted toward them, a look of frustration on his face and a clipboard clasped against his chest.

"Just what in Inferno is-" The man stalled as he looked at Erus. "Ah, sir. I apologize. I didn't realize you were here. Had to check to make sure we didn't have intruders."

"Indeed." Erus smiled at the man. "And it is good to know that all the correct procedures are followed in case of such an event. I was just showing Cedo some of our security measures."

As Erus smiled so too did the man. "Good. Good. It is an impressive building. Very secure."

"And it would be nothing without men like yourself," Erus said. "Please, go about your day and worry no more."

Unlike the previous factory they had visited, this one was lit entirely by artificial light, with no windows in either the walls or the roof. Lamps dangled from gantries which, on closer inspection, were hinged at the walls. High above them, sitting between the lip of the wall and the ceiling, were large gears, chains running around them and down to motors.

And there, in the heart of the gray, empty space, was what they had obviously come to see.

It looked like an elongated teardrop set on its side, three clawed feet planted against the floor. Fins stretched up from the tapered end, and on either side was a wing with a rotary engine attached to the end. A window wrapped around the bulbous edge, an array of guns nestled beneath it.

"We call it the Reaper." Erus' voice rang through the building. "It is a one-man unit, designed to cut down the enemy with rapid fire. This one is yours."

Cedo swung around to face his Master, shock tightening his body. "Excuse me?"

Erus looked at him, the odious sneer on his lips. "You heard me."

Cedo locked his eyes onto the beast of a machine, trying to take in every intricate detail. The Reaper was painted a burnished brass so dark it was almost black, with propellers many feet in length. It looked as deadly as its name implied.

"Come. We'll go and take a look."

He followed Erus to the hull, watching as Erus pressed a button beneath the wing. A door swung down, steps embedded in the opposite side. Climbing in, Cedo looked around, taking in the curved, enclosed space. The center comprised of a bomb bay, ready to hold all the munitions the craft would need. It also contained the burners for engines, bricks of obtainium stacked before it, ready to be flung into the hungry flames. To the front was the cockpit, a tall seat bolted before a sweeping control panel of dials and levers.

"There is no way I can fly this," he muttered.

"Piffle! Of course you can. And you will need to. It will be hangared at the house. That is what all the building work has been in aid of."

Seating himself before controls, Cedo wrapped his hand around the head of the yoke. Unlike their airship, it was a single stick, encased in wood that swept up into a wide ball. A number of metal buttons anchored to the head. His thumb swept over them, feeling them begin to depress beneath his touch.

"We were never intended to fly. If we were, we would have been given wings and feathers."

"Of course we are meant to fly," his Master said. "If we were not meant to, then we would not have been given the intelligence to create such machines."

From behind them, there came the sound of feet against metal, and Cedo turned to see a middle-aged man step aboard, dressed in the white lab-coat of a scientist.

Erus greeted him, "Doctor Cooke, so good to see you, sir."

"Good to see you, as well. I believe we're here for a flying lesson?" The man adjusted the spectacles on his nose.

"Indeed we are, and this young man will be your pilot."

Doctor Cooke offered Cedo a chain with a single brass key dangling from it. "This will start your ignition."

Cedo was not confident he could master the Reaper. It was clunky, the rotor engines swinging back and forth while the movable surfaces of the fins appeared to have a mind all of their own. How they were not plummeting toward the earth, Cedo did not know. The doctor sat beside him, steely voice instructing his every moment. Above them was the clear blue sky, the roof of the factory having rolled back to allow them to exit.

Cedo cursed beneath his breath, his hands tight around

the control column, panic tightening his body. The ground came and went, the craft rolling toward the sky before turning itself back to the greenery of the Downs. From the burners came the stark stench of the obtainium, the heat and steam funneled to the engines. Cedo felt his vision come and go, the motion of the machine making him feel ill. His stomach clenched, his earlier meals threatening to return. Grunting, he fought with the controls, everything feeling resistant to his movements.

"Take a deep breath," Erus commanded from behind him. "And focus on what is before you."

"You are not helping," he growled. "You come and do this if you think it is so easy."

Despite their yawing, his Master seemed perfectly composed, his voice crystal clear. "If you do not take a tumble, you will not know what it is like to get to your feet and try again. Now hold the control column steady and fly like your life depends on it."

The nose pitched forward, the ground suddenly roaring toward them. Taking a deep breath, Cedo held the column steady and eased it back. His feet pressed the pedals before the seat, controlling the movement of the fins. As quickly as they had begun to plummet, the Reaper eased up and began to fly in level line.

Cedo did not want to believe his luck had changed and kept his eyes straight ahead and the column in its beginning position. His feet held the fins in place.

"Try moving to the left," Doctor Cooke softly pressed.

Keeping his breathing steady, Cedo gently eased the column to the left, his foot easing the fins in the same direction. The Reaper instantly responded, sweeping to the left in a languid circle. They passed over the sea and the Downs appeared once more.

"Now try in the opposite direction."

Easing everything to the right, the Reaper swept into a

neat figure of eight before gliding into a circle. The engines roared, shaking the craft, and Cedo felt his muscles burn. His heart still pounded, fear rolling over him in waves. He knew that he had to conquer his fear, knew that it would translate into miscalculations and possibly death. There was a long way to go before he would be master of the Reaper.

It was not long before he began to tire, and Doctor Cooke took over. Leaning against the walls of the craft, Cedo surveyed the land below. They lifted higher and flew over the Downs, the country he had known already changed. Armaments strode across the gently rolling hills, large metal men and horses taking the place of the ones made from flesh and blood. While only a few were out in the bright sunlight, Cedo suspected that when the time came there would be hordes of them, all sighted on the skies and the sea.

Battle stations, lookouts, and guard stations swept along the rocky coastline, all patiently waiting for the moment that they would be needed. Large dishes, like those of the Sky Sweepers, scanned the air, sending and receiving messages from the cities. Where there had once been nothing, buildings and roads were now gorging on the green grass of his home. From their place in the sky, he could see people coming and going, preparing and plotting. It chilled Cedo to the bone to know that so many people were involved in trying to halt what was now inevitable.

In time, they returned to the factory, and the doctor neatly landed the craft. As they exited, the roof rolled back into place, motors thundering in the large, empty space.

"We'll deliver it in the next few days," said the doctor, "once we have confirmation that the hangar for it is ready."

Cedo felt a little ill following the flight, his head swimming and legs weak, but his Master nodded.

"It should be finished within the week. I shall send word once it is done and then it is yours to prepare."

The doctor shook Erus' hand. "Fantastic. Good day to you both. Cedo, it has been a pleasure meeting you. I hope that you shall never have use for the Reaper. But should you need it, know that you are going to be a grand pilot."

The doctor bowed his head a little and turned, his figure disappearing into the far shadows of the building.

They returned home with barely a word, Cedo pondering the enormity of the flying the Reaper. No doubt Erus was also thinking about the war, hoping that he had everything prepared.

As he suspected, upon stepping into the Witheybrooke house, Erus barely said a word to him before disappearing into his study. Cedo stared at the closed door before making for the stairs. Where he would have felt rejection in the past, he felt nothing now, understanding that Erus needed this time to prepare and ready himself.

Instead, Cedo walked to the bedroom in which Billy slumbered. Entering, he was happy to see his lover still cradled in the arms of sleep; his reappearance earlier in the day had not been a mirage. Light from the setting sun streamed through the window, turning the room a deep gold, its rays shimmering over Billy's hair. Curled on his side, his hair was spread over the pillow. Misty and Consiliatrix were long gone from the bed, having taken up residence on the window ledge, warmed by the light of the dying day.

Removing his shoes, Cedo slid onto the bed. Just being

close to one of those he loved was enough to send him into a state of euphoria, his body shuddering as he stretched over the rumpled sheets. Lying behind Billy, he draped an arm over his mate's body and buried his face in the thick drifts of hair. His lover smelled of the sea and the streets, of old dust and fresh sea breeze. He never stirred as Cedo held him close, fingers gently caressing him.

The steady beating of their hearts lulled him into restfulness. Easing the covers over them, he joined his lover in the land of slumber.

Darkness had fallen when he awoke, coolness seeping in on the wind. He longed to huddle beneath the thick layers and hold onto Billy. For dawn would bring them another day closer to when Billy would leave, possibly to never return. Sweeping the hair from his friend's shoulder, Cedo pressed a kiss to Billy's still-clothed body, fingers ghosting along his sides and over his stomach. Billy gave a grunt and moved to lie on his back. In the growing darkness, Cedo could see his open eyes, a smile beginning to curl his lips.

"'Lright, Cedo?"

Cedo allowed himself to be wrapped tightly in strong arms, warm lips softly finding his own. His fingers danced through Billy's hair, lightly tugging, reminding himself that his lover was real. Their kisses were slow, sensual, making him shiver with joy. Hands held him tight, running along his back, regaining the knowledge that they had lost.

The day dawned warm and full of promise, but for Cedo, it was a cold awakening, knowing that in a few days Billy would once more be torn from his side. He was determined to savor every moment, to spend time dwelling on the love which had been bestowed on him.

From the Downs, borne on the breeze, came the sound of preparation. Deep thuds and the distant roar of engines broke the otherwise beautiful day. Gazing from the upper window, Cedo watched a tall mecha-man stride across the horizon, flames bursting from its arms. In its wake came a convoy of smaller machines, rolling on tracks, long-barreled guns swinging between the sky and the earth.

"Which division will you be stationed with?" he cautiously asked.

"21st Svenfur Ground Division."

Cedo's eyes never turned from the display on the Downs. Another great machine had appeared in the skies above the mecha-man, its dark form turning in an easy circle before descending toward the ground, twisting propellers carefully powering it. "So you shall be driving the mecha-men?"

"Aye, I suspect so. Or somethin' similar. Or perhaps I'll just be a foot soldier. Don't know yet."

Cedo's heart felt heavy as he returned to the bed, allowing Billy to pull him close. Fingers stroked his face, sweeping over every curve before following the line of his nose. His mate's blue eyes shimmered, seeming to try and hold back a flood of emotions.

"Cedo, I know you're goin' to worry, but I want you to try not to. You're goin' to be playin' a big part in this war an' you need to try an' keep your 'ead about you. Stay strong. You've come a long way an' it would be stupid of you to be losin' all you've gained over me."

Cedo could feel a lump beginning to form in his throat and he slid a hand into the nape of Billy's neck. Staring

191

into his lover's eyes, Cedo gently kissed him, hope for the future flourishing with the simple gesture.

"I will try," he murmured in response. "Promise you will write?"

"I promise I'll write if you promise not to do anythin' stupid about what I say. Don't want to be comin' 'ome an' findin' you've burnt the place down in some fit of rage."

The words made him chuckle, a reminder of why he so adored Billy. The blond man had a way of making everything feel so much better. Even in the depths of their darkest hour, his jovial nature was alive and well, a man unwilling to dwell on what was to come.

A knock at the door pulled them apart. Rolling onto his back, Cedo said, "Enter."

Francis stepped into the room. His shirtsleeves were rolled up, spectacles slipping down his nose, and his eyes were ringed with dark bruises.

"Erus requests your presence. He's going to the city and wishes you both to go with him."

Cedo sighed; he did not wish to leave the room. He wished to remain there for every moment, not thinking of the short time they had left.

"I suppose we should make our presence known," he replied.

"Indeed." Francis looked to them. "I know that you don't want to go, that this time is precious to you. But please consider Erus. This time is extremely pressing, and I am sure that he finds your presence reassuring."

CHAPTER 15

The steam carriage rumbled through the streets of Svenfur, stopping and starting amid the heavy traffic. To Cedo, it felt like an age since he had last seen the city, and it invigorated him to be returning.

Billy sat quietly beside him, eyes watching the passing streets and buildings. Across from them, Erus also sat in silence. It seemed as though they had nothing to say to one another, either through fear of reaction or because their minds were turned to the stresses of the upcoming war. While one would help orchestrate it, another would fight, and Cedo was caught in the middle of a dangerous alliance between the two men.

Yet Erus' acceptance of Billy showed a great change within his Master. It told Cedo that Erus was finally warming to their relationship, seeing it as the support that they both needed.

Svenfur was changing. As they rumbled down the long, steep West Road, Cedo saw the subterranean railway station at the brow of the hill. It was a circular building of red brick, green-enameled tiles sweeping along the top, the roof made of matching rust-colored tiles. People streamed in and out, climbing from the ground like sightless beasts, blinking in the sunlight before continuing with their journeys. There seemed to be little fear of it now, if the number of people using the central station was any proof. The protests had moved on, the war a far more attractive subject of complaint.

Everywhere they looked there were signs of the war. Handbills on walls and boardings, headlines on newspapers, and a procession of dissidents snaking along the sea front. It was obviously the reason for the snarl of traffic, drivers and passengers venting their frustration. But the procession slowly marched on, the people draped in the black clothes of the grieving, their faces painted to resemble skulls. Some carried placards and banners, bearing messages opposing the war. A few carried ghastly ghouls, all draped in black, large skeletal hands outstretched and bone white faces grimacing at the assembled crowds.

It was a strange and unsettling sight, the opinions of the people greatly differing from those of the ones in power. The war was unwelcome, and would be for its entire reign. People would lose everything, and there was nothing they could do about it.

Loathing stained Cedo's soul. He had unwittingly been pulled into it and no amount of reassurance for his own safety would wash away the knowledge that others had no such assurance. At that moment, he wished he were back on the street, sleeping in the boarding house by night. If that were the case, he would not have the knowledge he now possessed.

The procession passed, as silent as the coming of death, and the carriage pitched left onto Sea View Road.

"Stupid people," Erus muttered.

Cedo dared ask, "Why?"

His Master glanced up at him, eyes dark, and Cedo could feel the man's wrath building.

"For thinking they know what is best. Did you not see the banners? They believe we are as good as dead, that this nation has already fallen, and that we are not doing enough to prevent the war. They call us murderers and child killers. Yet they gladly take when we offer them their freedoms. Do they not realize that sometimes these freedoms have to be fought for? That they have been hard won?"

Sighing, Cedo shook his head. "We have been through this, Master. They are allowed an opinion, just as you are allowed yours. It is what our country is built on. You should know that, as you have been allowed to become a successful industrialist through it."

"While this is true, I still loathe those who wish to stand in the path of change. These are the same people who believe that machines will rob them of their jobs. They are the ones who blame the machines for all that is bad in the world."

"An' perhaps they've got a point," Billy interjected. "They've seen the ones which go to the wars, seen 'em up on the Downs. You can't 'elp but feel for 'em. Perhaps they need more understandin'?"

Erus' eyes snapped to Billy. "You are very right, William. They need to be taught. Need to learn that these creations will only make their lives easier. That is something I had not thought of." Leaning back into the seat, Erus grinned, fingers pressed to his lips. "Tomorrow I shall speak to the main office. Have them draw up something which can be given to all citizens."

"Is that a good idea at such a time, Master?" Cedo asked.

Erus smiled. "It is always a good time, Cedo, war or not."

The foundry was on the outskirts of the Darker Quarter, a monolithic building belching smoke and ash from the multitude of chimneys that stretched along its walls. It was one of a number of such places spread around the city. Despite all being located in the poorer districts, even the upper classes complained about the thick smog that descended on the city every winter, hiding the sky and choking their lungs.

"One day I will create something to rid the city of the winter cloud," Erus murmured.

Seated in an air-cooled office, the sounds and heat of the foundry were a distant memory. Mr. Dickens, a well-built, middle-aged man with a tweed suit and a thick salt-and-pepper beard, had brought up the subject of Svenfur's winters.

Seated beside his Master, Cedo listened intently. Billy was to his left, his interest in the smelting process almost obscene.

"The big question is," Erus began, "will you be able to produce the steel we need for the armor? I understand you have already produced it for the many vehicles, but this particular line is rather close to my heart."

"You have a heart, Mr. Veetu?" Mr. Dickens raised an eyebrow.

Erus chortled and stretched his legs before him. "I know it is questioned often, but I certainly hope so, Mr. Dickens. Otherwise we are in dire straits."

"Interesting." The director of the foundry grinned. "I always thought your blood was pumped by a device of your own creation."

"And perhaps one day it will be. Who knows what the future holds?"

The office was spacious and overlooked the Downs. Already the view was being blighted by the slums that were growing in the wake of the Darker Quarter. The local government had, according to the newspapers, ordered them destroyed and replaced with affordable housing. Except that as soon as the slum housing was destroyed, it was quickly re-erected in the shadow of Night. For years, the fight had been battled between the Patron and the slum dwellers. Sometimes the man left his office and spoke to them personally, but it did no good. The dwellers preferred their ground-level wood and metal cast-off housing to anything the city could give them.

"Anyway, your armor," Mr. Dickens continued.

Opening his case, Erus took a sheaf of papers from a file and spread them on the desk. "I require something for the foot soldiers."

"But that's impossible! There will be millions."

"I understand, but we will start with those on the front line, on our coasts, and work our way in."

"Dear gods, Veetu." The director sounded exasperated. "Whatever has brought you to this?"

Seating himself, Erus stared the man in the face. "As I said, it is rather a personal action. This young man—" He gestured to Billy. "—will be fighting on the front line. He has become an integral part of my life, and I wish to see him safe. I also realize that many other people, all across this great land, will be feeling what I am feeling. They will be feeling shock, grief, and sadness, and will wish to see their loved ones return safely. This armor will help reduce the number of fatalities the government has predicted."

Cedo felt himself stare at his Master, his jaw slack, the shock almost numbing him. The words his Master spoke were ones he never thought he would hear. Yet they spilled forth, a declaration of Erus' quiet appreciation for the friendship Billy had given Cedo.

"Erus, this armor is awfully intricate. Are you sure it is the right thing to be doing?"

Even without looking at Erus, Cedo could feel his Master's anger rise. It rippled from the red-haired man like clouds over a mountain. Even though the anger was not directed at him, Cedo could still feel it, its claws sinking into his skin. Challenging Erus was never wise.

"Of course it is the right thing to do! Do you not wish to protect our men?"

"Of course I do," the director replied. "I am just questioning whether we have the workmen to make it."

"We have the workmen." Erus' voice was low, anger soaking through it. "We have the equipment. It will be made, and it will work."

The director surveyed the plans, carefully turning the sheets of paper. "What exactly does it do? Other than protect the human form."

The question appeared to relax Erus, and his attention returned to the small details. "It is has mechanisms built into the hinges. It allows the helmet to slide back at the touch of a button, allowing the soldier to speak freely, and returning it to its warfare position in a heartbeat. If the helmet and gloves are retracted and the enemy strike, the solider will be ready before the enemy has even blinked."

"And it is powered how?"

Cedo watched as a dark grin twisted his Master's lips. "Welcome to harnessing the body's own energy."

Cedo and Billy were afforded a period of freedom while Erus paid a visit to the Patron. Choosing to walk along the beach, they basked in the warm sun, savoring its heat on their cheeks. It was a perfect day of blue skies and sea, waves gently lapping at the shore. Beneath their feet, pebbles scuttled away. Standing in the shadow of the pier, they watched the cavorting beach dwellers, tourists and locals alike enjoying all that they had.

"I cannot believe him," Cedo said, voice just audible above the sound of the waves.

"I can't either." Billy stepped closer, running a hand along Cedo's spine as they looked out to sea, the feeling of freedom calming them.

How much longer would it last? Would the beach still be the same once the fighting had died away? Would the pier still be standing?

Cedo pushed these thoughts away and turned to look at his mate. Billy smiled at him, eyes twinkling in the sunlight. Hidden from view, he draped his arms around Billy's neck and stared into his azure eyes. He felt at peace with Billy beside him, the blond man acting as a bulwark between himself and Erus. And because of it, all of their relationships had benefited.

"Well, looks like we've got ourselves a pair of nancies here, boys."

The voice made Cedo still, his skin becoming cold. He dared not move, the words a venomous poison.

"Come any closer an' you'll live to regret it," Billy hissed.

He could feel his lover's body become tight, preparing himself for a fight. With his head feeling light, Cedo pulled away and faced the source of the voice.

A group of men, no older than themselves, had stepped beneath the pier. Dressed in the dirty clothes of metal workers, they all wore identical flat caps and thick-soled boots, faces filthy with grime. Their faces were writ with hatred, lips pulled back to reveal stained and rotten teeth.

"An' why would that be, nancy?" growled the speaker. "You goin' to take us all on? 'Cause I'd love to see that."

Cedo could feel his own body preparing itself, hands curled into fists, anger rising. Yet it was Billy who stepped between them, arms straining against his white shirt.

"You're nothin' but filthy perverts," the man continued, "an' you should burn in Inferno for bringing your kind to our town." He spat at their feet, face darkened with menace. "Filthy fuckin' perverts."

Barreling past his lover, Cedo swung a fist into the man's face, barely registering the sting to his knuckles. He managed to land a few blows before he was hauled away, thrown to the unforgiving shingle. Fists began to rain down on him. Amid it all, Cedo heard the cry that they should be hanged and a shout of agreement filled the air.

Terror swamped Cedo as he was hauled to his feet, struggling against the men who held him. His body ached and he could feel blood on his tongue. One eye was closed, too bruised to open. Through his remaining one, he could see Billy was in the same predicament and fighting against those who wished them dead.

They had done nothing wrong, yet in the eyes of the mob, they were on the same plane as murderers, good only for the gallows. And theirs would be below the pier Cedo had called home for so long. It seemed fitting that he would live on her boards and die at her feet, beaten and forgotten.

Cedo fought and struggled, freeing himself for a breath before the mob caught him. Rough-hewn rope was looped around his neck, scratching at his skin, and he gave a cry of terror. Amid it all, he heard Billy calling to him, assuring Cedo that they would be safe.

From above, the rope began to tighten, slowly choking him. Silently he prayed, pleading with the gods to save him. Why them? Why had they been chosen for such a fate? Of all the people who roamed the streets of Svenfur, why did it have to be them?

His arms were lashed behind him, ending his bitter and bloody struggle. Cedo felt all his hope fade away, dashed away on the waves. He was to die because he loved his own kind. A love that should never speak its name. Yet he felt a tiny blessing that he had known it, if only for a short time.

Cedo managed to turn his head and look to his beloved. Billy stood beside him, a rope around his neck as well, arms tied behind him.

"I'll see you in the next life, Cedo."

The words warmed him, if only for a moment, the heat of the sun having long ago forgotten him. "Promise?"

"Promise."

"Will you pair of nancies shut your traps?" the cry came from above.

The mob had clambered into the struts above the pier, hauling lengths of rope with them. Once more, the rope began to tighten and Cedo choked. Beside him, he heard Billy groan, the ropes creaking. Blackness began to descend as panic rose, clouding what was left of his vision. In the final moments, his thoughts were on those who loved him: Billy, Erus, the audiences of the music halls, his mother.

CHAPTER 16

Cedo gasped as bright sunlight blinded him and sweet oxygen filled his lungs. Arching his back against the hard ground, he choked and let out a rasping howl. Through his blurred vision, he watched shadows move, distant voices encouraging him to lie still and breathe deeply.

The shadows came in and out of focus, their voices distinctly male and female. Finally a feminine face came into view, stained with concern.

"You're breathing. Do you know who you are?"

Cedo nodded; everything ached and his body felt as though it were made of lead. "I am Cedo Reilly."

"And your friend?"

His mouth felt dry and breathing was painful, his throat still feeling the crushing tightness of the rope around it. The woman offered him a glass bottle filled with water and he gratefully drank from it. "William Burton. Alive?"

"Yes, yes, he's alive. My husband is tending to him."

Cedo tried to sit up, wanting to be with Billy, but the woman placed a hand on his chest and eased him back to the shingle. She sat beside him, her hand a reassurance against his cool skin.

"Home?" he rasped.

"Soon. We have called for physicians. The Black Rod Alliance unfortunately got to you both. But do not fret;

we are your friends."

He tried to smile yet his face refused to cooperate. He had heard of the Black Rod Alliance. They pledged allegiance to an all-seeing deity and their aim was to cleanse the country of anyone they deemed to be "unclean." The list of the "unclean" was long and included people like himself, those who preferred to dress as the opposite gender, and those who had children out of wedlock. The number of deaths attributed to the Black Rod Alliance rose on a yearly basis, yet those sworn to protect the citizens of the country did little to help.

The physicians came in a large carriage with bells heralding their arrival. Following a quick examination, they prescribed pills and ointments for pain and bruising before strapping both Cedo and Billy onto boards. With the boards secured safely in the back of the carriage, the physicians brought them home.

Cedo lay in Erus' bed, Billy beside him. Both were silent, their eyes on the ceiling, their minds elsewhere.

Why had he entered into a relationship with Erus, a man who beat and ridiculed him, making him feel as though he was not worthy to walk the planet? Why had he stayed for so long with someone who kept him so tightly bound, choosing his clothes and even dictating to whom he should speak? The root, Cedo realized, was security. Erus had made great promises to him, all of which he had fulfilled. He had placed Cedo upon the stages of the city's grandest theaters. He had given Cedo a safe home, security, and finances and had taken him away from the threat of life upon the streets. Because, even though Cedo had never wanted to acknowledge it, he had forever been one wet and dreary night away from life in the workhouse.

It still did not mean that he had to bow to each of Erus' whims, but life could have been far, far worse. Cedo could have found himself at the mercy of the workhouse masters, beaten and starved for a roof over his head. Erus fed him, and cared for him and, in his own way, loved him. Cedo was seeing far more of it, the Erus of old disappearing to be replaced with someone more tender and loving. It warmed Cedo to think that his Master, despite his protestations, could change. He remained the fierce weapons manufacturer, standing by his cause to protect his country, but behind closed doors, away from prying eyes, he was becoming a different person.

Yet there was one promise that Erus had yet to fulfill, and that was news of his mother. Taking up this position was supposed to have afforded him the luxury of finding her. So far, it had not, and a cold knot of grief once more wound its way through him.

Tossing back the covers, he rose, gripping the nightshirt tightly to him as he made his way downstairs. His body ached, the bruises becoming prominent, his throat still feeling as though it were closed, his breath wheezing and rattling.

Pushing open the door to the study, he stood beside Erus, watching as the flame-haired man grasped a piece of sharpened graphite, his hand all but flying across a sheet of paper. Upon it, Cedo could see the beginnings of a new machine, something large that rested on eight legs like a spider. Guns sat around its circular edge, giving it complete coverage of the enemy.

"Master?"

Erus ignored him for a moment more before placing the graphite aside and turning his emerald eyes to Cedo. His Master smiled and motioned Cedo closer. Clearing the blueprint from the desk, he gestured for Cedo to sit before him. Cedo flinched as he pulled himself up, pain flaring through him. He sat, head hanging, until he felt a hand against his knee. Erus looked at him, face filled with concern, and Cedo attempted to smile.

"I am so sorry for what happened today," his Master softly said. "I should never have let you go."

Cedo felt his smile grow and he reached out to stroke Erus' face. "You were not to know. I thank you for allowing us that freedom, no matter how short-lived it was."

"Nevertheless, the Black Rod Alliance is now being investigated by the City Guard."

Sighing, Cedo shook his head. "Nothing will come of it. They donate too much money to the charities of the Guard for anything to happen."

Erus' hand tightened around his thigh, holding his gaze. "Trust me, Cedo, it will happen. Because I can guarantee you that whatever the Black Rod have been giving, I have donated far more."

"But they're a countrywide group. Our Guard can do nothing to stop them."

His Master's hand slid higher, brushing against Cedo's groin. His voice became low, "Cedo, it *will* happen. We live in an age of enlightenment. Such people should no longer be allowed to roam our streets and cause misery. Do not worry; the Guard will eradicate them from this city. It will show other cities that we don't tolerate such actions from anyone, large donations or not."

Cedo wanted to roll his eyes. That was ripe coming from the man who had once willingly murdered his own countrymen on the orders of the government. Yet there had been a change. No longer did the experiments happen, at least not on Erus' direct watch.

"I did not come to speak of that," Cedo softly began. "I came to ask of my mother. When I first came here, you promised that there would be time to search for her. Yet I have not had that opportunity."

Erus nodded and looked to the window, his hand remaining on Cedo. He was grateful for the small touch, the contact making him feel wanted and needed in times of such stress.

"Before the whole debacle with the execution and the Dynasty, I asked the curators of the records office to look for me, to see if there was any mention of her."

Cedo felt his breath shorten and he strained forward to catch what was said, as though his Master's words were made of pure gold. "And was there?"

Erus shook his head, eyes filled with sadness. "Nothing. I am sorry."

Holding back the tears, Cedo managed a smile. "It is okay. At the very least it means that she is not dead."

"Aye, it does." His Master became thoughtful. "Did she go by another name? I have never asked you, and I do not know why. Was Reilly her married name?"

Cedo shook his head. "No, Reilly was her maiden name. She reverted back to it once my father left."

"What was her married name?"

"Faulkner."

The color drained from his Master's face and Cedo felt the hand loosen against his leg. "As in General Faulkner?"

Confused, Cedo replied, "Yes. Why?"

Erus let out a deep sigh and rubbed the side of his nose. "We shall have to make some arrangements. He is one of the four Generals who shall be staying below ground with us."

Cedo felt his stomach churn and his blood boil, the anger quickly rising. "Excuse me?!"

Gazing at his lap, Erus shook his head. "Cedo, I am sorry, I did not know. He has remarried since he was with your mother and his records gave no indication of either of you." Green eyes, filled with pain, looked at him. "Can you forgive me?"

Balling his hands into fists, Cedo glared at his Master, his jaw tight. The heat of what he was feeling flared through him and Cedo pushed himself from the desk, storming toward the door. He ignored the pains of his failed hanging as he made for the stairs, determined to escape Erus.

"Cedo!"

Swinging around, he snarled, "Do not speak to me."

His Master leaned against the doorframe, looking dejected and lost. "Cedo, I am sorry."

"I do not want to hear it!" He wrapped a hand around the banister of the stairs, preparing to flee to his room.

Erus moved toward him, his face still writ with the horror of the discovery. "Please listen to me."

He did not give his Master a chance to say another word, his balled fist swinging into Erus' pale face. Erus stumbled back, clutching himself, but did not react. Instead, he just gazed at the floor, hand against his face, chest rising and falling with deep, labored breaths.

"I deserved that," his voice was quiet, cracking with emotion.

Cedo stared at him, a sliver of guilt finding its way through the wall of anger, yet he refused to acknowledge it. The damage had been done, and the anger of knowing his father still lived clawed through him in sharp slashes. Erus lifted his head. Blood trickled from his nose and pooled at his upper lip.

"I am sorry for what I have done," Erus said. "My research should have been more thorough. I did not mean to put you in such a position. I hope that you will not leave."

"What else am I supposed to do?" he spat in response. "How can I stay here when that dog of a man will also be laying his head here?"

Erus closed on him, yet Cedo did not flee, determined to stand his ground. With his jaw tight, Cedo raised his chin, daring Erus to strike him. Instead, hands came to rest at his waist, drawing him into an embrace. Erus' billowing black clothing draped around him, hiding him from the world. For a moment, Cedo struggled, the hands tightening in response. One came up to stroke along his face, an attempt to calm him and drive the demons away. All it did was anger him further, making him flail to free himself.

Stepping back, he stared icily at his Master.

"I shall never forgive you for allowing that abomination of a man into this house. After all he has done, he does not deserve to breathe the same air as me."

Cedo watched as the words cut into Erus like cold knives. His Master slumped, the cowl-like clothes enveloping his body. His shoulders shook and he lowered his head. Guilt and pleasure swirled through Cedo as he realized his Master was crying. Crying for him, for the man he had anchored himself to. It was a sight Cedo thought he would never see, one that pleased and repulsed him in equal measure.

Leaning against the banister, the wooden claw and mouse set at his shoulder, Cedo waited. He had long ago stopped hoping that Erus could show any kind of emotion. Yet here he was, decades of self-built walls crumbling. Finally, Erus lifted his head, eyes stained red and cheeks damp with tears, the blood whispering down to his chin.

"Forgive me, please," he murmured. "I knew not what I did."

Cedo laughed. It was an unpleasant, rasping sound. "Do you think I want to see the man who disowned me? Or decided I was worthless because I did not want to follow him into the military?"

"Perhaps he will see you in a new light?"

"Because I live here?" Cedo snorted. "Despite his love of all things moneyed, I am still the artisan he loathed."

"Because you are changing," Erus replied. "Soon you will be the voice of the nation. There is no higher accolade for an entertainer."

Shaking his head, Cedo began to climb the stairs. "There is nothing you can say or do which will heal this. Leave me be."

The two cats sat at the head of the stairs, obviously awoken by the shouting. With his eyes on them, Cedo made for his room.

"So be it." Erus' quiet voice reached his ears, yet he refused to stop.

"You all right?"

Cedo shook his head. His aching body slumped to the bed and he allowed himself to be wrapped in his lover's arms. Sighing, he laid his head against Billy's chest.

"He is an idiot."

A hand brushed over his hair, fingers tracing the bruises his body bore. "At least 'e apologized."

"It still does not stop what is happening."

He stared at the fingers that touched his face before reaching out to take them. Holding Billy's hand, Cedo placed it against his chest, enjoying the momentary silence. He suspected that it would not last for long, that soon Erus would storm upstairs and demand an apology for the altercation. All of which he would hold Cedo accountable for.

"I know it don't, but you've got to give 'im credit for actually tryin' to mend things."

Beside Cedo, the cats purred, one deep and rumbling, the other a metallic drone. Gently he stroked them both, feeling thick white fur and smooth metal. Their presence comforted him yet the revelation that the man he abhorred would be beneath their roof still stung. Billy's words slowly made their way deep into Cedo's mind, the truth beginning to ease his pain.

"You are right, but I want him to have time to think."

"You give 'im enough of that every time you throw a fit. Go an' talk to 'im now. 'E's 'urtin'. Didn't know what 'e was doin'."

Cedo's neck cracked as he tilted his head back and he smiled through the pain. "I know you are right. You always are. But I do not want to talk to him at this precise moment."

Billy tightened the grip on Cedo's hand. "You need to go an' talk to 'im. You know you do. Don't put it off, 'cause you know what 'e's like."

"No. It can wait. Let us see what he does. He may do nothing."

"Or 'e may kick you out."

A cold chill rippled through Cedo. "He would not do that."

"I would not put it past 'im, 'specially if you're lettin' 'im sit downstairs an' dwell on it."

Sighing, Cedo sat up, every joint aching. "You are right." Peering over his shoulder, he smiled at his lover. "You are always right."

Billy returned his smile, his face lighting in the way Cedo adored so much. "Not all the time."

Cedo was just about to stand when a knock rattled the door. The sound stilled his heart.

He called, "Yes?"

"Cedo, I need to speak to you."

The pain in his Master's voice made him shiver.

Walking to the door, he opened it and stared out at Erus.

"I am sorry. Truly, truly sorry."

Stepping into the hallway, Cedo closed the bedroom door. "I know," he softly replied. "I should not have reacted as I did."

Erus shook his head, curls of red hair falling before his face. "No, you have every right to be angry. I know that this is the man you are trying so hard to not be like. I want you to know that you are succeeding."

Frowning, Cedo stared at him. "Pardon?"

The blood was gone from Erus' face, a dark bruise beginning to replace it. "You are nothing like your father. You are kind and understanding, traits that I rarely seem to see these days. Others may have come and gone but they all wanted one thing, and that was fame and fortune. They never stayed long enough to even begin to get to know me. You have done that and it is a great quality, one I adore in you. I now know that I must lay myself out before you and allow you to truly know me. And I must begin by apologizing."

Cedo felt himself ache with a need he had long thought lost. Once it had been an ache of lust, driven by the strange feelings Erus had awoken. The delicious mix of pain and pleasure, praise and humiliation had tied him to the flame-haired industrialist.

Over time and barely noticeable to the outside world, Erus had changed. His temper had lessened and his adoration had grown. Slowly, Cedo could feel his anger abating. It was no fault of Erus' that his father would be coming to them.

Linking his arms around Erus' neck, Cedo pressed a soft kiss to his Master's cheek. "I accept your apology, and thank you for your kind words. Never did I think I would hear you say such things,\ and they have warmed me greatly."

Erus held him, lips touching Cedo's head. "And I thank you. I never meant you any harm." His voice was still strained, still trying to hide the pained emotion that lay within. "We shall solve this little problem and I promise that you will not have to face him should you wish."

"I know you never meant any harm," he murmured in reply. "I should never have reacted as I did."

"You had every right to act as you did. It was an unpleasant shock."

They stood for several moments, pressed close together. As in the earlier stages of their relationship, Cedo could feel their hearts beating as one, hearts that had called across time and sea to one another. Eventually Erus pulled away, his eyes misted with emotion.

"Go to Billy and savor the time you have with him."

With a weak smile, Cedo gave his Master a gentle kiss and slipped back to his room.

CHAPTER 17

The night was one of little sleep, their aching bodies causing them to rise several times. Cedo was glad when dawn finally came. He dressed and retreated to the kitchen. The cats had already made their way to the warm room, Misty gobbling down all that was offered as Consiliatrix sat atop one of the work surfaces and surveyed his new domain. Francis had worked tirelessly to fill the cupboards with food. Cedo helped himself to a simple breakfast, the *Svenfur Tribune* he had collected from the front door spread out before him.

War On The Rise, the headline screamed, a photo-plate of the machines upon the Downs taking up most of the front page. Around it, the news story told of what was to come, begging all young men to join up and help protect the country. They were assured the greatest of protections with all weaponry, vehicles, and armor coming from the newly reformed Veetu Industries. Having seen the error of his ways, the story continued, industrialist Erus Veetu was returning to his place as the man who was assisting the military in winning the war.

Draining the cup of tea, Cedo leafed through the pages, each page carrying yet another story of what was to befall them. Around them were tiny stories of local interest: a new theatrical production, a robbery at one of the banks, protests against the war on the steps of the town hall. All wove a tale of a seaside city trying to remain as normal as possible.

Francis walked in, refilling the kettle and hanging it above the never-dying fire. A moment later, Billy entered.

"Mornin'."

Glancing up from the newspaper, Cedo smiled. "Good morning."

Francis responded with a hoarse, "Morning."

"You do not sound so well." Folding up the newspaper, Cedo placed it to one side.

Preparing a teapot, Francis shook his head. "I don't feel well, either, but we must keep on going, for the sake of normality at least."

"What counts for normal 'round 'ere, anyway," Billy replied.

"True. How are you both doing? I've heard about the terror which befell you."

"Sore," Cedo replied. "My back aches and my throat still feels constricted. I do not know about Billy, but it has definitely filled me with fear."

Billy shrugged. "I'm fine. Been in worse scrapes."

"Yes, but I expect that you have never found yourself at the end of a noose."

Preparing himself a plate of bread and meat, Billy replied, "I've been worried for my life more than once. An' it's not the first time I've been threatened with a noose. The Guard 'ave done that more times than I can count."

The kettle began to whistle and Francis removed it, filling the teapot with scalding water. "What was that for?"

"Bein' stupid mainly. Givin' 'em cheek, runnin' riot. I was a bit of a tearaway when I was a lad."

Settling himself at the end of the table, Francis changed the subject, "The wireless set arrived yesterday."

"Oh aye? What's it like?"

Francis sipped his tea before glancing at them. "When you've finished in here, you can come to the study and see for yourself."

It was not much to look at: a plain, unvarnished wooden box with a decorative grille at the front and a large handle on one side. It sat on one of the nearly bare shelves, a crudely printed schedule of who would be speaking and when pasted to the top. A part of each day was set aside for local broadcasts. A dial sat in the center of the front, a needle pointing to one of the many numbers painted around it.

"Have you listened to it yet?" Cedo asked, one hand running over the unfinished surface.

"Not yet, although I plan to later. It'll be interesting to see what is being said. Why don't you come and join me?"

"I may just do that."

"I'll come an' join you too." Taking hold of the handle, Billy cranked it several times, the tick of winding clockwork filling the room. "Will take my mind off everythin'."

"How do you feel about going to fight?" Francis asked.

"Don't want to, but got to do it for King an' country. It's my duty to go out there an' look after us."

Cedo smiled and laid a hand in the small of his lover's back. Billy smiled down at him, hand leaving the wireless to stroke Cedo's face. "An' got to make sure this one 'as a country to keep callin' 'ome."

Cedo gave Billy a kiss before turning his attention back to the contraption beside them. It was strange, unlike any other device he had seen. The other musical devices could be explained more easily, their sounds coming from a wax tube or disk. The amplification contraptions of the theaters and the underground club had been attached to the instruments. Yet the wireless set had nothing to produce its sound, instead capturing it from thin air before turning it into something they could hear. It was most odd, and a little disconcerting.

On the study's large desk lay a number of colorful handbills and posters, emblazoned with slogans such as *Your Country Needs You! Sign Up At Your Local Recruitment Office Today; Waste Not, Want Not. Reuse and Repair!; Housewives, Make Sure To Finish Traveling By 4pm. Leave Public Transport Free For Our Boys;* and *Hold Your Tongue! You Could Be Speaking To The Enemy.*

Sifting through them, Cedo frowned. Beneath them lay a map and, careful not to disturb the carefully stacked pile, Cedo pulled it free. It showed the world, the countries colored either in red or blue, no key indicating what it meant.

Francis came to stand beside him, his fingers tracing over the map. "Blue are the allies. Red are—"

"The enemy," Cedo cut him off. "And they know this so early?"

"They have always known it. Through the mists of time, every country has always known her friends and enemies. They may change from one day to the next, but they have always been there."

England, France, Prussia, the Americas, the Africas, India. The only one of the Great Eight not colored blue was the Orient. Instead its borders were the brightest of red, a damning insight to their view of the rest of the tradesmen.

"They hate us," Cedo murmured. "We all do so much for one another and still they hate us."

"They hate you because they see you as stubborn." Taking the map, Francis placed it back beneath the posters. "They believe that the Dynasty should be allowed to be a part of the Great Eight."

"From what I've read, they ain't very nice to people. Nor to animals." Billy had sprawled himself on the loveseat, feet swung over one end. "You know you can tell 'ow people will treat one another when you look at 'ow they treat their animals."

"The French eat horses, yet we do not dislike them," Cedo interjected.

"True. But would you want to live in a country which eats its cats an' dogs an' anythin' else that moves? An' if the stories the 'papers put out are true, then what Erus 'as done to people is nothin' compared to what they do. I mean, at least Erus 'ad the decency to shoot people when 'e was done with 'em. The Orient likes to chop 'em up an' then leave 'em to die to slowly. An' if someone wrongs 'em, they get the person to disembowel themselves."

"Enough!" Cedo cried. "I do not want to hear any more."

Walking across the room, Cedo straddled Billy's hips and stared down into the sea-blue eyes. Hands came to rest at his hips, gently caressing him through the layers of clothing.

"Why do you tell of such things?"

"'Cause if they're true, I want to know why we're allowed to trade with 'em. I mean, we won't let the Dynasty trade with us 'cause of their reputation toward 'umans. So why the Orient?"

"Because," Francis said, "it has always been one rule for one and one for another. They're allowed to keep their trade rights because of the progress they are making. The Dynasty hasn't made such progress. In fact, in the last hundred years it has slid further back and will keep on doing so until the president is unseated. His lust for power has ruined our once great country. Anyway, I believe you both require some time alone, and there are duties I must keep."

Looking over his shoulder, Cedo watched as Francis left. He had been meaning to ask him about leaving the Dynasty behind and the feelings that arose from it. Did Francis feel any more freedom? Did the passion of revenge still run through the bespectacled man?

The door clicked shut and Billy's fingers tightened around him. Returning his attention to Billy, Cedo watched him smile.

"Sorry for scarin' you like that."

"You did not scare me. I just dislike hearing about such things."

"I know. We just got to keep on top of these things. Got to keep up with what's goin' on in the world."

Easing himself forward, Cedo gently kissed his mate. "I know. But there are times I would much rather forget them. Like now. Now I would rather forget that such a vicious world exists."

He felt Billy grin against his lips, hands sliding to his back. "Oh, I can make you forget, all right."

Chuckling, Cedo kissed him harder. He wound one hand into Billy's thick waves of blond hair as he plunged his tongue between soft, willing lips. Beneath him, Billy writhed, raising his hips to give Cedo a taste of what was to come.

They tore at one another's clothes, stripping each other naked, not caring if anyone saw them. Hands slid across naked flesh, touching what had long been missed while mouths hungrily explored, nipping at throats and chests. Flashes of pain flared through Cedo, the heat quickly turning to pleasure. When Billy turned him over his lap, he gave a cry of laughter, never flinching as a rough hand slapped his rear. Cedo's laughter changed to deep sighs, the slight movements making his hard cock twitch with anticipation.

"That is delicious," Cedo purred.

"This?" Billy once more swatted his backside.

The sting flared through Cedo, making him moan and wriggle. It truly was delightful, far more than he thought it would be.

"Yes, that."

"Good," the blond-haired man replied.

Once Billy had finished reddening his rump, Cedo slid to the floor, the sharp warmth making him tingle with delight. Kneeling before his mate, Cedo smiled up at him before impaling his mouth on Billy's erection. Above him, Billy groaned, hands balling into Cedo's hair, moving and encouraging him. Cedo did as was silently asked, opening his throat and swallowing all his lover had to offer. For so long he had waited to once more do such things, to show Billy how much he adored and appreciated him.

Holding his lover's gaze, Cedo wound his tongue around Billy's erection, memorizing the velvety flesh. When Billy tugged on his hair, he pulled away, the taste of his lover still on his lips. Standing, he allowed himself to be bent over the low seat, his rear teasingly in the air, legs spread wide. Fingers delicately began to probe him, dipping between his buttocks and ghosting against his entrance. Glancing over his shoulder, Cedo smiled, admiring the powerful lines of his lover's body.

"Ready?"

"For you?" Cedo purred. "All the time."

A hand slid over his buttocks, cupping and squeezing. "That's what I like to hear."

Strong fingers wrapped around his hips, and Cedo felt his body go rigid as Billy slowly entered him. His long, thick cock teased him, making Cedo gasp. Gripping the red velvet seat, he began to move with his mate, thrusts deep and deliberate, his own cock aching for attention. Cedo had missed their lovemaking, missed the exquisite feelings Billy was able to draw from him. They were feelings that made him tremble and moan, made him beg for more. Cedo loathed the thought that soon they would be gone, whisked away with Billy to the front line.

"Will you write?" he murmured.

Lips touched the back of his neck, crushing his sweat-dampened hair to his skin. "'Course I'll write. Not gonna forget you. An' I'll visit when I can."

"And if you are stationed away?"

Billy kissed his way along Cedo's back, teeth nipping at his skin. "There'll be ways. I ain't goin' overseas."

"Not that you know of, anyway."

Billy gently tugged on his hair, lifting Cedo's gaze.

"Let's not talk about this, Cedo. Not now. I just want it to be about us. At least for now."

His body felt weak and he tilted his head, meeting Billy's lips with his own. Lowering his back, Cedo gasped as Billy pressed against the spot that made him shake with pleasure. Their kiss deepened as Billy picked up the pace, his voice becoming a deep growl. It was a sound that made Cedo shiver, knowing he was eliciting such a response. Wrapping a hand around his own cock, he rocked with his lover, groaning and calling to him until their orgasms washed over them.

At a quarter to five that afternoon, Francis entered the study, a tray balanced on one hand. Glancing at the men entwined on the floor, he smiled and shook his head, placing the tray upon the desk.

"Five o'clock. There is a broadcast from London. I'd

make yourselves presentable if I were you, because Mr. Veetu will be wanting to listen as well."

It was an effort to tear himself away from Billy and leave the warm kisses and teasing fingers. They had spent themselves a number of times, the floor becoming a place for them to play. Cedo was surprised that they had not been disturbed before, but he assumed that Erus was giving them the space they needed.

Dressing, Cedo took the offered cup from Francis and drank deeply of the rich tea. Billy's arms looped around his waist and kisses were placed on his neck. He chuckled and picked up another cup, offering it behind him. The arms disappeared, and he heard Billy gratefully drink.

The tray was covered with an array of cakes and sandwiches. A few moments later Erus entered, the cats following in his wake. Smiling at the small gathering, he seated himself behind the desk.

"I trust our little wireless box works?"

Offering him a filled cup, Francis replied, "Of course. What more would you expect?"

"That it has put fear into the hearts of the nation, I suspect. Not the intention when it was conceived, but I'm sure some will see it as witchcraft."

Seating himself on the loveseat, Cedo patted the thick fabric. Misty jumped up beside him and Consiliatrix followed suit, curling his metal body into Cedo's lap. He seemed as real as any cat Cedo had ever had the joy of owning, his rhythmic breathing perfectly timed and a deep purr rumbling from his chest. Green light flashed from beneath the expanding and contracting plates, his skillfully crafted ears twitching back and forth.

Silence fell over the room as Francis turned the wireless on. A low hum filled the air followed by crackling as the dial was rotated. Finally it settled on a on a low hiss.

As the clock struck five, a tinkling melody played from

the strange box. Somewhere, wherever the broadcast was coming from, someone was playing the piano. A moment later and it was replaced by a voice.

"London calling. This is London calling," the clipped female voice stated. "We welcome one and all to this broadcast on the country's brand new wireless system. Over the coming weeks and months, you will have the joy of hearing a great many broadcasts. Some will be informational and some will be entertainment. The aim of the service is to keep the country going during our darkest hour.

"You may be curious as to how your wireless device works. Like sound waves, radio waves are invisible. They are also completely harmless and can only be picked up by the specially crafted device you are listening to. As you will have noticed, there is a dial on the front of your wireless. The numbers associate with local frequencies around the country. In a few days, you will receive a pamphlet which will tell who is broadcasting on which frequency. Numbers zero-zero-one through to zero-zero-five are reserved exclusively for the London broadcasts.

"As you know, our country is on the brink of war. The president of the Dynasty has decreed that our country has wronged him. Yet we will show him otherwise. We will not be defeated and we shall not stand down. It has been requested that if you are male and of fighting age that you go to your local conscription office and sign up to fight this coming evil. Ladies, you are also being asked to play your part. With our men on the front line, there will be a great many jobs in factories and armories. It is requested that you go to these and put down your name to take up the job of one of our brave men. Only with your help will this country remain great.

"Many broadcasts will come from London and will feature the talents of the music halls, as well as speeches from members of parliament, the military and, most importantly, the King. He is greatly concerned with all of the citizens of this great isle, and his prayers are with you in these times. Ladies and gentlemen, boys and girls, we will win this war.

"Until tomorrow, this is London calling."

The disembodied voice stopped, leaving only a low hiss in her wake. Cedo stared at the device, a shiver running along his spine. "It is so strange."

"What is?" Erus asked.

"To hear someone who is calling from so far away."

"One day, Cedo, it will take over the world. Mark my words."

Francis switched the box off and the hiss died away. "It was most definitely different. I'd liken it to the system the president has running through the country."

"The numbers stations?" Erus asked. "They're most certainly interesting and something we will be adopting in the coming weeks. The challenge of trying to break the codes helped to keep me sane."

Francis smiled and tilted his head to one side. "At least he helped in some little way."

Erus laughed. "There are not many in which he can."

"Well, I liked it," Billy said. "Fascinatin' stuff. Can't wait to see 'ow they use it."

"We have many uses planned for it." Picking up the pile of papers, Erus rose and placed them on a shelf. "You will find it easier to communicate on the front line, and soon we will be able to send coded messages to all of our allies. Receivers and transmitters are being installed on all ships, both civilian and military. Who knows where this technology will take us. Perhaps one day we shall speak to the stars and moon."

A wistful smile played on Erus' lips and he moved to stand before the window, hands clasped behind him. "I long to discover whether there are civilizations beyond ours. I hope to live long enough to see that day."

"Do you think there are others beyond our planet?" Cedo asked.

"Oh indeed." Erus did not turn to look at them, his attention drawn to the beautiful day beyond the glass. "We are making startling discoveries about our galaxy and just how far it stretches. You cannot tell me that there is all that space and we are alone in this universe. There has to be much more to it than what we see."

He turned to them. "Francis, Billy, could you leave us for a moment, please?"

The two men nodded and left, the door clicking shut behind them. Returning to his desk, Erus gestured to the desk. "Sit."

Easing himself onto its leather-covered surface, Cedo watched his Master. Pale hands slid across his groin, their heels rubbing against his cock.

"You've been used today." It was a statement rather than a question.

"Yes, Master." Closing his eyes, Cedo felt his cock begin to swell, the fingers teasing him to submission.

"I thought that it would be the reverse, what with him being yours."

The agony was delightful, the rough fabric of Cedo's britches rubbing against his silken flesh, and he panted softly.

"We switch," he managed to reply.

His toes curled into tight fists, his heart racing as Erus released the buttons of his lower garments.

"And you don't mind?"

"Not at all." It was becoming difficult to speak, and Cedo knew he could not give Erus the real reason as to why he lay with Billy. "I see it as my duty to pleasure one of our future soldiers."

Warm lips and soft breath brushed against his own. "Indeed."

Erus' fingers slid into his britches and around his erection, slowly moving against his hardened flesh. Gasping, Cedo felt the will to hold himself upright slipping away, his body giving in to the pleasure.

"And you enjoy what he does to you?"

He managed to nod, a movement that sent fingernails into his flesh.

"I expect a verbal answer," Erus hissed.

Cedo took a deep breath. "Yes. I enjoy what he does very much."

He could feel his cock throbbing against his Master's hand, the need to reach orgasm growing once more.

"What else does he do to you?"

Behind his closed eyes, Cedo could see their afternoon of debauched pleasure playing like one of the new moving picture films.

"He enjoys placing me over his lap."

"Does he enjoy reddening your flesh with his hand?" His Master's voice was deepening, its tone becoming husky.

"Yes, he does." Cedo wriggled against the desk, his orgasm closing in on him like the bright white light of a newly born star.

"And do you enjoy it?" Lips again touched his, whispering and gifting him with gentle kisses.

"Very much so, Master."

A silence fell, one which was broken by their quiet pants. Erus' hand tightened around him, stroking faster. Biting his Master's lips, Cedo groaned, raising his hips and forcing his cock deeper into the welcoming hand.

"Perhaps I will see if he will allow me to watch," Erus replied. "I would enjoy that very much."

His throat felt dry, his voice barely able to speak.

"I shall ask him, Master." He groaned, his whole body aching with the need to reach orgasm. "Please. I need to spend myself."

The hand quickly drew away and his eyes snapped open. Erus' normally pale skin was flushed pink, his lips dry.

"Get down and bend over the desk," he commanded.

Cedo did as was asked. His britches were pushed down and his legs forced apart. Gripping the far edge of the desk, he raised his rear, presenting himself to the one he obeyed. Staring into the flame of the desk lamp, he gave a deep, satisfied groan as Erus entered him, hands gripping his hips. His Master's thrusts were quick and rough, sating their joined lust. It took only a few moments before they both came, Cedo spending himself against the dark wood of the desk.

CHAPTER 18

It arrived the following morning, a dark shadow against an otherwise perfect summer's day. Standing in what remained of the garden, Cedo watched as the Reaper lowered into the cavern of the hangar, the rudders moving back and forth to stabilize it. Mounds of earth surrounded the garden, hiding the hangar from view, the once-green grass torn into a thick, brown quagmire.

There was no emotion for what he was feeling as the ground rumbled beneath his feet, the air filling with the biting scent of obtainium. No smoke emitted from the flying craft, the new fuel doing its job perfectly.

As it settled into its new home, the hangar doors rolled shut with a deep clang and the ground became flat once more. In silence, Cedo stared at the gray doors. They were so prominent, so permanent, a reminder of what had been, what was to come, and what would be. Never would the beautiful garden be the same again, its tranquility torn away. Life as they knew it was gone forever.

With a heavy heart, he returned to the house. Walking through the quiet servants' quarters, Cedo made his way to the war rooms below. Still no news of their servants had reached them, their identities washed away. Perhaps they had been released to be with their families, or to join the forces. Perhaps, as had been mentioned before, they had been banished to the prisons on the Downs, harsh places where names were replaced with numbers, people becoming slaves to supply the country with cheap goods. Their names were ones he would add to the list so that once the time was granted, Cedo could search for them as he would his mother.

Below-stairs, the arrival of the military had begun. Standing at the freshly reinforced door, Francis checked names against a list, directing uniformed men to their stations and quarters. The house was no longer their own, having been handed over for surveillance and to direct the battalions along the south coast. The news was that the Dynasty armies were approaching, marching through Prussia and destroying all in their path. Soldiers had already been sent to assist the armies of Prussia and France. Great flying gunships had been seen leaving the coast, loaded with ammunition and primed to put a halt to the advancing enemy. Whether they would succeed or not, Cedo did not know.

Francis lifted his eyes from the list. "You may want to see if Mr. Veetu requires anything."

"Why do you say that?"

Tapping the graphite against the paper, Francis glanced into the open doorway. "He is becoming—how do I put it? Troubled by all the new arrivals."

"Well, that is no surprise." A strange need to laugh began to rise, triggered by the situation and the image of his Master rushing around, making the bunker ready. "He does not like it when things are changed."

"Yes, I seem to remember that from his time in the Dynasty. I believe most of his anger was at his change of environment rather than the distress of being locked up. Although I'm sure that caused him considerable anguish as well."

"I am sure James played a part in it too," Cedo added.

"I'm sure he did. Mr. Veetu is in the bunker. Go and

see him before you disappear."

Cedo entered the bunker, briefly resting a hand on Francis' shoulder as he passed. People were moving around, carrying sacks of clothing and unpacking the boxes. Straw and equipment were spread over the tables as it was sorted and primed. Some were simple items: paper, bottles of ink, and spare pens. Others were more intricate: items made from brass and glass with metal arms extending above them, muslin balls clasped in claws.

The men in their smart red uniforms ignored Cedo as he roamed from room to room. All were occupied with what was to come, making the most of their subterranean world. They would not see sunlight for weeks, perhaps months.

Eventually Cedo found his Master in one of the pump rooms. Hidden from the rest of the bunker, the beam engine stretched high above them. Presently, it was not yet needed and so sat silent and unmoving. Blocks of obtainium were stacked in protective cages and electric lights illuminated the tall room. Erus stood on a ladder, hands working at the machine's innards.

Finally his Master spoke. "Cedo, would you be so kind as to pass me the ratchet? The one on top of the box."

Glancing down, Cedo spied a large, wooden box at the base of the ladder. Atop a pile of tools lay the wrench Erus required.

Holding it up, he said, "How did you—"

"Know you were here?" Erus took the tool from Cedo. "You're the only one who doesn't come in barking instructions and questions. You're a mouse compared to the hordes who are now here."

"How many will be below ground?"

"Fifty. We could take more, and perhaps we will need to at some point. Those who are here are the only ones who are required at present."

A low wall ran around the base of the engine. Seating himself on it, Cedo watched Erus. He was pressed close to the machine, his right arm buried to the shoulder. From within it came the low clicking grind of the ratchet.

"How long do you think we will be down here, Master?"

"We are at liberty to remain above ground until first landfall. Whether that is from the air, or by foot, the first sign of enemy invasion is when we retire down here. The army will be locked in from tonight, watching and listening."

A nut tumbled from the opened panel, and Erus cursed quietly. Cedo retrieved it and held it out.

"So we are a listening post?"

"In essence, yes. We shall also run all of the southern coastal battalions, and I shall be keeping an eye on how well the weapons and machines work. There are many new inventions out there and, while I hope that they're perfect, they won't be. There will be fatalities and I want to know how I can make them better, faster and stronger. If a tiny adjustment can save even one life, then it is worth it. I do not want our men dying because of shoddy workmanship."

Cedo felt his heart swell with a happiness and pride he never thought he would feel. "It makes me happy to hear that, Master."

Above him, Erus paused and glanced down, a confused look on his face. "And why would that be?"

"When I first met you, there did not appear to be any kind of empathy within you. All you wished to do was be the best, even if it meant trampling over all before you. Now." Cedo smiled. "Now you have changed, something I never thought I would see."

Erus chuckled and gave Cedo a wry smile before returning to work. "As I told you, Cedo, it can take time to peel away the layers and discover what it beneath. We are ever-evolving creatures and sometimes it takes another to show us the error of our ways. It took me a long time to learn, and a trip to the execution chamber, before I realized that the person I was was a person I no longer needed to be. His time had passed and the anger he felt needed to go. I still feel some of that anger, but I no longer allow it to rule my life."

Erus shut the panel door, wiped his grease-covered hand and looked down at Cedo. "You've obviously come for something. Why did you seek me out?"

Cedo took the ratchet and returned it to the box. "I was wondering whether you needed any help. I did not want to face my father on his arrival, so I was going to stay in my room, but I wanted to make sure you did not need me first."

Erus look around the tall room, the green and red engine a sight to behold. "Well, I could use some help in here. Once we've finished, there's a new restaurant in the city I'd like us to try." His green eyes sparkled as he turned to Cedo. "You, Billy, and myself. How about it?"

Collecting the box of tools, Cedo nodded and smiled. "I would like that very much."

The sun was just beginning her descent as the steam-carriage left the village, the smell of grass, grain and the sharp scent of the sea engulfing them. The atmosphere in the carriage was one of relaxation and happiness.

Dressed in their finest, Cedo and Billy watched the rolling Downs pass by, the carriage's engine bubbling away behind them. Streams of steam rose from twin exhausts and danced behind them, the driver seated somewhere above them. Across from them, his legs crossed at the ankles, Erus read through a file of papers.

"I don't understand half of this new gadgetry they've brought with them."

"You mean you could have done a better job?" Cedo chuckled.

Erus lifted his eyes, a grin forming on his lips. "Precisely what I mean. Weather, poison, and fire monitoring I can understand. But do we really need a rat-catching device?"

"I can see why they'd want it," Billy replied.

Erus shrugged. "I suppose. Although we will have two cats down there with us. Admittedly, one won't eat them, but he most certainly will catch them. And what the blazes is a *Four-Wick Candlelighter*? Oh, for goodness' sake! That is just plain idleness. We have electrical and gas lamps. If they want candles they can do what every other person does and use a lucifer or a taper. Having a device for it is just superfluous to requirement. Do they think we have endless space?"

The steam-carriage rattled over a bridge, momentarily shaking them.

"We built an extension for the hangar," Cedo said.

"Yes," Erus replied, "but it is a hangar for the Reaper, not a dumping ground for pointless gadgetry."

The Rain Emporium was a new establishment, having opened only the week previously. It was a long-roomed restaurant with tables placed along both walls. Beside the door was a bar. Over it and each of the tables hung a tree canopy, cultivated to keep the occupants beneath it completely dry. Along the center of the restaurant ran a trough, and the climate of the room matched that of an exotic island.

Seated beneath one of the canopies, Cedo closed his

eyes and shivered as droplets of water pattered against the leaves. He could have been across the oceans, seated beneath a wide-leafed tree and listening to the beginnings of a tropical storm. Instead, he was seated in a building in the heart of Svenfur. It was most peculiar. Yet at the same time, completely normal for their city.

The waiters had umbrellas attached to their suits, leaving their hands free to carry plates and trays of delectable food and drink. A speaking tube was attached to each table, allowing them to speak quietly to the staff rather than disturb the ambiance that enveloped them.

"I'd like a bottle of champagne and three glasses."

He opened an eye to see Erus replace the speaking tube. Sitting across from Cedo and Billy, Erus smiled and folded his hands on the table.

"Well, it's certainly different, isn't it?"

Cedo felt himself smile. "It certainly is. A delightful little wonderland."

"I thought you would appreciate it." Erus rested his elbows on the table and leaned closer. "I have had another renovation made to the house. There is now a staircase leading from the bunker to the mirrored room. The forest remains in there and, provided the fighting does not come too close to the house, you'll be free to use it."

"Thank you."

"Hopefully it will make you feel a little more comfortable, especially with my recent blunder. It will give you some space to escape from the madness that will ensue." Sighing, Erus gazed down at the table. "Because it will be madness down there, a hothouse of tension. Tempers will be frayed, and I don't want you to become caught in the crossfire. I fear they will not see you as a worthy member of the company. That is something which has been worrying me greatly of late."

Reaching across the table, Cedo laid a hand on his

Master's arm. "It will be fine. Whatever happens, happens. I am just happy to know that I will be safe and that I will be able to not only help my country in its hour of need, but will also be able to watch over the ones I love."

Billy's fingers stroked at Cedo's hair and he looked up to smile at the blond man. Their wounds still ached, the bruises dark against their skin. Yet he had never felt more alive. Soon he would have to release his lover to the arms of the military and hope and pray that Billy returned safely. Every moment leading up until then was precious, moments to be savored and turned into memories.

"You will have time to do that. The army postal service is working well, and will continue to function during this time. I hope that you will both correspond with one another and keep what you have alive."

"Aye, I plan on it." Billy's voice was soft, tinged with what Cedo suspected was fear. Cedo could not blame him for feeling scared, knowing that he would feel the same in such a situation. Wrapping his hand around Billy's, Cedo held onto him, silently telling him that he would never let go.

Cedo caught the gaze of his Master. "Things have changed in you. For the better. It is wonderful to see, and I have never felt happier. Thank you."

Erus smiled and shrugged. "Whatever for?"

Smiling, he gestured around himself. "For this. For what has come of us. For allowing Billy and myself to remain together. I know that was especially difficult for you."

"It would be difficult for anyone, Cedo. To see the one they had taken in whisked away into the arms of another. I'll admit that it hurt, but I knew that it needed to happen so that I could learn a lesson. I knew that if you both stayed, then it would all work. If you did not, then it was never to be and I would face this war, and life, alone. I now believe you were sent to me for a reason. I never particularly believed in the gods and spirits that our people worship and what little belief I did have died when Papa Brokoveich died. I do wonder if things happen for a reason. I am glad that all that has happened has."

The champagne arrived, encased in a leaf-encrusted bucket of ice. Erus filled the glasses and handed one to each of them.

Holding his own aloft, he announced, "To a safe and happy future."

The toast was made and they drank, the rich liquid cooling Cedo's belly. Around them, the rain continued to fall, steadily growing heavier.

Their food was ordered and arrived on green and gold plates. Slabs of tender meat and mounds of colorful vegetables, it was a feast like none of them had seen for a long time. Deep down, Cedo knew it would probably be the last time they saw such luxurious food. He had read about wars in other lands, and had seen it with his own eyes in the Dynasty. Countries ripped to the bone with barely enough to go around, the leaders hoarding any finery for themselves. The mere citizens were afforded little more than scraps tossed to them by the wealthy. But soon, even the wealthy starved, the conquering army pushing them to their knees.

Attacking the heavenly meat, Cedo said, "How is your return to citizenship coming along? You have spoken very little of it."

"I'm proud to report that I once more have full citizenship." Erus grinned, eyes sparkling. "My time as a non-person is over, and everything that the Guard removed has been returned. It is being stored in the study in the bunker." The red-haired man sighed. "The only things that have not been returned are the servants. I still know nothing of their whereabouts."

Silence fell over them, a moment of respect for those who were missing from their lives.

"So 'ow 'ave they put it to the people?" Billy had been oddly silent, yet Cedo had sensed no unease or discomfort. Maybe he was savoring every moment, taking it all in before he took his first steps into life within the armed forces?

"There is a report coming soon which will be published in the newspapers. They'll use it as propaganda against the enemy, saying that everything was faked so that I could go covertly to the Dynasty and see what they were doing."

"Which you did." Cedo took another piece of the thickly sliced meat, sighing softly as it all but melted against his tongue.

"Yes, I did, even though I was, in reality, sold to James for other reasons. Perhaps I will reveal that one day, perhaps I won't. We'll see how I'm treated."

"By the Patron?"

"By everyone." Erus took a drink, green eyes glaring over the rim of his glass.

"'Ow do you mean, by everyone?" asked Billy.

Erus sighed and tapped the tip of his knife against the edge of his plate, a painful sound attacking Cedo's ears. "I mean anyone in power. The Patron, the King, the prime minister, any of the Generals who'll be below ground with us. How they treat me is endemic of how they treat the rest of the nation, that I am sure of now. If you do not have money, or status, then you are a nobody, a number in a ledger, meant only to be used and abused until the day you die."

"You are going to try and remove them from power?"

"I may. As I said, it all depends on how they treat me. Yet there is greed and corruption on a massive scale, all of which has started at the top."

Cedo felt himself smile. "Yet, you were once one of those people."

"Indeed I was. But, as I have said, it is time for a change, and if I can change the country as a whole, for the better, then I shall."

"Do you have a manifesto for this new country?"

Erus eyes snapped to Cedo's. "Indeed, I do."

Around them, the restaurant began to darken, the windows becoming black and the lights dimming. From somewhere thunder rumbled, and Cedo smiled. The restaurant was a delightful place, somewhere to relax. Unlike others he had visited, which had relied on noise and light to enchant their patrons, the Rain Emporium encouraged them to relax. It was why, he assumed, there were no prices on the ornate menus. Such pleasure came at a price, one which if it had to be asked for, the person could not afford.

"There's somethin' I want to ask," Billy said softly, his voice barely audible above the sound of the rain.

"Go on," Erus replied.

Beside him, Billy took a deep breath, eyes looking everywhere before they returned to the flame-haired man across from them. "I wish to 'ave the life serum."

Cedo felt himself go cold before the warmth began to return, a tiny tremble whispering over his skin. "Are you sure?"

Billy turned to him and nodded. "Very sure. I know it won't 'elp save my life in battle but, should I survive, I don't want to get to an 'undred years from now an' be sayin' goodbye to you."

Cedo's heart missed a beat and he draped an arm around his lover's waist. Laying his head against Billy's shoulder, he whispered, "I will love you no matter what. You do know that?"

"I do. But I don't want to leave you. Not now, not

ever. An' if I can 'ave a chance of stayin' by your side forever, then I'll take it."

From across the table, Erus spoke. "That is not a problem. We have spares of it at back at the house. I'll be sure to administer it before you leave."

Cedo felt Billy relax against him. "Thank you. I appreciate it."

Tea arrived, served in a large, curling pot. Three cups hung from the side of the pot. Nestling down into the deep seat, Cedo wrapped his hands around the cup, waiting for it to be filled. None of them spoke, enjoying the atmosphere. It had become like a tropical island at night, thunder still softly rolling through the air, the rain coming and going. It would become heavy before easing off and stopping. Then it would come again, pattering from the leaves and splashing to the floor. It trickled into the trough and from there it went to goodness knows where. The seats were deep, their backs curling up and hiding them away from whoever else was in the restaurant. It really was the perfect place to get lost and to share a few, fanciful moments. Gazing through the low light, he smiled at Erus before taking Billy's hand. His lover's strong fingers wrapped around him and he leaned closer, placing a kiss on Billy's shoulder.

"I must say," Erus softly said, "that it is nice to see you both together. I'm glad that we've all been brought together in this way."

Reaching across the table, Cedo took his Master's hand, lifted it and pressed a kiss to his knuckles. "And I am glad you allow us to be together. Your acceptance and understanding have not gone unnoticed. Your kindness will be repaid."

Erus chuckled. "I require no repayment. Just having you both here, and seeing how happy you are, is all that I need. Cedo, I will never stop loving you, and I thank you for sharing yourself with me. William, how do you feel? I don't want to forget you in all of this."

"I was uncomfortable at first. But you 'ave to do what's best for those around you."

Kissing Billy's cheek, Cedo murmured, "You must not forget your own happiness."

He felt Billy turn, soft hair brushing against his face. "I'm 'appy. Always 'ave been with you."

CHAPTER 19

They left the darkened restaurant to step into a world where night had fallen. From beyond the buildings came the steady thump of engines. A moment later and the sky was filled with the illuminated mass of one of the flying gunships. Its flat expanse filled their vision, lights searching the ground below. Above them, amid the shadows of the flying craft, arrays of engines, guns, and inflated airships could be seen, all stacked neatly along the edges. It was a flying city like one the world had never seen and, Cedo suspected, would never see again.

As it moved out to sea, its lights died and it ascended to the clouds, making it invisible to those on the ground. Only the roar of the engines gave it away.

"The Flying Fortress." Erus laughed. "Can't believe it actually works. Marvelous!"

With that, he strode off into the night, whistling a tune from the music halls.

"Whatever 'e's takin', I'll take a lifetime's worth," Billy muttered.

Chuckling, Cedo took his lover's hand and they followed Erus' rapidly disappearing form.

They walked through the night, taking in the bright lights of the pier and the excitement of the bustling summer crowds. People wandered the streets, jostling one another and calling apologies. There was no malice in the air, just the happiness of a warm evening. Whether visitors or locals, they were all dressed in their finery, brightly colored clothes and glittering jewels, strutting like peacocks. They made for the pier, the gin houses, and the music halls. All around them were the sounds of a city at play: music, shouting, laughing, and the cries of street vendors and theater touts.

"I'm not ready to return to the drudgery of that house," Erus called. "What do you boys fancy doing?"

Rose Avenue was not so much an avenue as a wide road lined with small, specialist shops. Each sold something different, something exotic, something that called the imagination. Stopping before one that sold fanciful costumes, Cedo looked at the beautiful window display. A life-sized fairy sat on a red spotted toadstool, toy animals playing at her feet. Iridescent wings clung to her back and, he suddenly realized, they moved ever so slowly. Lights hidden within the fake grass caught their purple and glitter decorated cells.

"Would either of you like to take a walk beside the sea?" Cedo asked. "I would very much like to see it before it disappears beneath the wheels and feet of war."

Erus' being was reflected in the window, little more than a ghost to the naked eye. "I highly doubt that will happen, but just in case it does, let us go and spend time there."

The street fed directly out onto West Road and, taking a right, they made their way toward the sea, and all the secrets she held.

It may have been night, but that did not mean the fun had to stop. People swarmed the beach, many of them in the costumes of parties, their feet rattling the dry shingle. They laughed, sang, and made merry, glasses and bottles of drink held aloft. Cedo was handed a bottle by a member of one of the cavorting groups. Nodding a thank you to them, he took a deep drink and flinched as a burning liquor scolded his throat. Shaking away the tears of pain, he handed the bottle to Billy, who followed suit, only to gasp and pass the bottle to Erus.

Before long, they were joining the throngs of the revelers singing bawdy songs. Cedo, Billy, and Erus wove their way into the coffee house beneath the road, grinning at one another as the words of another loud song reached their ears. Despite the late hour, the coffee house was as busy as ever, the long-aproned waiters moving around the cramped tables. After a short wait, they were finally able to seat themselves in a corner, the table still piled with empty mugs and crumb-covered plates. A waiter dashed up to them and moved the dirty crockery away before returning to take their order.

"Three liqueur coffees." Erus smiled at the man, chuckling as he blushed and moved away.

The harsh liquor coursed through Cedo, warming him and making his head swim. He had the urge to laugh, to dance and enjoy the night before them. It was still young and demanded their attention, urged them to grasp it and make merry. Wrapping his arms around Billy's waist, he buried his nose in the waves of wind-ruffled hair and inhaled his lover's heady scent. He smelled of all things masculine, strong and courageous, while beneath it lay the cool, salty fragrance of the beach.

"Will you join us tonight?" he whispered, lips finding Billy's ear. Gently he tugged at the soft lobe, tongue stroking along it. "In the bedroom?"

Hands stroked through his hair, knotting in it and carefully pulling him back. Billy's cheeks were reddened with the breeze and the alcohol, his eyes sparkling in the bright lights of the coffee house. The warmth and the welcoming smell of coffee pulled them into its embrace, adding to their excitement. Behind them, the large, ornate coffee machine gurgled and spluttered, turning out perfect cups of the hot, black liquid.

"You want me to come to bed with you both?" Billy's face glowed with a smile. "I thought I said I wouldn't, but I'm sure I can make an exception to the rule."

The dull pain of having his hair pulled roared through Cedo, reminding him of what he enjoyed when his skin was bared. "You will make an exception for me?"

Billy tightened his fingers and Cedo gasped as his throat was exposed, pulse thudding beneath his skin. His breath came in short, sharp pants and he could feel his vision becoming relaxed.

"Yeah," Billy said. "I'm goin' to make an exception for you, 'cause I want to see what'll 'appen. Besides, I've done far worse over the years."

"Really, now?"

Billy's lips touched his temple. "Yep, really."

The front door crashed against the wall and they stumbled in, singing, swaying, and clutching one another. Cedo could not remember the last time he had had such fun. The bottle of liquor had long ago run dry, the empty vessel abandoned for the street cleaning machines.

They were a new addition to the city, designed by Veetu Industries, and introduced while Billy and he had struggled through the Dynasty. Standing beneath a street lamp, Cedo had watched, fascinated, as one had scuttled along the pavement, collecting rubbish and depositing it into a hopper on its back. Much like the assassin crabs, even Cedo's foot trying to topple it had done little to deter it from its job. It had hunkered down, shook itself off, and continued along its path, extended pincers reaching where no human hand could.

Clutching Billy, Cedo roughly kissed him, fingers tangling in his hair as they made for the stairs. The alcohol still sang through Cedo, the promise of pleasure only heightening its affect. Billy grunted beneath his onslaught, struggling to guide him up the stairs, bruised lips and warm tongue attacking his own.

The gaslights of the bedroom rushed to life as they staggered through the door. Cedo felt a hand tug at his hair and he leaned back to accept a kiss from his Master. Hands pawed at one another, clothes becoming a forgotten memory as they were cast away to the floor. Swaying upright, Cedo laughed and pushed Billy to the bed. Heat rushed through him, for once a heat of excitement rather than embarrassment. He felt liberated, alive, defying all that people said. The class wars told him he should be subservient, begging for freedoms and money. Instead, he'd cheated them at their game, chasing the dreams he had been told he should not have.

Kneeling on the bed, Cedo straddled Billy, his cock already hard. Brushing his hands over his lover's sun-fed hair, he pressed his lips to Billy's cheek. Hands clasped his back, easing him closer, their lips finding the others. The need to hurry had died and they quietly enjoyed one another, mouths opening in silent gasps, fingers and tongues exploring.

A hand brushed his cheek and Cedo lifted his head, gazing up into his Master's lust-darkened face. Erus' eyes were hooded and glazed, a smirk playing on his lips. Stretching back, Cedo wrapped an arm around Erus' neck and pulled him close. Their lips slid together, Erus panting into his mouth. Groaning, Cedo shuddered, his cock throbbing against his stomach. As they kissed, fingers wrapped around him, slowly stroking, and he glanced down to see Billy gazing up at him.

Finally, his Master pulled away, gesturing behind

himself as he did. "I shall be over there." His voice was weak, yet his body told a different story. "For now I want to watch."

Erus sat, legs spread, his own excitement evident in his britches. Returning his attention to Billy, Cedo kissed him, gently moving along his body, his lips finding the curve of his chest and the velvety flatness of his stomach. Curling between Billy's legs, he kissesd his lover's strong thighs, nudging them apart. Cedo's mouth watered at the sight before him. With his hands balled into the bed sheets, Billy panted, body tense with need. The blond man's erection lay against his stomach, his balls full and pulled tight. He quivered when Cedo ran a finger from his lover's rosy entrance and along his cock, Billy mewling softly when his fingers tugged at the swollen head. Cedo could feel his own breath coming in short bursts, the need to make his lover reach orgasm growing. Yet he knew he needed to take it slowly, to enjoy the moment. For they did not know when they would get such a time together again.

Pressing his tongue to Billy's cock, he licked along it, lips encircling the head and drawing it into his warm mouth. His mate tasted exquisite, a mix of sweet and salty, flesh smooth to the touch. Closing his eyes, he impaled himself on Billy, throat willingly opening and drawing him deep. Cradling his lover's balls, Cedo rolled them against his palm, enjoying their weight, until Billy pulled him away.

Darkened blue eyes looked up at him, his lover gasping for breath. "Any more o' that an' I'll be done."

Catching his breath, Billy sat up, easing Cedo from the bed and to his feet. The look on his face changed from one of bliss to one of mischief. "Think you've earned yourself somethin' for that."

Trying to contain his own excitement and desperation,

Cedo grinned. "And what would that be?"

Billy's lips twisted into a smirk. "Oh, you know what it'll be, all right. 'Cause I know you enjoy it." Cedo allowed himself to be pulled closer, a hand resting at the top of his thighs. "You enjoy it when I put you over my knees an' spank you, don't you? Makes you scream and squirm."

Billy pressed a kiss to Cedo's flat stomach, eyes gazing up at him. "You know what I wanna do?" he murmured, voice deep.

"What would you like to do?"

"I wanna take you down to the stables, bend you over one of those wooden saddle 'orses, and thrash your pretty ass with a ridin' crop."

The thought made Cedo's knees go weak and he leaned into Billy's hands. "Do it," he whispered.

"Do what?"

"Thrash me, Billy. Please. Make me scream and beg."

"Here? Or down there?"

He could feel his flesh begin to flush, growing warmer by the moment. "Here. We can go down there later."

Moving himself from the bed, Billy seated himself in one of the chairs. His golden skin was already tinged with pink, his erection standing proudly. Cedo longed to impale himself on it and pleasure them both. From the corner of his eye, he could see his Master, eyes intense as he watched every minute movement. As he walked to Billy, Cedo could see himself in the reflection of the window, the dark night turning it into a mirror. He stood tall and proud, shoulders pulled back. Having two men watch his every move only aroused him more.

He trembled with anticipation as he lay across Billy's lap, hands and feet flat against the floor. He could just make out Erus shifting in his seat, one hand slowly rubbing across his lap as he leaned closer. Closing his eyes, Cedo let his head hang down, hair brushing against the carpet. Billy's warm, rough hands slid over his buttocks, making him gasp and shake. They squeezed his pert rear before a finger touched his puckered opening. It moved back and forth, teasing Cedo, pressing close and making him moan. Billy knew how to tantalize him, how to make him quiver and beg, how to bring him to the edge of release before pulling him back. Every movement was calculated, every touch following a map only Billy knew.

The first slap shocked him from the pleasured trance he had fallen into, making him cry out, his body tensing. Yet even before the second one landed, the stinging pain was roaring through him, awakening every nerve ending and thundering to his groin. Bracing himself, Cedo pressed himself to his lover's lap, their cocks forced together and their skin sliding deliciously against skin. The second blow landed against the backs of his thighs, Billy's free hand pressed into the small of his back, holding him still. Again, Cedo howled, the pleasure evident in his voice. With each smack, his body would tighten, the heat racing across his beaten flesh.

Cedo could not describe the pleasure he gained from such an act. Even the simple act of lying sprawled over his lover's thighs, his rear teasingly in the air and his arms and legs as straight and as solid as rods, aroused him. Not knowing when he would be struck only added to it, the pauses and gentle touches between each one only accentuating the hazy mix of pain and pleasure.

Billy's hand landed again, his palm striking the peak of his buttocks. Cedo trembled, lifting his head briefly as he took in a deep breath. Across the room, he caught his Master's glazed gaze, the green eyes having darkened several shades. Erus had his hand against his cock, touching himself as he watched his companion taking a punishment.

247

There was a pause and Billy's hands returned to Cedo's rear, gently stroking in languid circles. "You look so good like that," he heard his lover murmur. "So beautiful with your skin goin' all red. Could look at this forever."

Catching his breath, Cedo allowed himself to relax for a moment. "Perhaps we should have some of those new photo-plates taken. Then you can carry them with you forever."

Billy chuckled, both of them shaking with the movement. "Now that I'd love. Somethin' to look at when I'm in the 'eat of battle. Somethin' to remind me what I 'ave to come 'ome to."

There was not a chance to take another breath as Billy laid another stinging smack. Crying out, Cedo bucked against the hand that held him down, but it was of little use. His mate was far stronger than he would ever be and Cedo could imagine his arms flexing, holding him still as the erotic pain was meted out.

"I'm goin' to think up an 'undred other ways of doin' this to you." Another slap, another rush of pain that made Cedo's cock twitch and his body come alive. "I'm goin' to get ropes an' chains. Perhaps I'll go an' make some paddles like I've seen in those periodicals. An' I'll make some gags as well. Want to see you completely an' utterly 'elpless an' at my mercy."

A million images bounded through Cedo's head as Billy continued to talk, his rear becoming redder by the moment. The thoughts were ones he would have once considered mad, the people who thought them needing to be in an asylum. Yet now they seemed perfectly normal, ways of handing out the pleasure they found so delectable.

Over and again Billy swatted him until Cedo felt as though he was fit to burst. Only when Billy had run out of things to say was he eased to his feet. Dazed and dangling from Billy's arms, he grinned toward his Master.

Erus looked as flustered as he felt, pale flesh stained red, his cock still hard in his hand. Lifting the free hand, he gestured them to the bed.

"On your knees, Cedo." Erus' voice was barely there as he spoke between deep breaths.

Easing himself to the bed, Cedo lay on his stomach, his rear teasingly in the air. Glancing over his shoulder, he watched as his two lovers approached. The need to have them both swirled through his stomach, knotting just above his groin. He ached for release, his cock throbbing painfully.

Hands gripped his hips, tugging him toward the edge of the bed, Billy's fingers exploring between his buttocks. Cedo mewled and begged as they ghosted over his entrance, touching him, before one plunged deep into him. The pain was rich, but not unpleasant, and he pressed down against it, willing it to find the spot that pushed him closer to the edge. A cool gel was gently applied, his lover's fingers disappearing and returning, carefully preparing him.

Another hand stroked over his hair and he lifted his head to look into his Master's eyes. Following the movement, Cedo raised himself and kissed Erus' welcoming mouth. His Master's lips were as soft and as welcoming and Cedo had always remembered them. They teased one another with the barest of kisses, lips parting and gentle breaths sweeping their cheeks. Lifting a hand, he stroked it along Erus' face, coaxing him closer until he joined Cedo on the bed. The kisses, the gentle touches of their tongues, only goaded him on more, making him want what lay in their minds. The pleasure, the excitement, the thrill of chasing the heady rush, the moment when the body stilled, caught in the most primal of acts.

Behind him, Billy entered him, his thick cock stretching Cedo wide. Clasping Erus' head, he groaned into his

Master's mouth, teeth tugging at his full lips. His Master responded, the kiss becoming more passionate, their lips bruising and blood touching their tongues. As Billy began to thrust, Erus grabbed at Cedo's hair, pulling him back and forcing him down to his own, swollen erection. Cedo was only too happy to do as he was silently bid, his mouth closing around his Master's cock and sucking him. Billy's movements pushed him on, first pulling him back before driving his mouth deeper on Erus. The enjoyment of the moment echoed through Cedo, clutching his body in its claws and begging him to push it to the edge.

Relaxing his throat, Cedo impaled himself on his Master's cock. Delighted, he inhaled Erus' scent, one which, like Billy's, resonated of masculine power. Cedo delighted in what he did, the flesh plush and silken against his tongue and throat. He could feel it tremble and throb, moving and growing to the attention he gave it. All the while, Billy rutted into him, his thrusts fast and hard, pushing Cedo closer to the moment he longed for. He moaned around his Master's erection, his tiny sounds transferring to the bodies that pleasured him. Erus' hands were tight in his hair, tugging and pushing, forcing him to suck and swallow before coming up for a breath of air. Behind him, fingers dug into his buttocks, Billy growling, his heavy, full balls slapping against Cedo with every wicked thrust. In his mind, Cedo could see him, standing behind him, face twisted into a snarl, strong thighs and arms flexing as he thrust into the man who bent before him. It was a thought that excited him, made him shudder.

Pulling his head back, he feasted on the head of his Master's cock, lapping away the fluid that pulsed from the slit. It flowed down his throat, and Cedo knew that it would soon be followed by something far more forceful. Sliding a hand between Erus' legs, Cedo cradled his balls, rolling them against his palm, enjoying their weight and heat. Above him, Erus grunted and once more tangled his hands into Cedo's hair, forcing his mouth back down. Willingly Cedo swallowed, the tip of Erus' cock sliding down his throat.

A hand left his hip only to wrap around his aching cock. Cedo's cry was muffled by his Master's cock and he began to move faster, rocking on his knees. His cock throbbed against his lover's palm, his own fluid turning it silky and smooth, easing it over Billy's flesh. Behind him, Billy gave a deep yell, thrusting in as deep as he could go, fingers scratching at Cedo's flesh as he emptied his hot seed into him. Erus' hand tightened in his hair, grunting as he reached orgasm, his cock spurting into Cedo's mouth. Again and again, the liquid splashed against the roof of his mouth and he gratefully drank each drop. Riding out his orgasm, Billy continued to thrust, his hand tight around Cedo until the bright light flashed behind his eyes and his body became rigid. He growled around his Master's softening cock, lips clasped around the head as he sucked him dry, his own orgasm eclipsing him. He shook and spent himself against the bed, his cock aching with his powerful orgasm.

Panting, he collapsed to the bed. Nestled on the bed, Erus gently clasped Cedo's head and lay it in his lap, fingers stroking over his damp hair. Drawing in deep breaths, Cedo moved and gazed up at his Master, taking in the relaxed look that had settled over his face. It had been a long time since he had last seen such a look on Erus' face. Smiling, he reached up and stroked along his Master's strong jaw.

Billy settled next to him, head resting in the crook of Cedo's arm. His skin was damp with perspiration, his blond hair ruffled.

Sleep soon came, whisking them away in her arms, allowing them, for a few hours, to forget about the bleakness of the future.

CHAPTER 20

The following morning, a Master of Still Portraiture was summoned via a pneumatic message. They gathered in the study to await his arrival. With pots and cups of tea cluttering the desk, Erus reached into a drawer and drew out a long leather wrap. Once spread out, it revealed a glass syringe, several long needles and three vials of the blue, time halting drug.

Leaning against the desk, Cedo watched as Erus assembled the syringe, the needle twisted on to its opening. Erus removed the lid from one of the small glass bottles and carefully drew the liquid up into the chamber. Finally, his Master tapped the syringe, tiny pockets of air bursting.

Laying the syringe before him, he looked to where Billy was seated. "William."

Rising from the window, Billy approached the desk, caution in his step. Motioning him closer, Erus took Billy's arm in his hand, thumb gently massaging the flesh. Slowly a vein began to rise, thick and blue beneath the skin. Walking around the desk, Cedo took his lover's free hand, Billy's fingers tightening around his own as the needle slid home. Billy became tense as the drug entered his bloodstream, a low growl rumbling from his chest.

Resting his head against his mate's shoulder, Cedo whispered, "It will pass. Give it time."

Rae Gee

Billy did not reply, and Cedo did not expect him to. He remembered all too well the pain that had passed through him, the aching head and blurred vision.

From the corner of his eye, he watched Erus rise, gesturing Francis closer. "There is more, should you want it."

"And I thank you, Mr. Veetu. In this instance I shall be valiant and instruct you to keep it for others."

"Francis, there is much more where this came from. We'll never go short. So should you want it, it is yours."

Francis paused before nodding. "In that case, I shall accept. It'll be an honor working with you all."

Looking to his Master, Cedo raised an eyebrow, confused at Francis' final comment.

"I have asked Francis to act as one of my advisers," Erus said. There was the low *ting* of a fingernail repeatedly striking glass and he gestured Francis to him. "Francis knows much more than we do when it comes to politics. His time with James, and as a revolutionary, are valuable. Because of him, we know of James' plans, of what he wants to do, not just with this country but with the world."

Seating himself beside his lover, Cedo chuckled. "And you believe you can run this country."

Emerald eyes glared at him, strands of red hair falling before them. "If you can run a business, you can run a country. And I intend to give James an extremely good run for his money. He will suffer greatly once he arrives here and I will not give up until he is either dead or on his knees begging for forgiveness."

"And if he does not?" Cedo asked.

"He will," Erus hissed, obviously angered, not just at the questions but at the name of the one who had tormented him. His Master had once thought that he had the adoration he so longed for, only for it be turned against him and used for evil. The wounds, Cedo could see, were still raw.

Busying himself with packing away the syringe, Erus continued, "He will stumble and fall. He will pay dearly for all that he has done. He will never take us, dead or alive. This is our country, our soil, and it will remain ours forever more."

Cedo left it at that, the sound of the doorbell giving him good reason to leave the room. At the door stood a youngish man, a tweed suit clutching his tall, skinny frame and a pile of boxes at his feet.

He held out a hand. "I'm Mr. Greene."

Relieved, Cedo smiled and took his hand and shook it. "Cedo Reilly. Come in."

Collecting the boxes, he shuffled through the door, looking around as he did. "Where do you want me?"

"First door on the right," Cedo replied.

Mr. Greene continued to shuffle forward and Cedo moved to take some of the boxes from his grip.

"And is he?"

"Is he, what?" Cedo asked.

"Like the 'papers portray him as?"

Chuckling, he showed the tall man into the study. "Well, you will find out for yourself."

Much to Cedo's relief, Erus decided that best behavior was needed, especially with someone who would be handling what could be potentially incriminating images of them.

Mr. Greene had brought an array of different props with him and had transformed the study into a small studio. Cedo opened the curtains to allow the sunlight to stream in and, from a pair of poles, hung a backdrop depicting a forest scene. Trees and flowers were painted upon it, the sunlight that touched it making it seem almost real. Before it he had placed two plaster of Paris pedestals, artificial flowers draped over them, the loveseat moved between them.

His camera, a large wooden contraption with a glass lens at the front, stood on three wooden legs. Above it was a device Mr. Greene described as *the flash-lamp*, a long piece of metal he filled with a mixture of magnesium powder and potassium chlorate. It was a device, the gentleman continued, which would only be used once the room become too dark.

From where he was sitting on the desk, Cedo watched as the portraiture man rubbed a hand across his gently perspiring forehead. "So, what can I do for you gents?"

"One of our group, William, will be joining the army soon and we would like some portraits done before he leaves."

Mr. Greene smiled. "Well, that's not too difficult. If you'll all—"

Erus cut him off, "Some of them may be of a slightly intimate nature. Are you okay with that?"

The man looked at the three of them, a blush beginning to rise to his cheeks. "I can do that, yes."

"And you'll keep the plates in complete confidentiality?"

Mr. Greene looked around himself, clearly flustered, before returning his gaze to Erus. "Once I've made the prints, I always destroy the plates. Unless I'm working for the Guard or government."

"Very wise of you, Mr. Greene."

A hand touched Cedo's back and he glanced over his shoulder. "Shall we do this, then?" Erus asked.

The first few plates were of a completely standard nature. They sat and stood together, carefully positioned and told to be still. The camera was adjusted and their image was captured forever. Seated between Erus and Billy, Cedo stared at the large glass eye. In it he could just make out their reflection, all of them still, their backs straight and faces unmoving. They had been ordered not to smile, nor to laugh. It would, Mr. Greene had informed them, ruin the final image if there were even the tiniest amount of movement. Between plates, Erus mused on how he could make the equipment better especially, as he said, that they now had the technology for moving pictures and transmitting sound.

It was a long and laborious process, one that Cedo found almost painful. Eventually another plate was removed and a fresh one loaded.

Mr. Greene coughed softly to catch their attention. "I believe there were, well, certain other prints you wanted made?"

"Indeed." A smile broke Erus' formally stony expression. "If you two would like to make use of your plan, now is the time."

Standing, Cedo eased out his cramped muscles before he looked to Billy. A mischievous smile curled his lover's lips. "I'm game if you are, Cedo."

For a moment, he stared at the camera and the man standing beside it. He would see all, yet Cedo had shared far more with both Erus and Billy. Capturing what they had was just another way of preserving their memories.

Pushing away any doubts and embarrassment, Cedo removed his clothes and placed them to one side. Erus had joined Mr. Greene at the camera, lounging against the bookshelves. Billy's hand slid over his shoulder and he whispered, "You're goin' to be just fine."

His mate was as nude as he was, a state which never seemed to bother him. Letting his eyes slide over Billy, Cedo felt his excitement begin to rise. His lover was so perfect, a sculpture come to life. The strength that lay beneath Billy's golden skin shimmered and flexed, making Cedo's breath shorten. Stepping closer, he ran a hand over his lover's flat stomach and gently curving chest, his fingers winding around Billy's muscular arm. Blue eyes sparkled and Billy smiled, one hand creeping to the back of Cedo's neck and cradling the back of his head. He melted into the touch, his hands skimming over Billy's smooth skin, his lover's deep scent exciting him further. His cares for the camera faded and he touched his mouth to Billy's, smiling when he responded. Billy's hand tightened around Cedo, his free one sliding along his back and over the swell of his buttocks. From beside them came Mr. Greene's voice, quietly commanding them to be still. Cedo did just that, unwilling to be parted from the arms of his mate. Billy's spirit felt as though it was one half of his own, lost to the winds until they were finally reunited after the war.

There came the soft thud of the camera's shutter and Mr. Greene telling them to choose another pose. Mischief tickled Cedo and he placed a hand on Billy's chest, pushing him to the curving seat. Laughing, Billy made himself comfortable, his eyes glistening with happiness. Kneeling over him, Cedo wrapped his hands around his mate's shoulders and touched his lips to his jaw.

"Shall we do it?" he purred.

Hands clasped the small of his back, fingers tracing tiny circles. "Do what?"

"You know."

"Do I?" Billy's eyes twinkled, their color deepening to that of the midnight sky.

Giving him a soft kiss, Cedo moved away and spread himself across Billy's lap, stomach against his cock, hands and feet pressed to the carpet. Lifting his head, he grinned, shivering as Billy's hands cautiously made their way over his naked skin. With one hand pressed to the small of Cedo's back, Billy raised the other and the man of still portraits told them to hold the pose, Cedo gazing up at his lover. A few more were taken of the same situation, Cedo and Billy miming as though they were carrying out the act. When he finally stood, he ran a hand over Billy's erection.

"One more," he said. He tapped his fingers against his lover's thigh. "Stand up."

Billy did as he was told and, kneeling before him, Cedo moved his hands up his legs until one rested on the swell of his buttocks, the other resting against his swollen cock, fingers just curling toward it. He gazed adoringly up at his mate, love and passion surging through him. Cedo knew he could spend the rest of his life worshiping the man before him. Placing a hand on Cedo's shoulder, Billy returned his gaze, a tiny smile crossing his lips.

The shutter clicked for the final time and suddenly they were back in reality and standing in the study against the backdrop of a forest. Cedo dressed in silence, his back to Erus and the camera. Cedo did not want them to see what their posing had done to him, his cock hard against his stomach.

He was just about to make for the door when a voice halted him.

"Veetu?" it roared, its deep tones resounding through the house. "Veetu?! I know you're up here."

Erus' eyes settled on him, and Cedo shook his head. Holding up a hand, his Master gestured to them to wait before he exited the room. Even with the door between them, Cedo could still hear the conversation.

"Yes, General Faulkner, what can I do for you?"

"It's those damned pumps, Veetu. They're not working."

"Well, of course they're not working. The air pumps only come on when there is a threat of poison or contamination. The vents are currently open but, should that threat arise, the pumps will automatically turn on and begin filtering the air."

"So the bloody things can tell when there's something in the air, can they?"

"Indeed, they can."

"I'll tell you now that there's a bloody stink down there at the minute. Thought it was going to kill me."

"You may want to check what you're feeding your troops, General. You may find that is the problem rather than what is on the outside."

"And you're perfectly sure of that, Veetu?"

"Perfectly sure."

Cedo could feel his skin become cold, a shiver crawling across him. "Who the 'eck's that?" Billy asked.

He could barely lift his eyes to his lover's, his whole body feeling heavy. "My father."

Billy's hand came to rest on his shoulder, and Cedo found himself finally able to lift his head. "Sorry," his lover murmured.

The barest of smiles pulled at his lips. "It will be okay."

The door opened, and Erus walked back into the room. Shutting it behind himself, Erus leaned against it. "I wonder what the judge would give me for poisoning the lot of them? As of this moment, it is awfully tempting, and I'm sure that no court in the land would convict me."

The comment was enough to make Cedo smile and he began to relax. "Just whose silly idea was it to have them here?"

Brushing hair from his face, Erus replied, "The military's. I built the bunker specifically to keep myself and whoever else was here safe from an attack. When the military found out, they started copying the idea, building strongholds beneath the Downs, mountains and, most importantly, beneath the homes of the country."

"Why the homes?"

"Because very few people will think to look under them. Plus you have dwellers ready and willing to defend their home. You'd have to get past them before you could even think of getting beyond the fortified doors."

"But why here specifically?" Cedo asked.

Erus finally stepped away from the door and walked back to his desk. Around them, Mr. Greene was beginning to take apart his elaborate set, no doubt listening to all that was being said.

"Because I'd already made the ready provisions. They could station the southern coastal units here with no real worries. All they had to do was copy the idea for the rest of the country. As you've seen, it is like a rabbit warren beneath the country. And what you saw in London is just the tip of the proverbial iceberg. I don't think there's one inch of land that doesn't have some kind of underground works beneath it or near it. There are clues, of course."

"To what?"

"To their existence." There was a passionate glimmer in Erus' eyes.

Leaning against the desk, Cedo grinned. "Do tell."

His Master winked. "Later."

Mr. Greene left, promising to return the finished portraits to them via the normal postal service. "I could place them in pneumatic tubes," he had said, "but they will be a nuisance to unroll."

Having first visited the kitchen and made trays of food and drinks, Erus had summoned Francis from wherever he had been working, and they lounged in the study, awaiting the day's wireless broadcast. Beside him, Billy twitched, and he placed a hand on his knee.

"Are you okay?"

"Aye," Billy replied. "I'll be fine. Just getting' used to the idea that, in a couple o' days, I won't be 'ere."

Cedo closed his hand around his friend's leg and leaned

closer. "It is going to be fine. You will have special armor and be with the finest men in the country."

"I know." Billy pressed a hand over his, fingers warm and reassuring. "I just worry, that's all."

"And that is completely natural. You will worry about your family and yourself."

"An' you. I'll be worried about you all, locked under there. What if somethin' 'its the 'ouse? What if it buries you alive?"

Taking a deep breath, Cedo stared into the distance. It was true. What if something did happen? What if neither of them could get word to the other? Would the wireless transmitters and receivers continue to work? But what if they were too badly injured to use them?

"We just need to hope and pray, Billy. Hope and pray that all will be well."

Francis stood to turn on the radio and, exactly at the hour, it came to life.

"London calling. This is London calling," the clipped voice began. "Reports are beginning to arrive that the Dynasty's army has crossed their border and are now venturing across Prussia. Reconnaissance craft have over flown the area and report that the army spans many thousands, possibly into the hundreds of thousands. We are currently waiting for them to return with the photo-plates they have taken. The last reports, which came in at fifteen hundred hours, stated that the reconnaissance craft are just crossing into France. In the coming days, we will send gunships to intercept the Dynasty's army.

"No one should hold any fear in their hearts. We are well prepared. Our army is one of the strongest in the world, spanning many countries. By comparison, this is the first time the Dynasty have crossed their own border in decades. They have always had defenses in place, using them against anyone who should dare try and cross them.

"Our allies are rising and preparing their own armies. They will help us to defeat the Dynasty. This evil will not be allowed to rise. It will not be allowed to rule the world. We will conquer it.

"If you are a civilian, you will soon be receiving a pamphlet which will outline how you can help the war effort. If you grow your own foods, you will be asked to support others. If you are not enrolled in the armed forces, you will be asked to take a job that has been vacated by someone who is now on the front line. There are many roles to be filled and we ask that you all support the war in any way you can.

"If you are a housewife, you are asked to finish traveling by 4pm and leave the transportation free for those who are working. In the coming weeks, revised timetables for transportation will be issued and sent to you by your local government.

"That concludes our current broadcast. Please tune in again tomorrow for more reports. London calling. This is London calling."

The voice vanished, leaving a hissing sound in its wake. Erus stood and turned it off.

"Well, it appears that our wireless system is working perfectly." His voice was wistful, one hand stroking across the smooth wood of the box. "Such a fine invention and I'm so glad I have been able to be a part of it." He turned toward them. "You should all be proud of yourselves. You will all be playing a vital part in the war and all you do will earn you gratitude. Before me are three brave men, all of whom are willing to play their part. I hope that others see you and take inspiration from all you are doing."

The words stabbed at Cedo. While Billy would be away fighting and Francis would be advising Erus, his job seemed so much more mundane. Despite what his Master said, being the voice of the nation did not hold much appeal. It felt as though it were a token job, invented purely for him.

Taking a deep breath, and with his heart pounding, he said, "I wish to go to the front line."

All eyes were suddenly on him, astounded voices filling the air.

"Absolutely not!" Erus bawled.

Billy draped an arm around him, pulling him close. "You can't do it, Cedo."

He looked at his lover, staring into the endless blue eyes. "And why can I not do it? You are."

"You can't go out there, Cedo. You're needed 'ere. An'." Billy stalled.

"And what?" Cedo demanded. "Am I not man enough to fight for my country? Am I too weak to do it? Why should I not be standing shoulder to shoulder with my fellow men, showing the enemy that I will not live in fear of them?"

He lifted his chin, daring Billy to try and talk him down. His lover's arm tightened around him, warm breath passing over his face.

"An' I won't allow it, Cedo. It's bad enough that I'm goin' out there without you goin' too. If they don't call you up, you don't go. Simple as."

"You are going to stop me?" He felt his heart ache at Billy's words, longing to stand beside him on the Downs and watch the enemy fall.

"Aye, I'm goin' to stop you. Because I love you, Cedo, an' if the army 'ave been told that you're doin' your bit 'ere, then you'll stay 'ere an' do it. I'll return to you, don't doubt my words. But I don't want you goin' out there. Don't want to be the one that 'as to get the letter that says you're no longer alive. No. I forbid it."

"Am I—" he began before Billy placed a finger over

his lips, silencing him.

"You are man enough, Cedo. Trust me, you're all man. But there's not an 'ope in Inferno that you're steppin' out that door to join the army. Please, stay 'ere. If you don't do it for me, then do it for the people you'll be talkin' to. You've got the chance to reach a whole country an' tell them 'ow good they are, 'ow well they're beatin' the enemy. An' if you don't do it for them, then do it for the relationships you've built. Look at 'ow far you've come. You're not the scared young man I first met. You've grown an' changed an' become somethin' amazin'. An' you're goin' to be amazin' for your country. You'll be doin' your job, don't you doubt that."

Cedo shook beneath Billy's arm as he tried to prevent the wave of emotions from rising. He so desperately wanted to do something useful, something physical. Yet he needed to be below the roof of the Witheybrooke house, broadcasting to the nation. Cedo would be doing his piece for the war effort, even if it pained him to be away from his loved ones. It took him great strength to stand down, to not keep arguing with Billy, knowing that arguing would lead to nothing more than anger, resentment, and hatred. He had learned that building a relationship could be a painful process, and he no longer wanted to hurt his loved ones. Arguing that he wanted to go and fight was a pathetic way to end the day, an argument that did not need to happen. It was over something pointless and needed to not be followed.

Leaning into Billy's touch, he laid his head against his lover's shoulder. "Okay, I shall stay. I shall stay for all of you, and for my country."

"Good." Billy laid a kiss in his hair. "I know it 'urts you, but 'opefully it won't be for long. 'Opefully we'll all be reunited before the year is out. 'Opefully I'll be back 'ere for Wintermass."

"I hope so too," he murmured.

"Good," Erus said from across the room. "And now that you have gotten that daft notion from your head, it is time I let you be for a while. I have a feeling that someone in the bunker will want to shout at me sooner rather than later, so I shall bid you farewell for the moment and go and fix whatever they have managed to break this time."

Sleep evaded Cedo, the pain of his failed hanging and the agony of knowing that Billy would soon be leaving hovering over him like specters. Still, he took the pills the physicians had prescribed, hoping to chase away the aches and bruises. Their recent activity had done little to help the strain on his neck.

Beside him, Billy slept, the cats curled at the foot of the bed. A faint green glow illuminated the room, moving with Consiliatrix's steady nocturnal breathing. Erus was elsewhere, most likely locked below-stairs in the bunker, tinkering or scolding. Cedo loathed the thought that he would soon be there, locked away while the world perished, kept safe while others died for him. He prayed to the gods that all would be kept safe, that the armors would protect them from harm. Yet he suspected it would be far beyond their imagination. Soon their world would change beyond all comprehension, the places they loved wiped from the face of the planet. Darkness was descending, crushing their collective soul.

And knowing that he would be trapped beneath the earth with his father did little to help. The idea made the sickness rise, clenching around his stomach and chilling him to the bone. The man had humiliated his family, but had still been allowed to rise to such an esteemed position. Yet it was not surprising, the sordid details no doubt buried in the past, hidden by his superiors. The world worked in mysterious, and often unfair, ways, and his father was proof of this.

Did he already know that Cedo was here? Had he been told? Or would they just one day happen upon one another? Cedo loathed the thought and tried to chase it away. But, like the ghosts of the past, it remained, hanging over him and haunting him. The cruel words of the past lingered in his mind. To his father, he was nothing, little more than a hindrance to his life. As far as his father was concerned, the sooner Cedo faded away from the world, the better. And all because he had refused to live up to his father's expectations.

His mother flickered through his mind, her smile still radiant. Yet her memory did nothing to warm him, instead making him feel worse. The thought was there, barely forming before fading away. Had his father had a hand in her disappearance? Was that why there was no record of her?

Closing his eyes, Cedo begged the questions to die, his mind to become silent, if only for a few moments. He wished to rest, to sleep, but they would not fade, thundering through him and awakening his brain.

With a blanket around his shoulders, he slipped from the bed and crossed the floor to the window. Outside, a full moon hung over the land, bathing all in her path with a bright light. On the Downs stood lines of mecha-men, larger than any building Cedo had ever seen. All pointed listening dishes toward the sky and the sea, great pieces of concave metal that silently swept back and forth, searching for the sounds of either flying craft. The mecha-men were a warning to all who dared come too close, positioned around the coastline. On their last visit to Svenfur, Cedo had seen the beginnings of the Sky Searchers, their long legs stretching for the heavens, waiting to receive the armaments that allowed them to keep a watchful eye on the air above. So many weapons, so many people, and all to stop one man on his murderous journey.

From below the window, he heard the sound of metal moving. Pressing his cheek to the window, he watched as a group of steel horses were led into the yard, men walking at their heads. They almost glowed beneath the moon, sleeker than his previous horse. Each was carefully stabled, the doors shut and locked, the men who had brought them melting into the darkness. Cedo's mind flashed back to their arrival, the carnage that had been wreaked across the garden, and he pondered on whether his Master had discovered who had killed their horses.

He watched Billy sleep, hair tossed across the pillow, body tucked beneath the blankets. He was their savior, one of the brave souls who would step forward and face whatever was coming. It was a fearful prospect for even the boldest men.

Slowly, the moon began to set and the sun to rise, heralding the beginning of a new day. One day closer to his loss, and one closer to all Inferno breaking loose. As the sun's rays began their journey across the Downs, Cedo returned to bed. Draping an arm over Billy's waist, he buried his nose in his lover's thick waves of hair and finally allowed sleep to spirit him away.

Yet, even in the darkness he was not alone, the nightmares of previous months once again rising. This time, the deaths below their own streets were gone, to be replaced with deaths on the Downs. Machines equipped with cannons and long, chiseled arms roamed the land. The unlucky ones were plucked from among the ranks and pierced with spikes before they were lifted into the air and torn to pieces by the bipedal machines. Their screams were not just of pain, but of loss, anguish, and fear. The grass beneath their feet turned red, rivers of blood running off the Downs and toward the sea. The air was filled with the stench of burning and smoke, the once blue sky turning a billowing black. The beach, once a place of pleasure, was a place of pain, dismembered bodies strewn across the shingle, entrails and rotting flesh lying among the stones like the debris of the sea.

CHAPTER 21

Cedo's sleep was broken by a knock at the door. It opened slowly and Francis walked in, a tray of food balanced on one hand. Shutting the door behind him, he placed the tray on a table and sat on the end of the bed, a worried look on his face.

"I would not go downstairs if I were you." Slowly his accent was disappearing, replaced by one of their own isle.

Sitting up, Cedo leaned against the headboard, Billy stirring beside him. "Why not?"

Dark ruffled hair fell into the bespectacled man's eyes and he pushed it away. "Mr. Veetu appears to have come to the end of his tether."

A chill snapped along Cedo's spine. He had seen such events all too often. "Whatever has gotten into him this time?"

Francis shook his head and Billy finally awoke, sitting himself upright. "What's 'e done now?"

"It isn't what he has done," Francis began. "More it is what is happening below-stairs. I believe he is regretting his invitation for the army to join him."

"Did he even have a choice in it?"

For a moment Francis stared at him, eyes unfocused. "I do not know. But he is angry. It may be wise to stay away from him today."

There was no time to think, nor to reply, as the door crashed open. Erus glared at them, his hands gripping the doorframe, hair untamed and eyes bruised with dark circles. He looked as though he had not slept, and Cedo suspected that he had not, quickly returning to the person he was before their foray in the Dynasty. Instinctively, Cedo huddled down into the bed, a cold fear rising.

"Why?" his Master demanded. "Why are they so obstinate? Why do they have to make changes to things they do not understand?"

He entered the room and slammed the door shut in his wake. Leaning against it, he surveyed them as though searching for an answer. In time, he answered himself, "It's because they believe themselves to be better than anyone else. They believe that they are the answer to everything. Because they have been dragged up in families with money and status, they think that everything that falls from their mouths is correct."

Erus joined them on the bed. Pouring tea into a cup, he stared at it. "I need something much stronger than this. It is a long time since I drank on a daily basis but I feel that they will push me to it. I shall have to place an order with Mr. Sainsbury later. Because if I have to spend several months with the monsters below-stairs, then I wish to do it in a permanently inebriated state. It will be the only way to survive."

Cedo sighed with relief and tried to hide the minute smile. Erus' humor was a trait that had rarely made itself known. Now it showed itself on a daily basis, his Master's complaints peppered with self-deprecating comments.

Francis leaned against the windowsill, cup clasped in his hands as he watched them.

"I will allow you to do that on one condition," Cedo said.

Erus turned to him, the paleness of his skin more

evident in the warm, morning sun. "And that is?"

"That you do not come crawling into bed at all hours, pawing at me and expecting me to rise to your demands." He smiled, face alive with merriment. "I have seen what alcohol does to you and I refuse to be a part of that on a nightly basis."

His Master's face lit with a smile of his own, eyes sparkling. "I shall try, Cedo. But I'm not making any promises."

After dressing in a light suit of cotton, Cedo encouraged Billy from bed. A darkness had fallen over his mate, the threat of the coming hours hanging over him like the angel of death himself. Both Francis and Erus had melted back into the house, Francis to continue with his duties and his constant attention to the house. Cedo hoped Erus had finally gone to bed, but he was most likely back in the study or bunker. The coming weeks would be a nightmare if his Master was in a constant state of exhaustion.

Helping Billy into an outfit of black trousers, white shirt, and black waistcoat, they made for the outdoors. The sun was high and warm, birds circling overhead. A light breeze sang through the grass and the trees, ruffling flowers and leaves. The air was fresh and clear, filled with the scent of the sea.

Walking through a copse of trees, Cedo took Billy's hand in his own. Sunlight filtered through the trees, turning everything green. The warmth was welcomed, touching his skin. All around them were the sounds of peace: birds singing to one another, the light rustle of leaves, the breaking of twigs beneath their feet. The calming scents of summer surrounded them.

"I will always love you," he murmured, not wanting

to break the perfect stillness.

Billy's hand tightened around his own, fingers lacing through his. "An' I'll love you, you know that."

"Are you scared?"

His lover fell silent, as though he did not want to speak about what was in his heart and soul. When Billy spoke, his voice shook, "Far more than you can imagine."

They were words Cedo knew he would hear and yet they still made him feel ill. "I will always be here for you. Even when all this is over, I will still be here."

"Aye, I know. I just 'ope I'm 'ere to come 'ome."

"You will be. And know that, to me, your honor and bravery are an inspiration."

They walked in silence, birds darting from tree to tree and unseen animals rustling in the undergrowth. From a fallen tree hung a white feather. Plucking it from its resting place, Cedo stopped and gently drew it along Billy's cheek. His mate shivered beneath its soft spines, his blue eyes falling shut. Drawing it over Billy's lips, Cedo leaned closer and gave him the gentlest of kisses. A hand crept over his hip and along his spine before cupping the back of his head, holding him close. In the silence of the forest the only noise was their own, their lips sealed together in a heated kiss.

Winding the feather into Billy's hair, they continued their walk until they broke free of the copse. Standing atop one of the rolling hills, they looked down into the carnage that stretched across their green and pleasant land.

Trenches had been dug, running for as far as the eye could see. Before and behind them stood armed mecha-men, cannons pointed sea and skyward. Some strode back and forth, their heavy footsteps resonating through the ground. Domes could be seen in the ocean, waiting to electrify the water. Camps had been built, springing up like gray forests. Along the coast, Cedo could just make out the railways, now hidden behind layers of steel fencing. Beneath the protective metal layer, he could see trains running back and forth and he suspected that many new stations had sprung up, temporary stopping places for troops and supplies to be unloaded. And, no doubt, for prisoners of war to be collected. Somewhere, in the surrounding hills, there were encampments, places where those who did not fit into society would be sent.

It had been something Erus had told him. While his status as a person had been returned, those who were deemed unsuitable for society were stripped of theirs and sent to the prison camps. Those who were the most heinous were used to test the new weapons on, the need to use the forgotten and the homeless finally erased. It was where they suspected the members of the Veetu household had been sent, their lives hanging in the balance, constantly aware that if they failed the camp's reeducation tests they could be taken away to have deadly experiments run on them.

It sickened Cedo to think that those who had trusted their lives to their country were having their lives ended in such bloody ways. Erus had suspected that this unfortunate fate had befallen the staff of the house. He had said it with great sadness, his eyes downturned, his words soon turning to the affection he felt for those who had lived and worked with them. He missed them and all they had done for them and hoped that, one day, the staff would rejoin them rather than meet a bloody death.

"I cannot believe it has come to this."

"You ain't the only one. The sooner it's over the better."

Dropping Billy's hand, Cedo wound his arm around his lover's waist, hugging him tight.

"Are you scared, Cedo?"

He took a deep breath, unable to take his eyes from the sea of metal before them. "I am. Fear does not even describe what I feel right now."

Hand in hand, they silently watched the maneuvers below them. Steam-powered vehicles, as small as insects in the distance, moved around, collecting and unloading people and supplies. The occasional whistle of a passing train could be heard. Other than that, there was complete silence, the warmth of the sun and the gentle breeze their only company.

Eventually hunger drove them from their vantage point and back through the copse. Time seemed to be slipping away at a great rate, minutes disappearing in the blink of an eye, hours feeling as though they only lasted a moment.

With the sun becoming low in the sky, they ambled through the trees, not wanting to break the moment, not wanting to return to the house and all that was happening beneath its eaves. As they walked, Billy ran his thumb over the back of Cedo's hand, a gesture of quiet reassurance.

Upon their return, they found the house to be in chaos. Raised voices could be heard behind doors, while doors deeper in the house were thrown closed, the sound thundering through the building. Francis sat on the stairs, elbows on his knees and his fingers touched together beneath his nose. When the front door closed, he looked up, shaking his head as he looked to Cedo and Billy.

Standing in the hallway, Cedo listened, shock stilling him. "Whatever is happening?"

From somewhere beyond the stairs, a voice was raised, bawling at another, unseen, person.

"It appears that there are things wrong with the bunker," Francis replied.

"What kinds of things?"

Francis shuddered as another door was slammed shut,

face visibly tightening. He took a deep breath. "Apparently things have not been calibrated correctly. From what I can gather, the periscopes do not work properly, and neither does one of the broadcasting devices."

Joining Francis on the stairs, Cedo glared at the study door. From beyond it, he could hear his father's voice, its deep tone screaming obscenities. Billy sat at his feet and together, they listened.

"Surely they can be re-calibrated? It cannot be that hard?"

"I'm sure it isn't," Francis replied. "But you know what the army types are like. If it isn't exactly to their liking then it is broken and cannot be fixed."

Inside the study, something crashed against the wall and Cedo felt himself flinch. "But why all the hysterics? It cannot be that bad."

"Oh, it's not. Far from it. I think that the stress of all that is happening has gotten to people and this is just the tip of the iceberg."

"And my father?"

Francis nodded toward the door. "As you know, he's in there. However I don't think he knows about your presence. As awful as it may sound, Mr. Veetu has done his best to keep you hidden. I'm sure your father knows about your forays upon the stage, but I'm sure he does not know who was behind you."

Cedo felt a sigh of relief wash over him. He was not yet ready to face his father, and when he did, he did not know what would be said. Would Cedo vent his anger? Or would he meekly stand before his father, hands clasped and head lowered? Cedo wondered if his father ever thought of his mother, wondered if the man who'd abandoned them knew where she was. His father had probably never had another thought of Isobel, instead turning his attention to his new wife and family. Cedo wondered if the man had had more children and, if so, whether he now had the son he had always wanted.

Standing, he touched Billy's shoulder and looked to Francis. "Come. Let us go and eat. I refuse to dwell on that man."

The kitchen was warm, almost unbearably so. Cedo did not feel like eating, his earlier hunger having faded. But he knew that he needed to. Above the fire, a pot bubbled away. Cedo fetched three bowls and ladled thick soup into them. It smelled heavenly, chunks of meat and vegetables lying among the stock. After placing them on the table, he collected cutlery and sat.

As if by magic, the cats appeared, Misty jumping onto the table and Consiliatrix sitting on the floor. Two purrs, one natural and one metallic, filled the air. Smiling down at Consiliatrix, Cedo shook his head.

"You cannot eat this."

The mecha-cat gave a deep, mechanical meow and Cedo picked Constiliatrix up and placed him on his knee. Obediently, the metal cat sat, front paws resting on Cedo's knee, eyes forever on the table. Misty wandered between the three men, nudging hands and accepting soft strokes, watching every mouthful of food that was eaten. Eventually Francis rose and filled a plate with meat and the thick stock and placed it on the table for her. It was gone in minutes, and then Misty returned to her rounds, trying again to tempt the weary men to part with their meals.

She still made Cedo smile, her personality warming his heart. Through everything he had been through, she had remained by his side. Whether it was because she knew he would feed her or from genuine love and friendship, he did not know.

As the sun sank lower, they confined themselves to the upper floor, listening as footsteps thundered and voices continued to shout. The noises died as darkness took over, the silence almost painful. Fingers whispered over switches, turning on the gas lamps, the curtains closed against the night. For a while, they sat on the bed, listening and waiting, wondering if the storm would return. When it did not, Cedo slipped from the room.

"You're goin' to find 'im?" Billy sounded shocked.

Holding the door open, Cedo looked over his shoulder. "Yes. I want to know what is going on."

Francis asked, "And you are willing to test his wrath?"

"Yes. I will go and face it." He could feel his heart pounding, thumping against his ribs.

With that, he stepped out into the hallway, closing the door behind him.

Rapping his knuckles against the study door, Cedo waited to be admitted. When his Master's voice finally called out to him, it was with a heavy heart that he walked in.

Erus was slumped over the desk, a pen clutched in his hand. The desk lamps gave the only light, shadows stretching away from them and engulfing the rest of the room. To one side of Erus lay an empty plate, a few crumbs the only signs that he had eaten.

Stepping before the desk, Cedo asked, "Are you coming to bed?"

Erus shook his head but did not look up. "No, I must correct what is wrong."

"What is wrong?" Cedo knelt before the desk, hands

folded on the warm wood. He knew that he was treading a fine line, stepping into his Master's personal space.

"Everything," Erus sighed. "Everything is apparently wrong, and none of it will be fixed in time."

"Why do you not just tell them that everything is fine and that nothing needs changing?"

Erus snorted, the sound sending a shiver down Cedo's spine. "Do not think I have not already tried that. As I said earlier, they do not listen."

Erus lifted his head and looked at Cedo, skin still pale and the darkness around his eyes deepening. His face was dotted with the beginnings of whiskers, his hair ruffled and in dire need of a wash. Erus looked haggard and tired, exhaustion refusing to leave him.

Cedo stretched his left hand across the desk and clutched his Master's fingers. "Come to bed. Please?"

The anger and hatred that had hung over the room melted away, and a whisper of a smile played on Erus' face. "Later. I promise."

CHAPTER 22

Erus, for once, was as good as his word, Cedo waking as he eased into bed. His Master's arm was cast over his chest and a warm body pressed against his back. In the darkness, Cedo smiled.

As promised, their portraits arrived the following morning. Laid out on the dining room table, Cedo felt himself blush as he took in the images. They were far racier than he had first thought and he could only imagine the cajoling Billy would receive if they were discovered.

Mr. Greene had printed them in several different sizes, some small enough for Billy to secret away inside a book. Leaning against the table, Cedo inspected them more closely, the black and white images with carefully picked out colors an art form in themselves. His embarrassment slowly disappeared, erased by his sense of marvel at seeing their images caught forever.

"Amazing," he murmured, fingers dusting across one of the three of them. Cedo straightened up. "I do think we should have had one with Francis as well. It seems wrong that it is just the three of us after he has done so much."

From across the room, Francis chuckled. "Don't worry about me."

"Besides," Erus said, "there will be plenty of time for more once this war is over."

Cedo picked up one of the small prints and stared at it. "True."

It was with a heavy heart that he allowed Billy to spirit them away to the bedroom, tucking the images into the leather-bound notebook Cedo had gifted him with so many months before.

"I'm goin' to write," he said. "Every day. Goin' to keep a journal type thing of what it's like out there. See if I can draw some of what's 'appenin' as well."

Cedo chuckled. "They will be having you for a war reporter before long."

Placing the knapsack on the bed, Billy gave him a wistful smile. "Would be a damn sight better than bein' in those trenches."

"Who says you are going to be in the trenches?" Seating himself on the edge of the bed, he pulled the green fabric bag into his lap, holding it open for his lover.

"'Cause that's where people like me wind up. I ain't goin' to 'ave a nice job. I'm goin' to be on my 'ands an' knees in mud."

Cedo felt disheartened, his normally merry lover dwelling in a pit of darkness. There was nothing he could do to help pull Billy out. Only leaving and finding out what lay in store for him would help. And it would either excite Billy or kill him. Cedo truly hoped it would be the former.

There was a knock at the door and they both looked up to see Erus walk in to the room. His Master looked better for having had some rest, a little color touching his cheeks. Yet he seemed quiet, as though his thoughts were too heavy to deal with. His hands were clasped before him and, though he had been wearing a suit of blue the previous day, he had now returned to his loose, robe-like clothes.

"I have news." Even his voice sounded distant and Cedo slipped from the bed, the pain of the moment before being replaced with concern.

Resting his hand at his Master's elbow, he asked, "What sort of news?"

"News from the War Department. It concerns William's placement."

Cedo felt his skin prickle, the fear once more rising, clutching at his chest and cutting off his air.

"William, you will not be in the trenches."

"What?" The bag was pulled shut, its strings knotted before it was returned to the bed. "What the 'eck are you on about?"

"I spoke to them," Erus began, "and explained that you were the mind behind the kinetic armor. Everyone who is on the front line will be issued a set of that armor. You have been moved from being a foot soldier to being an overseer of one of the mecha-men. I just apologize that I cannot get you a desk job somewhere."

"I'm sorry. I ain't quite with you on this one." Billy had stopped what he was doing, instead leaning against one of the bedposts.

"You will be in command of it, in charge of a group of three other men. It will give you more protection than simply being on the ground."

Guiding Erus to look at him, Cedo gazed up into his eyes. "Master? What is the meaning behind this?"

"I had to do it." Erus swallowed and returned his attention to Billy. "You have to return alive, for the sake of this household. I cannot bear to have to grieve for you, and I know that will be magnified a million times for Cedo."

"You shouldn't 'ave done it," Billy mumbled, eyes on the sack as he sorted through it. "You shouldn't 'ave interfered. Now I'm goin' to be singled out."

"No, you won't," Erus replied. "That I can promise."

Billy looked up, eyes blazing, and Cedo took a step back, an angry energy rippling through the air. "An' what is your promise worth, 'uh? You've made 'em before an' never 'onored 'em."

Shaking his head, Erus gazed at the floor. "It is worth a lot more than it was a year ago. Please, William, accept it, and do not worry. No one is going to single you out, nor will you be seen in any other light than for the brave man you are. No one other than the General in charge knows, and no one will find out. As far as they are concerned, you have been given the role of an overseer and you will be accepted on that basis alone."

Billy slumped to the bed and refused to look at either of them. With his soul aching, Cedo sat beside him and laid a hand against Billy's back. Through the thin fabric of his clothes he could feel Billy's heart beating, a steady rhythm that he would miss.

"Please accept it. I do not want you to leave here angry. I want you to leave with hope in your heart and a song on your lips."

Billy's body sighed beneath his hand, shoulders rising and falling. He tucked strands of hair behind his ears, eyes still on the floor. Leaning closer, Cedo pressed a kiss to his shirt-clad shoulder.

"I'll go, an' I'll make the best of it. An' I'm goin' to come back."

Cedo smiled. "Thank you. And I know you shall. I am already looking forward to your return. Do you want to go and see your mother before you leave?"

Billy shook his head, the hair he had pushed away falling free and once more hiding his face. "No. She knows, an' she's proud. I've sent 'er a couple of notes, just to tell 'er 'ow I am, an' I'll write while I'm away. She thinks I'm goin' to be good for my country."

"You will be, that I know."

Finally Billy looked up, blue eyes glazed and watery, struggling, it seemed, to hold back the emotions that ran through him. Silence fell over them and his lover moved closer, pressing a kiss to Cedo's head.

Time never stopped, always seeming to gather pace. Meals came and went, the sun rising and falling again. Those in the bunker fell quiet, arguments and complaints fading to nothing. The door had been shut and never re-opened. A dial on the door shone with a red light, the only indication that it was locked. In the deep room before the bunker, a hundred assassin crabs had been laid, waiting for the command to come alive and add another layer of protection to those behind the heavy door.

Gazing at the door, Cedo wondered what life behind it would be life. Would they live? Would they die? Would their work be beneficial? Or would it all be in vain? He hoped that his path would not cross his father's and, that if it did, he would be able to stand his ground rather than wither away. He wanted answers and he refused to allow his father to bully him again. For too long, Cedo had lived in that man's shadow, worried and angry. Below ground, and in the darkness of war, his own personal war would end, once and for all.

As the sun set on Billy's final day with them, the four of them gathered in the dining room for one last meal together. The papers, maps, and boards had disappeared, no doubt whisked away to the war rooms. Instead, candles flickered in their candelabras, casting pools of light on the freshly washed linen. Each place was immaculately set, cutlery polished and the finest china fetched from the kitchen. Flasks of wine formed a line down the center of the table, small dishes of condiments marching along beside them. Tall glasses sparkled beside each place setting, the flames of the candles dancing through them. The table was set for their final hurrah.

Francis wheeled the food in on a wooden stand, each shelf groaning with food. A joint of meat as large as the head of any man took pride of place on the uppermost shelf, its smell divine.

Placing it in at the center of the table, Francis announced, "Soup to start, with main courses of venison, pork, beef, and chicken, followed by a dessert of trifle, with coffee and pastries to finish. Are we all suitably pleased with what is on offer?"

He smiled a smile Cedo had never seen, one that was wide and filled with the joy of the moment. It told them to enjoy what was happening, to not think of the following day, nor to think of the darkness that would cover the country.

"Wonderful, Francis," Erus said. "You have done us proud, and I thank you."

"In that case." He collected a tureen of meaty smelling soup. "We shall begin."

The food tasted as glorious as it smelled, meat melting on the tongue and sauces dancing across taste buds. The wine, rich and red, rapidly vanished, glasses being filled and refreshed, the warmth of the room sending the alcohol to their heads, giving them reason to laugh and joke.

"Francis," Cedo began, "wherever did you get this food from?"

Francis' eyes twinkled in the low light. "Ways and means. Everyone is after rich foods to try and remember what they had before the war arrives. Many are stockpiling food and this will soon be outlawed. You'll only be able to have whatever is issued to you by the government. For now, we can have it and every shop is heaving with it, raking in money while they can. Because soon, they will only be able to give out government-issued foods."

"And they will be?"

"The basics, I assume. We have had the same in the Dynasty for many years. You are issued a small book, and it lists what each person is allowed. Mostly it is milk, eggs, sugar, tea or coffee, fats for cooking with, bread, flour, and a small amount of meat. You are, of course, allowed to grow your own foods, and I'm hoping to do the same here."

"It can be arranged," Erus said. "We don't have to be below ground all the time, unless a suspected poison attack is imminent. Anyway, enough of that. We're not here to talk death. We're here to celebrate life."

Sweeping up one of the flasks of wine, he refilled their glasses, raising his own in a toast. "To life and liberty."

The four words reverberated around the room, all filled with happiness and glee. Any dark thoughts were pushed away, becoming nothing as they talked and told jokes, Francis reciting poems from the Dynasty, while Cedo repeated racy rhymes he had heard while on the stage.

CHAPTER 23

Sealed in a heated kiss, they stumbled into the bedroom, Cedo kicking the door shut behind himself. Pressing his lover against the wall, Cedo roughly kissed him, lips bruising and their hands riding over the other's body. Billy growled against his mouth, teeth nipping at his lips, need riding high. The air was charged with their passion, goading them. Cedo could feel his cock hard against his stomach and he pressed a leg to Billy's groin, his lover's arousal further exciting him. He was wanted, desired, needed even, and it all came from someone he held dear.

Forced away from the wall, Cedo allowed himself to be tossed to the bed, Billy pinning him down, their kisses becoming more frantic. Blood touched his tongue and he swallowed it, relishing the metallic taste. Wrapping a hand in Billy's hair, he bared his teeth and tugged Billy's head back. Billy's eyes were dark, glazed, and his expression mirrored Cedo's.

"Take me," Cedo hissed. "Take me and do not stop. I want to feel you, really feel you."

Billy grinned and sniggered, crushing his erection against Cedo's. "You mean I 'aven't made you feel it before?"

Arching his back from the bed, Cedo growled. "You know what I mean."

"Oh, I know what you mean, all right. An' you're

goin' to get it just 'ow you want it." Billy's tongue licked along his throat until his lips wrapped around his ear. "Long and slow."

Howling, Cedo forced himself upwards, pressing Billy to the bed. Billy laughed when Cedo forced his strong hands above his head. Sliding along the other man's lithe body, Cedo pressed their groins together, sighing as he felt the electricity between them. Kissing Billy, he rocked, his lover twitching beneath him. Lying together, they each teased the other, hands tugging at clothes and sliding beneath hems, finding naked skin.

Fingers carefully picked buttons undone. Jackets, waistcoats, and shirts slid from slender bodies, constraining cravats fluttering to the floor like snow. Fingers snared the waistband of Cedo's britches, drawing them down over his buttocks and legs, leaving him exposed in the warm air of the summer evening. Hands skimmed over skin as they rolled on the bed, each battling for dominance. Lips sought out throats, fingers, feet and chests, each sighing with a deep contentment.

Finally, Cedo lay face down on the bed, a mound of pillows lifting his hips, the soft material tormenting his erect cock. Billy's hands moved over his back, working at tight muscles, sending Cedo into a rich state of relaxation. They worked at his shoulders before ghosting down his spine and over the rise of his buttocks. Purring softly, Cedo stretched himself along the bed, encouraging the fingers to work deep and further.

"Likin' that, huh?" Billy pressed a kiss to his spine, mouth moving along the peaks of his bones.

"Very much so."

"Still want me to take you?"

"Yes, please," his voice sounded distant, as though it were coming from another world, a haze of delight wrapping around him.

Behind him the bed depressed and hands were pressed to either side of his shoulders. Billy pushed himself in, Cedo letting out a low moan. He did enjoy being with Billy, enjoyed everything the blond man did. It was something he had never thought he would find in another.

Pushing himself into the luscious rise of pillows, Cedo moved in time with his lover, shivering as fingers caressed every inch of flesh, memorizing every curve and line. Sending Billy away on a high meant a lot to him, and Cedo hoped it would be these memories he carried with him as he stood in the shadow of the enemy. His hands crawled along Billy's curved back, gentle touches coupled with tiny kisses. Cedo sighed softly before drawing his arms around his lover's neck and pulling the blond man down to him. Nestling his head against Billy's shoulder, Cedo moved with him, hoping that his lover would carry this moment with him.

Shifting his hips higher, Cedo purred and glanced over his shoulder. His reflection shone in Billy's darkened eyes and he stretched an arm behind himself to sweep his hand along his lover's face.

"Us," he whispered.

Brushing his lips against Cedo's hand, Billy replied, "Always us."

He would wish the war away, send it back to the dank pit it had crawled from, all so that they could remain together. Cedo never wanted to leave the room, the gaslights casting soft-edged shadows across their skin. Shadows that danced and flickered, their heat kissing the two lovers, encouraging fingers and lips to find each trembling nerve and to seek out every inch of soft skin.

Resting his head against Cedo's shoulder, Billy sighed, hands shimmering over his ribs. Cedo chuckled and shuddered beneath his lover's teasing fingers, his minute movements making Billy sigh deeper. Lips touched the flesh beneath his arm, raising goosebumps along his skin. "Never want to leave you."

Melting against the welcoming mouth, Cedo draped his arm around his lover's neck. "Me neither. Never ever want you to go. Always want you beside me."

"An' I will be." His lover's lips began to count off his ribs, his hips still swaying, thrusts long and slow, just as he had promised. "I'll always be in your 'eart, even when I'm not 'ere."

Billy tantalized every part of him, driving him to the brink before pulling him back. Over and again, they rose and fell, Cedo begging and Billy refusing to give in. Sweeping against the pillows, his cock throbbed, the temptation of orgasm a knot at the base of his groin.

Pulling away, Cedo shifted onto his back before kneeling up and pressing Billy to the bed. The blond man laughed, hands wrapping around Cedo's hips. Letting his head fall back, Cedo impaled himself on his lover's cock and softly sighed with pleasure. Rising and falling, he shuddered as pressure was applied to the spot inside of him. Billy's fingers wrapped around his cock, sending everything into sharp focus. Cedo gasped and lolled, body sagging before he picked up the pace once more. Beneath him, Billy groaned.

"Come on, Cedo. You want this as much as I do."

Roughly Cedo kissed his lover, his teeth tearing at Billy's lips. Fingernails drew along his skin, making him hiss, the pain sending the pleasure spiraling around him, the hand around his cock tightening. Everything closed around him, his body suddenly the center of the universe. Calling his lover's name, he came, body shaking as his seed coated Billy's hand. A heartbeat later and Billy joined him, body tightening and warmth flooding through Cedo.

Cedo had begged it not to, but the sun still rose, creating another perfect summer's day. Perfect except for one thing.

Breakfast was eaten in silence. Even the cats refused to beg, instead sitting silently on the floor, guarding the precious last moments. No one dared to look at another just in case the emotions would spill forth. It was painful, a chilling time as they gazed at the crockery upon the kitchen table.

As the clock struck the morning hour of eight, the four of them rose, a strange and silent procession making for the front door. To Cedo, it felt as though they were about to witness an execution. His heart ached and his body felt heavy, his hand only able to brush against Billy's. It was with relief that Billy wrapped his hand around Cedo's, holding it tightly for the final few steps to the door.

Beside it sat the knapsack, its rough, green fabric bulging with Billy's worldly possessions. The blond-haired man swung it over one shoulder and turned to face them. Cedo could feel his composure beginning to fail, the strength he had secreted away crumbling to nothing. He wanted to sob, to hold him one final time. A whisper of a smile broke Billy's face and he drew Cedo close.

"I'll always be 'ere." He tapped at Cedo's chest. "In your 'eart an' in your mind. An' I'll be comin' back. I ain't goin' forever."

Tilting his head back, Cedo managed to smile, lifting a leaden hand to stroke along his mate's face. "I know. I know."

His vision began to blur, his body trembling against Billy's. His lover's voice, that deep and wonderful sound, told him not to cry, not to mourn, for he would return. But it was difficult to obey Billy's words. Cedo wiped his tears on the course material of his shirt sleeve before giving his lover one last lingering and passionate kiss.

Pulling away, he managed a smile, and Billy returned it, fingers sweeping over Cedo's nose and pressing to his lips. "You'll be fine. I know you will. Just keep me in your thoughts an' I'll come back sooner rather than later."

"Is that a promise?"

Billy's smile widened into the one that Cedo remembered so well, bright and full of life. "'Course it is. I'm not goin' to leave you alone for too long. Don't know who'll come along an' pinch you from me."

Cedo laughed, the ache in his soul slowly fading, and he leaned against the wall, watching as Billy held his hand out to Francis. Francis shook it.

"Thanks for everythin', Francis. You've been a real pal. You take care, okay?"

Francis swept stray strands of hair from his face. "I will. You too, okay?"

"Don't you worry about me." He nodded toward Cedo and Erus. "You just stop these two from killin' each other, won't you?"

Chuckling, Francis nodded. "I'll do my best."

"Cheers. I appreciate it."

There was only one person left who had not been acknowledged ,and Billy stepped forward, offering out his hand to Erus. For a moment it hung in the air, a cold silence lingering between them. Cedo silently prayed that nothing untoward would be said, that harsh words would be pushed away even for a moment.

Then Erus took Billy's hand in his own and shook it, the tension breaking as they both laughed. Clapping a hand to Billy's back, Erus held him before looking into his eyes.

"You are going to make a fine soldier, William, mark my words. Go out there, do your level best, and return to us a hero. You will get a welcome and a half in this house."

The grin on Billy's face finally chased away the last of Cedo's fears. Acceptance, true and perfect, lingered among them all, holding them together like bricks and mortar.

"Thanks, Erus. An' I appreciate all you've done for me. Really, I do. Wanted to say that before I left."

Erus still clutched Billy's hand in both of his own, their eyes locked together. "You'd have had the chance to say it on your return, don't you worry about that."

To Cedo it was a joy to see them both smiling, each clutching the other's hand as though they were the oldest of friends. In a way, they were. Together, the four of them had been to Inferno and back. They had battled their way across frozen wastelands and had looked the enemy in the eye. They had planned and plotted and, between them, had laid the foundations for a country of safety, a place where they, and those who needed them, would be able to shelter in the darkest of days. Their experiences had brought them together, and it would be what kept them together, standing shoulder to shoulder.

As the clock struck quarter past the hour, Billy stared at the door. Running his hand across its dark wooden panels, the workings within began to click and whirr before the locks thudded back. The door swung inwards and the beauty of the day flooded in.

"Well, it's a beautiful day for it, I'll give it that," Billy said.

He stepped outside, Cedo following in his wake. Behind him he could feel Erus and Francis, both pausing on the step, leaving them to walk to the end of the path. Sheltered beneath the two large trees, they waited quietly, Billy's hand seeking out his own. Holding it tight, Cedo lifted it to his lips and gave the strong fingers a kiss.

From the brow of the hill came the sound of rhythmic footsteps. With his heart in his throat, Cedo watched as the group of young men, all dressed in their best clothes, began their descent. Soldiers on horseback rode alongside them, calling for other men to join them.

Billy's hand slipped from his own, and Cedo felt the cold dread grip him. His lover took a deep breath and stepped onto the cobbled street. One of the soldiers pulled up before him, a sheaf of papers grasped in one hand.

"Name?" he demanded.

"William Henry Burton."

It took all of his Cedo's strength to remain on the path and to not join them. He knew his role was to be in the safety of the house.

The red-coated man nodded and touched his heels to his horse. With one long backward glance, Billy joined the throngs of passing men. Sagging against one of the trees, Cedo felt his breath come in short, painful pants, watching his lover depart.

As they rounded the corner, Cedo sank to the ground, knees drawn up and head resting against them. He felt broken and despondent, as though the life was being drawn from him. Something metallic nudged at his hand and he glanced down to see Consiliatrix sit beside him. Managing a smile, Cedo ran his hand along the smooth, cool head, feeling the mecha-cat purr beneath his fingers.

A deep thud filled the air and, turning his eyes skyward, Cedo watched as the blue sky disappeared behind a layer of blackness. Waves of gunships flew toward the coast, long gun barrels facing forward, the propellers along their sides beating the air. Each was the size of a small town, as black as night, and as fearsome as any death. Consiliatrix moved away and Cedo watched him walk to Erus, sitting at his feet, his angular head cocked to one side.

Glancing down, Erus nodded. "Consiliatrix, it is time."

With those few words, the metal beast stretched, claws

extending into the ground and ears flattening against his head. A shudder ran along his spine and the green glow from beneath his plates turned to a blazing red.

Cedo's breath was stunned from him, but then Consiliatrix padded back to him, and rubbed against Cedo's ankles. The creature looked as calm as before and, with a heavy heart, Cedo ran a hand along the mecha-cat's back. Turning his eyes toward the sky, Cedo watched as the flying craft continued to make for the coast, the sound of their engines filling the early morning. The world as they knew it was ending, and he was sure it was not for the better.

To Be Continued

CPSIA information can be obtained
at www.ICGtesting.com
Printed in the USA
FFOW03n1655051114
8509FF